"Is this your way of flirting with me?"

Reuben looked up from his task and she could see his white teeth. "I don't flirt, sugar. I don't need to."

"Then I don't get it. Why all the concern? You said yourself this game is about everyone for themselves."

"It is. Or at least it will be after we get a few others to drop out. But for now I need you."

"And when you're done needing me?" she asked.

"I'll break you like a bad habit." His smile grew wider even as he took her injured hand and began to wrap it up, this time in the white shirt.

"Good to know," she muttered.

"I play to win."

Talia lifted her chin, instinctively reacting to the challenge in his tone. "So do I."

Dear Reader,

This month marks the first anniversary of Silhouette Bombshell. And just when you thought the bookshelves couldn't get any hotter, we're kicking off our second year with a killer lineup of innovative, compelling stories featuring heroines that will thrill you, inspire you and keep you turning pages! Sit back, relax and enjoy the read....

Once a thief, always a thief? The heroine of author Michele Hauf's *Once a Thief* says no way! But when her archenemy frames her for theft, she's got to beat him at his own game to keep her new life, a new love and the freedom she won at such great cost....

When hijackers steal her billion-dollar satellite and threaten to use it as a weapon, a NASA scientist must work with a know-it-all counterterrorist expert to save the day. The heat is on in Kathryn Jensen's exhilarating *Hot Pursuit!*

A Palm Beach socialite-turned-attorney gets into a killer's sites when she's called on to defend a friend for murder, in *Courting Danger* by Carol Stephenson. It'll take some fancy legal moves—and a major society shake-up—to see that justice is served.

And how far might someone go to win a million dollars? The heroine of *The Contestant,* by Stephanie Doyle, begins to suspect that one of her fellow reality TV show competitors might have resorted to murder—could it be the sexy ex-cop with the killer smile?

Enjoy all four, and when you're done, tell us what you think! Send your comments to me c/o Silhouette Books, 233 Broadway, Suite 1001, New York, NY 10279.

Sincerely,

Natashya Wilson
Associate Senior Editor, Silhouette Bombshell

Please address questions and book requests to:
Silhouette Reader Service
U.S.: 3010 Walden Ave., P.O. Box 1325, Buffalo, NY 14269
Canadian: P.O. Box 609, Fort Erie, Ont. L2A 5X3

Stephanie Doyle

The
Contestant

Published by Silhouette Books

America's Publisher of Contemporary Romance

SILHOUETTE BOOKS

ISBN 0-373-51366-6

THE CONTESTANT

STEPHANIE DOYLE

is a dedicated traveler who has climbed Croagh Patrick in Ireland, snowshoed on Mount Rainier, crawled through ancient kivas of the Anasazi in Arizona and explored the badlands of South Dakota all in the pursuit of the next great adventure. A firm believer that great adventures can lead to great stories, she continues to seek new challenges that will trigger her next idea. Next stop: the Galapagos Islands!

Stephanie began writing at age fifteen. At eighteen she submitted her first story to Harlequin and by twenty-six she was published. She lives in South Jersey with her two cats, Alexandria Hamilton and Theodora Roosevelt.

For my sisters Mary Kay and Megan—the two strongest swimmers I know. Your unwavering support means more to me than you will ever realize. So much so you each get your own room at the beach house.

Prologue

Summer Olympics, Sydney, 2000

"What a crowd we have here tonight, Susan."

At the subtle request from the NBC sports commentator, the cameraman pulled the stationary camera back on its wheels and slowly scanned the crowd filling the aquatic center where the ten-meter platform diving competition was being held. The smell of chlorine filled the air and reflections from the brilliantly blue pool gave the impression of a water wonderland. After sweeping over the cheering audience, he returned the bulky eye to the pair of talking heads seated on the bench in the production booth, each of them wearing matching red shirts, khaki shorts and wide smiles. In his headset, he could hear chatter from the production people upstairs to the camera crew located on either side of the pool, preparing them for the next dive.

"Absolutely, John. The surprise standout, Talia Mooney from the United States, and Chu Lau from the ever-dominant Chinese diving team are really putting on a show for them."

"Would you agree that Talia especially has been in perfect form all day?"

"I do indeed agree. I don't think I've ever seen her perform at this level. Not at previous trials, certainly not on the world stage. And I have to say, John, that I know this young woman. Talia is not a real big fan of performing. She loves diving, and I think she likes testing herself against her peers—she's definitely a tough competitor. I just don't think she likes the attention that comes with doing it on a large stage. But she's not going to be able to avoid that now. This is her fifth dive. She's in a strong second-place position with only fourteen-year-old Chu Lau from China in front of her. Given the rest of Talia's dives, if she executes, she has the difficulty elements necessary possibly to overtake Chu Lau for first."

"Why don't you break down this dive for us?"

"It's an arm-stand back double pike. It's got a difficulty level of three point two. Talia will start this from a handstand position. She'll fall back into two complete somersaults in the pike position before entering the water. It's one of Talia's favorites. It's difficult, but it shows her gracefulness."

"*Graceful* seems to be the right word, Susan. Given her significant size over Chu Lau—probably six inches in height and at least twenty pounds—it's amazing that Talia doesn't create any more splash upon impact into the water."

"That's all about technique, John. It doesn't matter how big or small you are. If you're not executing the dive correctly, you're going to make a splash."

"It looks like Talia is next."

"And I love this part about her, as well. She's completely still on the platform. She's not shaking out muscles or doing anything that would detract from the overall impact of her long, slim body. She may not like being on stage, but she knows how to do it right to create an image of fluidness even before she goes into the dive. Remember this is a judged competition where every point counts."

Knowing the camera was steady on the heads, the cameraman tilted his neck toward the monitor on his right that was broadcasting the event. The production guys upstairs would know when to cut from the pool to the announcers and would in turn let him know. For now everything was focused on the girl on top of the sky-high platform.

Man, she was something. He couldn't help but admire the length of her body. Like one lean line wearing nothing more than a clingy blue tank suit. Her legs seemed to go on to forever and her broad shoulders suggested that she was just as strong in the water as she was flying through the air. Her hair was short and choppy and so icy blond that when it was dry it looked like a color only an angel might lay claim to. Certainly not a color any chemical could reproduce. And the way her nose curved up made her seem sweetly innocent despite the fact that she was a woman brave enough to fly thirty feet through the air.

Yes, she was a tall drink of water, as his long-dead father would have said. And he was too damn old himself to be having such thoughts. But what the hell, a man could look, couldn't he? Tearing his gaze away from the monitor he once again focused on the heads.

"Look at that handstand in the air," Susan noted. "Strong, straight, no shaking arms, she holds it, holds it, holds it, and there she goes."

Wow, the cameraman thought. *Good dive.*

"Wow," John said.

"Wow is right, John. She ripped that one. Beautiful quick rotation and another smooth entry into the water. Given the difficulty I wouldn't be surprised to see eights and nines on this…. And I'm right! Look at those scores. This is really exciting for Talia."

"Now wait a minute. What's that? Do you see the way she's holding her hand?"

"Uh-oh, that's her coach coming over."

This time there was more chatter in his headset. The production people were shouting quick orders to keep a camera on the girl and the coach no matter what. And the on-the-spot guy was being told to get into position.

"He's looking at it now, but she seems to be shaking her head at him. I can't see anything in the replay that looks as though it might have caused an injury. But she's moving away from her coach and heading for the whirlpool. I think she's okay. Either way, she's rinsing off and getting ready for the next dive."

"Did she even see those scores?"

"If she didn't someone is telling her now. Two more dives like that and Talia has a shot at the gold."

"While some of the other divers take their position on the platform, let's talk about diving. Susan, I don't think people realize how physically demanding this sport can be."

"Absolutely, John. Everyone remembers Greg Louganis smacking his head on the springboard, and falling almost lifelessly into the water. And that is a very real danger. Both on the springboard and the platform, the goal is to create height at the time of takeoff rather than distance from the board. As a result, divers' heads can come perilously close to the edge. In addition to that is the fact that their bodies are hitting the water at speeds up to thirty-seven miles per hour. That's a lot of pounding on a body over time. If you're off position even slightly, you can easily break a bone, dislocate a shoulder, wrench a knee. And no one is perfect all of the time. So many of these divers have experienced injuries at least once, if not several times over the course of their careers. Pain becomes a constant companion in their lives."

"I can see Talia climbing the steps to the top of the platform and she is really favoring that hand."

"Yes, something is definitely wrong with her right hand, but whatever it is it's not bad enough to keep her from these last dives apparently. Like I said, Talia is a tough competitor. She knows she's close. She's not going to let pain get in her way."

"What's this next dive?"

"It's a forward twisting three-and-a-half pike somersault. Again with the difficulty level this could bring in a lot of points, but I have to say if there is something wrong with her hand, it is going to be very hard for her to enter the water cleanly. Obviously, it's the hands that are first to make impact with the water. A diver's hands are pushed flat at the last second which creates an entrance for them and helps to lessen water movement when their bodies follow."

"And if she broke some fingers on that last dive?"

"I don't even want to contemplate the pain involved at impact."

"She's on the board now. Chu Lau made steady sevens on her last go-round."

"Again, still polished. Still very poised. John, if she's in agony right now then she deserves an Oscar, as well as a gold medal, because she sure doesn't look it. And here she goes... Excellent twisting motion, perfect turns... Oh no, look at that splash. Definitely not as clean as her others have been. I think, if I can see the replay, yes, John, she changed her hand position. She always does right hand down and grips with her left. This time she's put the left hand first perhaps in an attempt to shield her injury."

"What will this do to her scores?"

"We'll have to see. There is no specific rule that relates to the size of the splash. This isn't like figure skating where it's a set deduction. The judges should be looking for how vertical her entry was. But this is a subjective sport and the truth is the judges really like to see as little water as possible. Here are her scores now."

"They're not bad, Susan."

"They're not bad at all, John. Seven-and-a-half and eights. It was a really good dive, perfect form in the air, very vertical entry with just a slight imperfection at the end. Depending on what Chu Lau does with her next dive, Talia could still have a chance."

The cameraman's attention once again turned to the chatter in his headset as the production people gave the okay to cut to poolside. He was told that the on-the-spot guy was in position. He held up his hand and made the motion to the commentators that they needed to cut to him.

"Susan, let's see if we can talk to our correspondent, Chuck, who is down at the poolside now. Chuck, what is the situation down there?"

The cameraman again took his eyes off the two in front of him to watch the monitor. Chuck's face filled the screen. The camera guy downstairs was doing a good job of keeping the activity of the divers in the camera's view without letting it get too distracting.

"Well, John, Susan, I had it confirmed. On her fifth dive Talia did break two of her fingers, I believe the first two on her right hand, as well as dislocated the other two fingers at the knuckles. I got a quick glance at her hand before her coach covered it up with a towel and it's already starting to swell pretty badly. They're not letting reporters in the locker room, but I've been told they're going to try to pop the two fingers back into place and wrap the other two with tape. I'm also told that she will be executing her final dive. I'll let you know when I have more. Back to you, John."

Upon Chuck's lead-in the cameraman quickly checked to see that the heads were centered in the monitor.

"That's amazing."

"Why do you say that, Susan?"

"First that she had the will to dive in the first place knowing what it was going to feel like when she entered the water. And second that she was able to change the order of her hands, something that's probably routine for her, without really blowing it. I've never seen a diver able to switch technique midcompetition and be successful. Like I said before, Talia is a gritty competitor and she is obviously not going to give up without a fight."

"Here is Chu Lau up on the platform now. She can secure the gold with a total score of eighty-four-point-two points."

"Which, given her difficulty level, means she's looking for sevens and eights. But I do want to comment here, John. You can really see the difference in maturity between these two divers. Chu Lau is only fourteen compared to Talia, who is almost ten years older. She doesn't walk with any real confidence. I would like to see those shoulders back a little more. But when it comes to diving there is no one more precise with her positioning. This dive is an inward twisting two-and-a-half tuck somersault. There she goes. Man, she's quick in the air."

"Whoa. That's going to be tough to beat, isn't it, Susan?"

"That's going to be very tough to beat, John. She was

really perfect, in the air, in the water and…there it is. She's gotten what she needs. The gold is hers. Given the degree of difficulty on Talia's next dive there is no way she can overtake Chu Lau. Not even with tens."

"Do you think Talia will even bother at this point?"

"If I was her coach, I would tell her to sit it out and take a no dive. She actually has enough points that, even without the last dive and given her competition's next dive, she will probably still come in third. Bronze is a very respectable finish. She can't win gold, but she could do some real damage to her hand by going for the silver."

"Isn't that her coming out of the locker room?"

"She's probably just checking the scores. Figuring out what the situation is. That's her coach talking to her now. Telling her it's over."

"Is it my imagination, Susan, or do they look like they're fighting?"

"She's definitely shaking him off. And—I don't believe it—she's heading for the steps. I can see the tape around the first two fingers. She's climbing up. John, I'm shocked. She's going to dive."

"This is amazing. She knows she can't win. Her fingers are broken."

"Forgive me, but I'm actually getting a little choked up at this. I happen to know that this is Talia's last competition. She's waited to go to college, felt she couldn't focus on school and diving at the same time. She told me she would be attending Tulane in Louisiana this fall. I think she wants to finish this out. It's really a remarkable display of courage."

"You don't think she's looking to win silver?"

"I don't think she cares about the medals at this point, John. I think she simply wants to dive her last dive. She's on the platform. Her scheduled dive was going to be a backward three— Wait, I can see she's changed that. She's facing forward on the platform. She's not doing her listed dive…and look at that. She's going with the swan. The original dive, really…and perfect. Just perfect, John. Beautiful takeoff, absolutely elegant in the air, no splash at all. That's what a ten looks like, John. Only that wasn't for points. That was for her. I think we just saw Talia Mooney say goodbye to diving."

The cameraman watched as the girl climbed out of the pool. The guy downstairs was using the shoulder camera to follow her progress and once again he was getting the call from upstairs to tell the two announcers to cut to Chuck. He made the motion with his hand for them to stop talking and watched the monitor as Chuck raced to try and catch the girl. He knew the business was all about catching the right moment, but he couldn't help but think that they should just leave her alone.

"Talia, can you talk to us for a second?"

She turned around and everyone watching was able to see her reluctance, her pain and her strength in keeping it all together as she evidently struggled to hold back tears. It was a great shot. And it was going to make for some fabulous TV.

"Let me start with…how's the hand?"

"Uh…it hurts. I'm going to go get some X rays taken and see what the damage is."

"Talia, you were so close to gold. What were you thinking when you knew it had slipped from your grasp? And what prompted you to make that last dive?"

"I wanted to go out on my terms. And it's my favorite dive."

"You can see the scores, tens, but of course without the difficulty it's not a lot of points. Wait, I'm just now hearing in my earpiece that you did earn enough to win silver. Talia, you're an Olympic silver-medal winner. Congratulations."

"Silver's great," she smiled genuinely, brushing a tear from her cheek.

"And will this be your last competition?"

"Absolutely. No offense, Chuck, but I hope I never have to have a camera shoved in my face again."

The cameraman in the booth upstairs smiled.

Chapter 1

"Hello! My name is Evan Aiken and I am your host for what is going to be the adventure of a lifetime for eight lucky contestants. This is a game for the strong and for the determined. This show will go beyond survival and challenge each of these contestants' ultimate endurance. Okay, Joe, cut. That works."

Joe, the cameraman, whose large frame had been perched somewhat precariously on the bow of the boat, lowered the large battery-powered shoulder camera to his lap.

Talia Mooney was curious what would happen if she picked it up and tossed it over the side of the skiff into the Pacific Ocean. She had a hunch Evan wouldn't be pleased.

How the hell did I get here?

It wasn't the first time Talia had thought it, but now that

she was actually being filmed, it was starting to hit home that for the next several weeks, however long it would take to whittle down eight contestants to one, her life was going to be played out in front of a camera. Again.

She was going to kill her father when she got back. Despite the fact that she was doing this to save his damn hide.

"I'm in a wee bit of trouble, my dear."

He always liked to bring out the Irish whenever he was telling her bad news. He thought it softened the blow. The more *wee*s he added, the worse the news. She should have hung up after *wee* number three.

Instead she'd dutifully driven from her apartment in Miami to Islamorada in the Keys, to the marina and the boat she'd called home since her mother died of cancer when she was only ten. Her father had supported both of them by taking sport fishers out on day tours. And while growing up on the *Slainte* wasn't exactly a routine childhood, it had allowed her always to be close to her two favorite things: the water and her dad.

Of course she'd go to him in his hour of need, as he called it. She loved the rascal, despite his tragic flaw. The man was the ultimate dreamer. In truth it had been his idealism and hope that had urged her on throughout her diving career. She would have been content diving for fun. A competition here or there because she liked the challenge of testing herself.

But her father had dreams of Olympic gold.

An adult now, she could recognize that being an idealist and a romantic probably wasn't the worst flaw to have. If only it didn't make him such an easy mark.

"He had maps. Maps and charts and a diary. He

*knew the course the Spanish galleon was headed on
when it sank. And there were records of Spanish roy-
alty onboard. It would have been filled to the brim with
doubloons."*

"Did you see this map?"

"I—Well...I...was going to...eventually. I suppose."

Fifty thousand dollars. Fifty thousand dollars he'd
borrowed—not from a bank since no respectable insti-
tution would dare give him that kind of money, but
from a local loan shark, a muscle-bound goon named
Rocco. Then Colin Mooney had handed all that money
over to a man named Buck Rogers in the hopes of finding lost treasure and quadrupling his investment.

As if the name alone hadn't been a clue that the treasure hunter was a fake.

Mooney's Sport Fishing Tours barely made that
much in a season, let alone in enough time to make a
decent repayment that would keep the shark off Colin's
back. Of course, Buck Rogers was already long gone
with the fake maps and the cash. And the loan shark was
getting antsy.

Everybody in the small island community knew that
Rocco was a bad imitation of a mob thug, but when it
came to getting his money back, he wouldn't mess
around. If he didn't outright kill her father as a lesson
to others not to cross him, then he'd certainly take out
a knee or two. And without his legs, her father wouldn't
be able to make a living on a boat.

"You're my only hope."

Talia grimaced as she recalled his plea. She'd just
finished college at the ripe age of twenty-eight, she had

no savings, no job yet, and no way to bail her father out of this latest mess. She'd offered up her silver medal to auction off on eBay, but he refused to let her part with it. That's when he'd shown her the application.

Ultimate Endurance. A reality-TV game show where the prize was one million dollars. He'd sent in her information, her picture and a video of her competing. Apparently the producers had gone for it. If she could outlast just a few of the contestants, she could bring back enough prize money to pay off Rocco and save her father's knees.

She'd spent her life on the water and camping on various islands. Her mother had been Australian and had loved the outdoors, so they'd often vacationed on islands in the South Pacific. From an early age, her mother had taught Talia how to fish with her hands, make a fire, make shelter and stay away from deadly predators.

"A few weeks on a remote island competing against seven people who you know you can beat doing something you love to do…to save my very life. Is that so much to ask?"

As an added push, he'd reminded her that she wasn't having much luck finding a job in her chosen profession and that a little extra pocket cash might help to tide her over. Granted his reason for her failure to land a job was ridiculous. He'd said it was because no one interviewing her would ever believe she was an accountant.

But she was. Or at least she wanted to be. It was what her degree read.

She even believed that being a former Olympian

might give her an edge when it came to finding an entry position in an accounting firm, but now she was seriously considering removing it from her résumé. Each time she went in for an interview, the human-resource person would start asking about her hand—as if after four-and-a-half years it might still hurt—and end it with the question: *"Are you really sure you would be satisfied with a job where you do nothing but sit in a cubicle all day working on a computer?"*

Yes! That was exactly what she wanted. She wanted to wear business suits instead of bathing suits. She wanted to walk in pumps instead of bare feet. She wanted to have a normal job, in a normal company and have a normal apartment that didn't rock when the wind picked up.

It was during those moments of rejection that she wished her mother was still alive. Because as much as her father didn't understand her need to be taken seriously as a smart businesswoman, she knew her mother would have. Her mother may have married a dreamer, but she had been all about hard work and getting the job done whatever the cost.

But instead of being on another interview right now, here Talia was with her father's life in jeopardy, back to wearing a bikini and cutoff jean shorts, riding in a boat with a camera, en route to an island with a bunch of people who were all after the same prize. There was nothing normal about this.

She absolutely was going to kill her father when she got back.

For now there was nothing to do but play the game.

She sat quietly on the bench seat with three of the other players while a second speedboat, being piloted by a crewman who worked for the show, was behind them carrying the other cameraman, Dino—a short, stout, bald man with a round face—plus the other four contenders for *Ultimate Endurance.*

Ultimate Endurance? They had to be kidding.

Two of the contestants were well over fifty—Iris and Gus. One was a grandmother, the other a former military officer who looked gritty, but would that translate to real toughness on a deserted island? Then there was Sam, a soft-looking marketing executive who liked to smile and tell stories and who, Talia suspected, was closer to fifty than he let on.

Also appealing to the fortysomething demographic was Nancy. She was a last-minute replacement for the other fortysomething housewife who had dropped out. It was just luck that Nancy had decided to take a vacation to Hawaii and was available when the show needed her. A sweet-faced, overweight divorcée, from the moment she'd stepped on the yacht she'd alternated between some form of sheer ecstasy for having made it on to the show or wrenching tears at being separated from her children. The woman was an emotional roller coaster and liked to gather sympathy by telling everyone how her rotten ex-husband had dumped her for a younger, more adventurous woman.

However, Talia couldn't help but feel protective of Nancy. The divorcée was so far out of her element, Talia didn't know how she was still functioning. And it was only going to get worse.

Until this point they had been cruising on a luxury

yacht from Hawaii to the remote destination in the South Pacific just past the Vanuatu Islands in the Melanesian chain. Now they were on their way to the island they would be calling home, and Talia believed that the reality of the situation was finally beginning to settle in with everyone, especially Nancy, who had been suspiciously quiet during the trip.

Or she could have been seasick. It was a tough call.

Still, Talia had to be grateful that she wasn't sharing the short excursion with Marlie. An impossibly young, ridiculously skinny—especially since she was about to go at least a few days without a regular meal—wannabe starlet, Marlie was clearly more interested in fame than the million-dollar prize. She had spent the entire journey sucking up to—if not actually sucking off—Dino, so that when filming began he would always try to catch her from the right. It was her best side.

When she asked Talia what her best side was, Talia had named her backside. The others who had been nearby when she made this declaration had chuckled. It wasn't completely a joke. She had a pretty firm butt.

Sam, Marlie and Gus were on the second boat with Tommy. Another slim young gun with a lot of attitude and eyes that instantly made Talia think of a snake. He'd carried a blue backpack with him wherever he went on the yacht, claiming he wanted to be prepared in case the host planned a surprise drop-off. Since for most of the trip they were at least a hundred miles from any inkling of land, Talia thought that idea unlikely.

She suspected he had something in that backpack he didn't want anyone to know about, so he refused to let it out of his sight. Considering they were about to take part on a survival show, that probably meant he'd stocked food.

Not that Evan seemed to care a whole lot about the rules. His hosting duties didn't seem to extend that far. Also a late addition to the show, he obviously was struggling to learn all the nuances of the game himself, as he'd been useless at answering any of the questions from the group.

Tommy didn't worry her though. Cheaters rarely did. No, if there was one person in this group she needed to be worried about beating, it was the man sitting across from her.

Reuben Serrano was strong, with lean muscles along his body that didn't bulge but were defined well enough to suggest significant strength. He carried a little thickness in his middle, although she suspected that he'd packed on some of those pounds for the game. Not that the extra weight made him look fat or soft. Just more substantial.

From the beginning, he'd worn a stone-faced expression giving everyone around him the impression that he was someone who would fight dirty should the occasion call for it. And then there were the eight thousand other silent signals he'd sent out that said don't get close and you won't get hurt.

Except with her.

Getting close was all he seemed to want to do with her. Each night at dinner, he sat next to her. Each time the group gathered, he was at her side. Even if they were all sitting by the poolside or watching a movie or having a drink at the bar, it was a good bet where she was, he wasn't far behind.

Added to that was the way he watched her…. It wasn't sexual so much as it was predatory. Either he had guessed that she was his biggest competition and was plotting how to eliminate her or he was planning on knocking her over the head and dragging her off to the nearest cave to ravish her as soon as they got to the island.

Given that hint of primitiveness she detected in him, she couldn't help but wonder what type of woman in this millennium could handle dating such a caveman. Not that she knew if he even had a girlfriend, or a wife for that matter. He'd said nothing about his past, his job, where he came from or who he was. He talked only about the game and about winning.

Actually, it wasn't a bad strategy. Talia had decided early to take her cue from him. She'd never been a social butterfly—although she imagined she could give Reuben lessons on congeniality—but she knew it was smarter to play a little quieter than she normally would have. The less sharing on a game like this, with a group like this, the better. With each story that the others told, there was always a weakness to be found and possibly exploited.

To her surprise, Evan hadn't said anything about her past Olympic experience. Maybe he was waiting for the most dramatic moment, maybe he forgot or maybe he didn't know. He'd barely managed everyone's names when they had first come onboard. And since no one had mentioned anything about it, she'd said nothing about it, either. Nor had she told anybody about her life growing up on a boat or her experience with fishing.

Her father had gotten her into this because he needed the money. It was important that she not lose sight of that. If she was going to put herself, her face, her whole life in the spotlight again, then it was damn well going to pay off. To the tune of one million dollars.

"Joe, the camera seemed to be slipping a bit toward the end of that. Are you sure you still had me in the frame?"

Joe, the veteran of the two cameramen, gave his boss a dirty look.

"How long have I been doing this?" It was clearly a rhetorical question.

"Fine. Whatever. Just checking," Evan said and waved him off.

Talia tugged a bit at the constraints of her life jacket. She hadn't been forced to wear one since she'd learned how to swim shortly after her fourth birthday. For someone as comfortable in the water as out of it, she felt ridiculous wearing the bulky equipment. That and it rubbed against her shoulders that had been left bare by the bikini top.

Nancy, however, who was sitting next to her on the bench, in a T-shirt and baggy shorts that did everything they could to conceal her chubby body, was hugging the orange preserver close to her chest.

"Do you think we're going to have to swim?"

Talia considered the question. They were going to be stranded on an island surrounded by water for an unknown amount of time. It was a pretty good bet they were going to have to swim. But she knew that what Nancy was truly worrying about was the swim to the island. Talia tried to smile reassuringly. "Probably not too far. You can swim though, right?"

"Oh, definitely," Nancy answered. "I've been taking lessons at my local Y for months now. Just to get ready for this."

Months. Talia smiled, but didn't say anything and thought about the likelihood of Nancy being able to swim more than a mile to shore. Often Talia had been called upon to watch over casual sport fishermen, who liked to drink hard under a hot sun only to want a relaxing swim after a day of fishing. She couldn't count the number of times she'd had to pull one of those guys from the water or at least hold their heads up until her father could come to the rescue. So she was reasonably sure she could get Nancy to shore, but then she glanced at Iris, the grandmother, and considered the odds of getting both of them to safely to the island.

"What about you, Iris? You a swimmer?"

The older woman gave an affirmative nod. "All my life. One mile a day. Don't you worry about me. I'll get there in one piece."

Talia sighed inwardly with relief. Until she realized Reuben's intense focus was directed at her. She raised her eyes and met his stare, a silent dare for him to speak up.

"Hey, Pollyanna, the game is called *Ultimate Endurance* not *Love Thy Neighbor*."

"So you're saying we shouldn't count on you for help. I hope I'm not hurting your feelings when I tell you I had already reached that conclusion. No wait. I take that back. I know I'm not hurting your feelings."

His lips twitched. "All I'm saying is that it's not a team sport. Every man…and woman…is on his own."

There it was again. Something in his expression, the way he seemed to single her out, had the hair rising on the back of her neck. It was ridiculous. He was wearing dark sunglasses over his eyes; she didn't really know that he was looking at her. But she swore that she could feel the heat of his gaze through his shades. This guy was dangerous. She just wasn't sure in how many ways.

"I can take care of myself," Nancy proclaimed, apparently sensing that she was the weak link. She was right.

Talia reached out to pat her hand gently and caught Reuben's smirk. It didn't matter. The future was looming in the shape of an island that was growing larger on the horizon. It seemed to explode out of the clear aqua water, and Talia figured since it was probably nothing more than a big volcano island, that's exactly what it had done a couple of hundred years ago.

"Okay, Joe. Get ready."

Talia heard the host's commands and tensed. They were still a good mile or so from the shore. The water was shallowing out underneath the boat and she could see clear through it to the shadows of the coral reef below. She considered the predators, moray eels, gray reef sharks, tiger sharks and a sundry of fish that could bite hard enough to take a chunk out of a person. Not to mention the coral itself. If someone fell out of the boat the wrong way and impacted with the reef, it could rip flesh open, spilling blood into the water. Which would serve only to attract the predators they all very much needed to avoid.

"Are you sure this is safe?" Talia questioned Evan as the boat slowed to a bob in the water.

The host smiled, his stupid teeth practically gleaming in the sun. "Of course it is. If anything happens we can always pull you back on the boat. Don't forget the cameras will be watching you the whole time."

Talia wanted to ask who would be watching out for trouble in the water, but she figured Nancy was currently bumping up against a panic attack and there was no reason to suggest anything that might trigger it.

"What's the matter, Pollyanna?" Reuben jibed. "Getting scared?"

"What do you think?"

He didn't answer right away. Instead he smiled. "No, I don't think you're scared. Of the water, anyway."

His smile widened. It was the first time she'd seen his teeth since the trip began. They were almost as white and as straight as Evan's. Only Reuben's smile wasn't so much fake as it was menacing…and perversely exciting.

The second boat moved alongside and everyone nodded to each other, their expressions cautious, but also anticipatory. Both cameramen sprang into action, focusing in on the contestants one at a time. Talia did her best not to look away.

"Okay folks, here's how it's going to work. For the first part of this game we will be separating you into two teams. Not randomly though. This is going to be Darwinism at its purest. The first four that make it to the island, thereby the strongest, will be one team. The final four will be on the other. Once everyone gets to the island I'll explain how the first few days are going to work. Until then, this is a race and I'm the starter. Ready. Set. Go."

Everyone scrambled for the single backpacks that they were allowed to bring. They were only supposed to have contained some basic clothing, sneakers and, for the women, some feminine products. But the way Tommy was clutching his made Talia wonder if he hadn't included gold along with his illegal ration of food.

It didn't matter. It was time to focus on getting everyone safely to the island. She watched as the group from the second boat jumped overboard and began to swim. When she didn't see any lingering signs of a brownish fluid floating to the top of the water, she assumed that they had made it safely over the reef.

Nancy was about to fall backward into the ocean, when Talia stopped her. "No. You've got to watch what you're doing," she said pointing to the shadows underneath the surface. "Check out the other side."

Nancy bobbed her head and scrambled for the other side of the boat, while Talia stripped off her life jacket. Reuben had already stashed his glasses in his sack and dumped the jacket in the boat, but she could see he was cautiously assessing the situation rather than diving right in. Iris was also still searching for a safe spot.

"You need to the move the boat in farther," she told

Evan. "We're sitting on top of a chunk of coral reef. It's too dangerous."

"This game isn't about making it easier for you," he stated heavily.

"Idiot," she cursed under her breath. He was trying to make it seem dramatic, when the truth was if anyone got cut open, they would be in serious danger, if not from predators then certainly from an infection.

"There's a clear spot here," Reuben called to them, already in the water and treading in a way that told her there was enough depth for them to jump. Then he was off, swimming toward the shore.

Knowing she couldn't play the game as ruthlessly, leaving her competitors to fend for themselves, she helped Iris into the water, and then turned to Nancy.

"Let's go."

"Maybe I should take off the jacket, too."

"No, I think you'll feel more comfortable with it on." The woman had no idea the physical strength it would require swimming such a long distance in the ocean. She'd been practicing in a pool. It was the difference between driving on a highway versus racing a car in the Indy 500.

"But don't you think it will slow me down? This is a race."

A race that Talia had already given up the idea of winning. Someone was going to need to stay with the older woman for the duration to make sure she got to the beach. The fact that Nancy didn't understand that she needed help wasn't good, either. The last thing Talia needed to deal with was ego, as well as the trials of getting them both to the shore.

"Sometimes slow and steady wins it," Talia told her encouragingly. "Let's go."

She got Nancy over the side and into the water. Then she hooked the woman's backpack over one shoulder and her own over the other. The weight in both was trivial and Talia was easily able to manage them. She waited a moment as Nancy tried to acclimate herself and then jumped in behind her.

The ocean was warm and buoyant and for Talia it was like putting on a cozy sweater. She allowed herself to enjoy the feeling of floating, practically weightlessly in the salty surroundings. Swimming wasn't as much fun as diving. But it was a close second—head and shoulders above walking or running.

Why anyone chose another method of exercise that involved panting, sweating and pain, when swimming was all about being fluid, comfortable and relaxed, she would never know. But this wasn't a vacation. It was time for her to get to work.

Using a breaststroke helped Talia to keep the packs on her shoulders, as well as giving her a nice, easy stroke to conserve energy. She also was able to continually survey the group in front of her. She swam up next to Nancy, who was working her arms in a modified freestroke form. The divorcée was doing a lot of splashing, but she wasn't going very far.

Splashing wasn't as problematic as blood, but they definitely could do with less of it.

"Take it easy. We've got a long way to go. Just kick your legs nice and easy, not too deep, and move your arms like this."

In an exaggerated motion, Talia showed her the move she wanted her to emulate.

"O-k-k-kay," Nancy chattered with what only could be nerves as the water was a balmy temperature.

Together they moved, making slow but steady progress to shore. Talia used the time to study her opponents. Iris, as she'd indicated, was a sound swimmer. Seemingly in no hurry, she moved at an easy pace, lopping one arm over the other, her head twisting out of the water with each stroke to take in air. Currently, Tommy was the closest to the shore. He was doing a lot of splashing, too, but his momentum was carrying him forward at a fast clip.

Gus was swimming along behind him, but Talia could see that the former military man was keeping an eye on Marlie, who was basically dog-paddling her way to the beach. Sam was a few feet behind Marlie and struggling. He had chosen to leave his life jacket on, too, which was a good thing considering his uncoordinated moves. Fortunately, he was kicking strongly, propelling himself forward.

Not surprising, Reuben was the strongest swimmer. Maybe even as strong as she was. He was eating up the ocean stroke after stroke as cleanly as a hot knife cutting through an ice-cream cake. The thought made her mouth water slightly…the ice cream, not the man.

"How you doing, Nancy?" Talia called over her shoulder. The woman was a few feet back, but she was kicking her legs consistently. Not waiting for an answer, Talia dipped her head below the surface, eyes open as she surveyed the blurry perimeter. She could see the movement of creatures beneath the surface, not too clearly, but clear enough to make out the basic shape of the fish. Small fish. So far so good, she thought.

The sound of the small motorboats trailing them greeted her ears as she came up for air. Turning on her back to tread water, she watched the two cameramen focusing in on their natural prey—dramatic humans. Purposefully, she dipped beneath the water again when she saw Dino turn her way. Below the surface, she rolled her body over.

That's when she saw it. Out of the corner of her eye. A large shadow moving so gracefully, it would have made her gasp had she seen it safely from the boat.

Actually, it made her gasp anyway.

Purposefully, she kept her movements fluid as she surfaced for air. Raising her hand she tried to get the attention of one of the boats, but both were too far off in either direction to notice. Evan was steering Joe toward Tommy, who was going to be the first to reach the shore, and the crewman who had piloted the other boat was a few yards behind Reuben about thirty feet off to the right.

The shadow loomed to her left, but didn't seem to come any closer. There were no deliberate moves to indicate any sort of intent to attack so, theoretically, there was no need to worry. The trick was going to be alerting Nancy without panicking her.

Talia moved back and came up beside the older woman who was still making progress. "Not too much farther. Think you can pick it up a step?" she calmly suggested.

"Oh, I don't think I could go faster," she panted.

"But you don't have to wait for me. You're going to lose the race."

"That's okay," Talia said casually, her eyes searching for trouble. The shadow was out of view, but that wasn't a good sign. She would have much preferred having a bead on the big fish the entire way to the beach.

To keep the woman calm, and herself for that matter, Talia swam around Nancy a few times, checking the perimeter and chattering about her fellow contestants. "Looks like Tommy and Marlie are going to win. I don't mind if I'm not on that team. Too much talking, if you ask me."

The veracity of the statement made the older woman attempt a smile despite her evident unease. No one could deny that Marlie and Tommy loved to talk, mostly about themselves. They were perfect candidates for a show such as this as they believed they were worthy of having every word and every event in their lives filmed for the benefit of others' entertainment.

Glancing up again, Talia saw that Tommy had, in fact, reached the shore first. He'd had a pretty good head start. Then he walked backed into the water and tugged Marlie up to the beach with him, leaving Gus to fend for himself. But Gus was close enough, and so was Sam, that Talia didn't have to worry about either of them. Iris, too, was now standing in the shallow water and, even though it was a well-known fact that shark attacks often occurred close to shore, Talia figured there was enough interest in the deeper water to keep the big fish occupied.

Taking another dip, Talia studied the sea in front of

her but saw nothing. When she popped her head up, she could see that Reuben hadn't made it to the island yet, which was strange given his previous pace. He should have overtaken at least Gus and certainly Sam. Then she saw where his gaze was pinned. He started shouting for the boat, but it didn't seem as if the crewman could hear what he was saying.

"Oh! Oh, my goodness!"

Instantly, Talia turned around only to see Nancy freeze with sudden horror as a straight dorsal fin rose out of the water and swam directly in front of her, cutting between them.

"Don't move," Talia shouted. Judging by the shape and color of the fin, it was a gray reef shark, and not too big considering how long they could get. Maybe four feet. Maybe five. Its movements were still easy and unthreatening. At this point, he looked as though he was simply checking out the new breed of fish in town. If Talia remembered correctly from her mother, the gray reef would hunch its back before it attacked. As long as they avoided any unnecessary splashing or signs of distress that might incite the animal to think they were prey, it should just leave them alone.

"Shhh…shhhhaaar…"

"Keep it together. And no splashing."

Coming up along Nancy's right side, Talia wrapped an arm around the other woman's waist and tried to propel her forward, but when she tugged, she felt resistance. Immediately, Talia sank and discovered that Nancy had gotten her shorts caught on a piece of the reef that projected from the ocean floor.

Popping up for a quick breath, she couldn't miss Nancy's frightened gaze. The woman was on the verge of wigging out and once that happened there would be no reasoning with her.

"Nancy, I need you to listen to me. I need you to stay calm. No splashing. Just relax."

"But…I can't…it's— Did you see it?"

"It's just a fish, and you're bigger. Trust me when I tell you it doesn't want anything to do with you. But you're caught on part of the reef and if you move and get cut you're going to bleed."

Bleed had been the wrong word to use. If it was possible, Nancy's eyes grew rounder. But at least now she was so frightened that she wasn't capable of movement. Diving again, Talia went to work on the cotton material. It had been hooked over a piece of shell formation, much like a fish caught on a line. She hated to do it, but the easiest way out was simply to break off the coral. Considering it was a crime to tamper with the reef in Australia, she really hoped the camera didn't catch this on tape.

And that's when she felt him. Barely a brush of something large against her leg. Sleek, scaly and smooth. She stilled and slowly turned her head back and saw the pug face of the gray coming directly at her. But its jaw was shut and its position in the water was still unthreatening. It slid past her head, but she watched it as it turned around, coming back for another pass.

Like any skilled predator, it seemed to be waiting for her to make the wrong move before it pounced. She was doing everything she could to remain still, but her heart was pumping with adrenaline and the need for oxygen was becoming urgent.

Come on, you bastard. There has to be something tastier in the water than me. How about a turtle?

Suddenly, she saw a disturbance in the water to the far right. The motion caught the shark's attention and it went to investigate. Moving quickly, Talia snapped off the coral, then kicked hard to the surface.

Nancy, clearly having felt her release, was swimming with a purpose now, and Talia was right behind her. They were only a few yards away from the point where the water would be shallow enough for them to stand. With her fastest stroke, the freestyle, Talia gave it everything she had.

Finally, her hand touched the sand on the down-stroke and she pulled herself to her feet and onto the shore, the backpacks dropping from her shoulders to the sand. Just to her left, the group was pulling Nancy out of the water. Not surprisingly, she had broken into tears as soon as she realized she was safe. Both boats pulled up to the beach to make sure everyone was okay. Or to watch a hysterical Nancy do a bad interpretation from a *Jaws* movie. It was hard to tell.

Talia had other concerns. She scanned the water looking for Reuben and saw him a few yards down the beach crawling on hands and knees, his chest visibly heaving with effort as he sucked in lungfuls of air. She ran to him.

"You okay?" she asked as soon as she reached him.

"I was moving fast," he puffed, but after a few breaths he seemed to recover.

"You splashed deliberately? With a shark in the water? Not the brightest idea." Even though it had given her the time she needed to get Nancy loose and moving, it had still been a crazy move.

He smirked. "Yeah, well, I'm a city boy and it was the best I could come up with. So much for our protection." He pointed down the beach where Joe and Dino were both hovering while Evan knelt beside Nancy, patting her hand. Either the host was really rattled by what could have happened or he was a pretty good actor because he seemed truly shaken.

As well he should be, Talia thought. "These waters are dangerous. These people think it's a game, but—"

"But there be sharks in the water," he quoted in a bad imitation of a pirate. "Hell, I wouldn't be shocked if the damn thing was some toothless trained animal sent to drum up a reaction."

She gave him a doubtful look, but she could tell by his expression that even he didn't buy it.

"Guess it turns out you're a hero, after all."

"Don't get any ideas," he warned her. "I just figured if something was going to take a bite out of your ass it was going to be me."

He wiggled his eyebrows and she was forced to smile at his outrageousness.

Just like a predator. "There are tastier fish in the sea," she murmured, echoing her earlier thoughts.

"Somehow, I doubt that."

Talia ignored that and the fact that, for the first time, he was making his intentions known. Instead she concentrated on the personality revelation.

"You're not fooling me. I don't know why, given your surly attitude, but I had a hunch you weren't one of the bad guys."

A weak hunch, but a hunch nonetheless. And in a weird way, the role fit him better. He was still a hard-ass, but now she knew he was something else, too.

"Don't give me that much credit," he growled even as he got to his feet. "Once I saw Tommy and Marlie finish first I figured I would wait it out and take my chances with team two, even if it meant tangling with a big fish. Those two talk too damn much."

Chapter 2

"You okay?"

Reuben asked the question of Nancy as he and Talia approached the group. Almost in unison the rest of the pack turned their heads as if just realizing that there had been other people in the water with the shark. There were looks of guilt from some, but not from all.

Nancy bobbed her head in answer to his question and Talia crouched down so she could check the pupils of her eyes. A blanket from one of the boats had been wrapped around her in an attempt to prevent shock. Given that her eyes weren't dilated and she was no longer shaking, Talia reasoned that the woman was in pretty good condition, all things considered.

"It was really a shark, wasn't it?"

This time it was Talia's turn to nod her head in reply.

There was no point hiding the truth from her now that it was over.

"I was in the water with it. I was swimming with…wow," Nancy sighed. Then something akin to excitement lit her eyes. "Well, that was certainly dangerous and adventurous, wasn't it? And I got out of the water on my own. Wait until my husband and kids see that!"

Talia glanced over her shoulder at Reuben at the comment that Nancy had gotten out of the water alone. He merely shrugged and then fell into the sand butt first, his arms resting casually on his knees. He was in a T-shirt and bathing trunks, and the T-shirt was clinging to his skin showing off firm pecks and hardened little nipples.

She recalled his remark about biting her ass, and her body shivered a little. Not because of him, she told herself, just…because.

"Okay, if we are all recovered from our first adventure—" Evan began to say.

"*Our* adventure? I don't remember seeing you in the water, Evan," Reuben stated.

"Yes, well, I would have jumped in to rescue you all of course…had that been necessary. Thankfully, it wasn't. So let me explain the next phase of the game," he said quickly.

"As I mentioned, for some of the early contests, we will be pitting team against team. Team one—Tommy, Marlie, Gus and Sam—against team two—Iris, Nancy, Talia and Reuben. You all will be sharing one camp, but for the team that wins a game, each member of that team will receive one of the items you chose and ranked in order of necessity before the show began. The losing team will receive nothing.

"Remember, this isn't about politics. It's about Darwinism. Anyone on the losing team will have the opportunity to pull themselves out of the game citing that they are a weak link. If no one chooses to leave, then as a group you will vote to decide who the strongest member of the team is. Then that person, and that person alone, can choose to eject who he or she considers the weakest link. Or not. It's that person's call. It's a game of attrition, folks. Eventually, most of you will be broken to the point where leaving will be your only choice until there is only—"

"Hold it," Joe called out. "I'm low on juice." He lowered the camera off his shoulder and took a look at the battery gauge on the pack that was hooked around his waist. "Dino, focus in on Evan so we can get this last shot, will you?"

Dino, who had been circling the group trying to catch the riveted faces of the contestants, Talia assumed, steered his camera in the direction of Evan.

"We need that last line again," Joe told the host.

"Eventually, most of you will be broken to the point where leaving will be your only choice…until there is only one person left."

"Got it," Dino called. Then he also lowered the bulky camera from his shoulder.

Seeing both cameras turned off, Talia breathed a sigh of relief, then chastised herself. She was going to have to get used to this if she planned on sticking it out for the next few weeks. Or months.

Could it go that long?

She turned and saw Reuben leaning back on his elbows, his face toward the sun, almost ridiculously relaxed considering what they just had been through. He certainly looked comfortable in this element despite being a city boy. If he was telling the truth about that. In a game like this it was hard to know.

"Okay, let's head out," Evan suggested.

"To where?" Reuben wanted to know.

"There is an inlet at the other end of the island. We've put up some shark netting across the gap so it will be safe to fish. You'll camp on that beach," Evan explained as he directed everyone back to the boats.

"Then why in the hell did you drop us off here?" Gus questioned, clearly irritated with the host.

"The inlet is too enclosed," Joe explained. "There wasn't enough good light for filming and out here the water is clearer so we could get shots of some of the fish."

"TV reality as opposed to real reality," Talia muttered. She wasn't going to let it bother her. This was a game for entertainment that she was playing for money. Like *Wheel of Fortune*. If they wanted to film in good light, that was fine by her. "Are we going to have to swim again from the inlet to the beach?"

"Oh, I couldn't possibly," Nancy objected as she got to her feet. "Not after what happened."

"No," Evan told her. "We'll take you by boat. Then one boat will go back to the yacht, and the other that has our equipment, the radio and some emergency kits will stay on the island in another part. But it will be hidden and only I will know the location of the boat so don't think of trying to look for it or trying to get any information from Joe or Dino."

Talia rolled her eyes at Evan's attempt to sound menacing. The man was about as threatening as a schoolgirl.

They all loaded back into the boats, each team sticking together, and cruised around the island to where the beach jutted out and then into the inlet that Evan had described. The vessel slid over the netting and Talia could see everyone watching it, wondering if it would be enough to hold back a shark intent on getting inside. It was impossible to know. All they could do was have faith. A lot of it.

The gap between the two stretches of land was only about thirty feet wide. The shape reminded Talia of a horseshoe that was pinched at the top. And she now understood what they meant about the light. The foliage on either side served to shade the inlet, darkening it to the point that only beams of sunlight broke through. The water seemed a darker, deeper blue. More menacing than the previous site in many ways because you couldn't see beneath the surface.

At the base of the inlet was a stretch of white beach bordering the water. To the left it looked as if the water moved even farther inland creating what Talia imagined would be a lagoon, although she couldn't see it from her position. The pure white sand was guarded by the trees, bushes and brush. She noted the palm trees, banyan trees, bamboo shoots and massive ferns, all indigenous to the South Pacific. No need for any fake scenery here. It looked just the way it was supposed to look—a remote tropical island.

For the first time she considered that this place, this island would be her home for a while. She wasn't displeased. It was spectacularly beautiful. Turning away from the view, she studied the people in the boat, trying to assess their reactions, wondering if they saw what she did—a secluded beach protected from the harsh sun by shade and a lagoon that would make for easy fishing.

For her, it was a place where she could live for as long as she needed.

Iris was smiling softly. Nancy still looked a little out of it, no doubt envisioning how she would relay the story of her close encounter with the shark to her ex-husband. Reuben, predictably, was giving nothing away. But when he realized she was watching him, his mouth turned up in what she was coming to know was a half smirk, half smile.

"Looks a little bit like paradise, doesn't it?"

"It does," she replied casually.

"Then I guess that would make you Eve."

"And I guess that would make you the snake," she returned, refusing to fall for his crude charm.

Undeterred by her sharp tongue, he tilted his head back and laughed full out. Quickly, she looked to the view so he wouldn't see her own smile. If this was going to be home, then these people were going to be family. Learning to live with them would be as much of a challenge as surviving the elements. But dealing with Reuben, Talia sensed, was going to make those other two obstacles seem easy in comparison.

What in the heck was she going to do if it ended up just the two of them in the end?

Deciding that she was borrowing trouble she didn't

need, Talia instead focused on the immediate situation. The boats landed and everyone unloaded themselves and their belongings to the beach. Backpacks were tossed on the sand in a rough circle as a marker for the most likely camp. All except Tommy's, that is, which was firmly on his shoulders.

One of the boats took off for the yacht. "How far away are we from the yacht?" Sam asked Evan. "I mean, in case there is a real emergency."

"It's anchored about two miles off shore," Evan explained. "And I contact them daily by radio. Also if something serious were to happen, we're not that far from the coast of Australia."

"And what about you guys?" Tommy asked, pointing to the two cameramen. "Where do you guys stay?"

"That we can't tell you," Evan said. "It will be easier for you this way, so you're not tempted to find our camp. Joe and Dino will take shifts filming throughout the day. At night, for the most part, you'll be on your own. We'll leave you with a walkie-talkie that should be used only in an emergency. That's it. Any other questions?"

"Yes, where do I go to get my nails done?" Marlie laughed at her own joke, and so did Tommy. They were the only two.

"Okay, Joe and I will head back. Dino, you can film until your pack runs low and let us know when to pick you up." Evan turned over the walkie-talkie to the cameraman. "For the rest of the day I suggest you guys concentrate on building a camp. I don't have to tell you that fire is your first priority. And I'm allowed to tell you that not too far inland is a freshwater stream. The water should be boiled before drinking it, but there is more than enough for everyone. We've left a metal bucket at the stream for you to use. Tomorrow will be your first 'necessity event.' Oh, and you will all need these."

Evan reached into the boat and pulled out a waterproof sack. He unzipped it and Talia could see what was inside. Eight portable microphones. Reluctantly she took one. It had a clip that she could hook onto her shorts. She'd insisted on the jeans as strongly as her father had insisted on the bikini.

"After all, girlie, showing a little skin might get you some new endorsement deals."

Her last commercial after the Olympic games had been for Ace bandages. She'd taken half the money and paid a semester of college. She'd given the other half to her father, who turned around and used it to finance a search for a legendary pirate's sunken treasure in the Caribbean. He didn't find it. But he'd had fun.

"And isn't that what life is about, girlie?"

Maybe it wasn't too late, she thought sinisterly. Maybe she could still turn him over to Rocco and ask the loan shark not to be too rough. It was a definite possibility.

The rest of the group imitated her action with the microphone, then stood back as Evan and Joe got back into the boat and headed out of the inlet. Dino hefted the camera on his bulky shoulder and got to work.

"Okay," Gus began. "This is the part where we start telling each other what to do because we each think we know best. So before that happens and we all get pissed off, does anyone have any serious camping experience?"

Talia raised her hand. So did Gus. "Then how about we try getting a fire started," Talia suggested. "Someone else should go for water. And we'll need something to sleep on."

"Why?" Tommy wanted to know. "We can sleep on the sand. It will be soft."

"And filled with sand mites that will eat you alive. Trust me."

"I can get the water," Iris volunteered. "I'll take Marlie and Nancy."

"What?" Tommy said sneering. "You think girls can find water better than men?"

"No, she thinks you, me and Sam are the best candidates to get wood for the fire, and logs and ferns for us to sleep on," Reuben told the younger man. "You got a problem with that?"

And there it was, Talia thought. The first gauntlet being thrown. Reuben was immediately stepping into the role of alpha male and was all but daring Tommy to try and take it from him.

"Whatever," Tommy muttered. "Let the girls go find the water."

Round one: Reuben.

She wasn't surprised.

"How do you want to do this, Gus?" Talia asked him, indicating the method they would use to start the fire.

"I'm pretty good with two sticks."

Talia understood that meant scraping one stick that

served as a spear against the other that served as a shell to create enough friction to cause a spark.

"Then let's start looking for something that will work, as well as some dry brush," she concluded.

All at once people were moving. Deciding to follow the men or deciding to follow Marlie, it was quite obvious who Dino was going to film. Talia for one was glad to see him go. Meanwhile, Reuben pushed into the brush surrounding the beach, instructing Sam and Tommy on what they were looking for.

Gus found the first piece of the puzzle—a thick, dry piece of bark that was curved. Talia paired it with a stick that had a sharp point. Then they found some stringy remains of a palm leaf that would serve as kindling and got to work.

Talia held the bark in place and watched as Gus made quick back-and-forth motions with the stick. The tip snapped off but he continued to work it in staccato thrusts. In the meantime, Reuben gathered some significantly sized pieces of wood that he dropped near Talia for use when the fire finally caught.

She glanced at the pile quickly. "We want the driest pieces you can find."

"Oh. The dry wood. Sure, no problem. I'll just go to the dry side of the island."

She ignored his sarcasm and instead concentrated on the small pile of brush they'd placed where the bark and stick connected. She could feel the bark growing warmer, but that was a long way away from hot.

"I'm done," Gus panted. "I need a break."

They switched tasks and Talia worked the sharp

branch against the bark. The key was consistency. Hard, fast strokes delivered unceasingly would not only create the friction they needed, but also exacerbate it.

"That's it. Keep it going."

"I'm getting tired," she warned him, preparing him for the next switch. "Now."

Moving fast so as not to lose the momentum or the heat, they switched and Gus went back to work. After a time, they switched again and Talia was working the stick. Around them the men already had brought back enough materials to set up a mat to sleep on for the night and Iris had returned triumphantly with a pail of water.

Their tasks complete, the group focused on Talia and Gus. The tension was tangible considering the stakes. If this worked, they could boil water and have some warmth tonight. If they failed, everyone would suffer. As the sun started to set, and all of their clothes still damp from the earlier swim, it was clear that the group was starting to get a little cold and very thirsty.

Talia worked the stick in her hands, feeling it scrape against her palms. Blisters had already formed and burst making her hands slick with blood and ooze. Still, she worked, beyond the pain in her shoulders, beyond the stinging and beyond the fatigue.

Moving past pain was nothing new to her. She'd done exactly that each day of her training. It was expected, by her coach and by her. It might have been years since she'd pushed herself quite this hard, but the old routine came back like riding a bicycle.

"You're bleeding. Stop and let me finish." Reuben

was standing over her shoulder and evidently could see the blood coating the stick in her hands.

"I'm almost there. I can feel it. Gus?"

"There have been a few embers," he reported. "But nothing's caught yet."

"I said stop. You're hurting yourself."

She shot a glance at Reuben, which she hoped sent the message to back off. He was doing it again, laying down the gauntlet and expecting her to bend to his will.

Fat chance.

"If you don't stop, I'm pulling you off."

"What's your problem, man? Let her finish." This came from Tommy who was apparently already annoyed with his older, stronger counterpart.

"Yeah." Marlie backed up Tommy, her loyalties formed.

"Honey, your hands *are* bleeding," Iris commented.

"Oh my goodness, blood." Nancy, it seemed, was squeamish around the stuff.

Talia could sense that her time was running out. Despite the protests from the group, she understood, probably better than anyone, that Reuben wasn't going to be swayed once he set his mind to something. She knew because she recognized the trait in herself, which was why she couldn't stop when she was so close. With even faster strokes, she pushed the stick harder and…

There it was. Red embers catching against the dry strands. Then a small single blue flame dancing among the brush.

"You got it," Gus proclaimed.

She didn't need to be told. Gently she backed off the

stick. "Add a little more brush to the bark, not too much. You don't want to suffocate it. Fire needs to breathe."

But Talia could see that Gus knew his way around the process. Slowly they added bits of debris, blowing gently on the small fire to give it the oxygen it craved until there was a significant flame.

"Over here," Sam directed them. While Tommy and Reuben had seen to the bedding, Sam had stacked a tripod of wood and packed it with more driftwood and sun-singed palms that would serve as kindling.

Eight pairs of interested eyes, and one spectator with a third eye, watched as the fire caught and surged inside its new home.

"We'll have to take shifts so that it stays lit at all times," Gus told the group. "We don't want to feed it so that it gets too big, and we want to make sure that we can transport some of it if it rains."

Talia turned her hands over and studied her now dirtied and bloodied appendages. "Yes. I don't want to have to do that every day."

Reuben walked over to her and circled her wrists with his hands, holding her palms up for inspection. He grimaced, then tugged her toward the water. "I told you to stop."

"And I ignored you. You might have to get used to that from me. I'm not Tommy."

He pulled up short and glared at her. "That much I have figured out." Forcibly, he dunked her hands in the water.

Since rinsing the wounds had been her plan, she didn't fight him. She figured part of her strategy for dealing with him would be to conserve as much energy as possible. As long as they were headed in the same direction, she had no problem letting him take the lead. Then when it came time to buck him, she'd have the wherewithal to do it.

Together they bent over the salt water up to their elbows. Talia watched for any signs of smaller predators that might be attracted by the blood, but stopped worrying as soon as she saw her hands were clean.

"I don't need you getting an infection that would take you out of the game."

"Worried about me again." It was more of a statement this time. She shook her head. "First saving me from the shark, then from myself. Who's the Pollyanna now?"

"I have my reasons" was his only response.

She straightened and looked at her hands. Pieces of skin were missing but, other than that, she was fine. "I know you do."

He narrowed his eyes to study her. "What do you do? I mean back in the real world." It was unexpected. He'd been so insistent about keeping his own secrets that she felt taken aback by his sudden curiosity.

"What do *you* do?" she countered.

He scowled at her nonanswer. "I asked you first."

"So?"

He huffed then shrugged his shoulders. "I don't really do anything anymore."

"Then you'd better hope you do well in this game. It sounds like you could use the money."

With that she left him and made her way to the group.

The fire was gaining strength among the logs. Gus and Iris were creating a makeshift skewer that could hold the bucket for boiling water and would also be useful for when they started catching fish.

Reuben rejoined the camp and found his backpack. He reached into it and pulled out a sealed plastic bag then stepped in front of Talia cutting her off from anyone watching.

"Let me see your hands again."

"They're fine."

"Hey, camera guy," Reuben called out to the man who was currently filming the fire as if it were another contestant on the show.

"Dino," the portly man answered, supplying his name without stopping his filming.

"Right. Do we have a first-aid kit?"

"There was one in the boat."

That was answer enough since the boat was gone. Talia heard Reuben muttering under his breath, but couldn't make out what he was saying. He opened the bag and extracted two T-shirts. One white and one black. Both dry.

"Nice trick," she noted. All her stuff was wet from the swim. She planned to lay everything out overnight to dry and realized she should have planned better. A dry shirt to change into would have felt good. She couldn't help but be somewhat annoyed that Reuben had been one step ahead of her in that regard.

"Lucky for you I thought of it. We'll use them as bandages." He started to wrap one of his shirts around her hand, but she pulled it back.

"I don't need your help," she countered.

"They need to be covered. You scraped them raw and bugs will have a feast if you don't wrap them up."

He was right. She winced at the image of bugs eating the exposed flesh. But still she didn't understand his motivation.

"Is this another way of flirting with me?" And more importantly, was he flirting with her as part of some strategy to win the game? Or did he simply want to get her into bed?

He looked up from his task and she could see his white teeth. "I don't flirt, sugar. I don't need to."

"Then I don't get it. Why all the concern? You said yourself this game is about everyone fending for themselves."

"It is. Or at least it will be after we get a few of the others off." He took a step closer to her, invading her space. "But for now I need you."

Uncontrollably, her breath caught in reaction to his nearness. "And when you're done needing me?"

"I'll break you like a bad habit." His smile grew wider, even as he took a step back and reached for her other hand to wrap up.

"Good to know," she muttered.

"I play to win."

Talia lifted her chin, instinctively reacting to the challenge in his tone. "So do I."

"Should be an interesting game."

He finished and Talia noted the solid job he'd done with the makeshift bandages. The shirts were tied loosely enough so that her wounds would get some air, but securely enough to keep any critters out. The man understood the basics of first aid, it seemed.

They moved closer to the group, who were now circled around the fire. Clothes were being laid out to dry and everyone was picking a spot on the bed they had crafted. The men had done a good job of finding enough big logs and securing them together with leaves and vines to make what was essentially a large raft, then covering it with palms that had been rinsed in the water first. It wasn't as soft as sand, but it was definitely smarter.

Talia glanced down at the last two spots left to her and Reuben on the end.

"You'll take the inside spot," Reuben told her, dropping his sack to claim his place.

"Great," she murmured. She was going to be sandwiched between Gus and Reuben. On the plus side, she'd have the benefit of their body heat. On the downside, her body was reacting a little too warmly to the idea of sharing space with Reuben.

Eventually the sun finished its descent over the western horizon and Dino called to Evan for his escape. Building the camp had left them little time for gathering food or trying to fish, so the general consensus was that they would go hungry tonight and start early in the morning. At least they had been able to boil the water so that everyone had something to drink.

"Wow, my stomach really hurts," Marlie whined.

They were circled around the fire, no one yet ready to call it a night. The air was beginning to cool and Talia watched as a scattering of clouds drifted overhead, periodically blocking her view of the fabulously starry sky. She was dry, warm, a bit hungry, but overall quite content.

She'd forgotten how much she loved camping. As a family, she and her parents had taken trips several times a year before her mother had gotten sick. Then after she was gone, Talia and her father had continued the tradition. It had been difficult at first trying to pretend to have fun when they both knew how much they were missing the same person, but eventually she and her dad had been able to take comfort in each other. They'd developed a camaraderie that hadn't existed before and had become a unit of two.

Unfortunately as she'd grown into her teens, her training and competition schedule had left them little time for vacations. She made a mental note that when she got back to civilization she was going to rekindle this particular tradition. If she didn't decide to murder her father…then she would ask him to come along, too.

"You're just hungry," Gus responded to Marlie's complaint.

"Are you sure? What if it's some kind of parasite in the water?"

"No one else is feeling sick, dear." The soft words came from Iris. Talia could see she was rolling her eyes at the young woman. Iris and Talia shared a conspiratorial smile.

"But it really hurts," Marlie complained, this time with a high-pitched quality in her voice that had Reuben, who was on Talia's right, clicking his teeth together as his jaw clenched shut.

"Are you kidding?" he asked. "This is day one."

"So?" Marlie's lower lip protruded in a pout worthy of a three-year-old.

"So if you can't handle a few hunger pains, little girl—"

Talia reached out and patted his hand, stopping what she imagined would have been a blistering tirade. After all, it was day one. There was no point in him making enemies of everyone.

"I have an idea," Talia suggested. "Why don't we play a game? It will take our minds off how hungry we are."

"Good idea," Sam said, backing her up.

"What kind of game?" Tommy wanted to know.

"I don't know." She shrugged. "How about we go around the circle and say what each of us would do with the million dollars if we won?"

"I'll start," Iris began. "I'm going to buy a luxury condo in an over-fifty community. There's one I've got my eye on. It's got a pool and a community center that holds bridge tournaments every month."

"I don't know what I'm going to do with the money other than I hope it will keep me from having to be one of those greeter guys at the local Wal-Mart. I really hate those guys," Gus explained. "It's not about the money for me. I really came to see if I've still got it."

"You did a pretty good job with the fire," Talia pointed out.

"Yes, I did," he said, smiling proudly. "I think maybe I'd get a log cabin. In the woods somewhere near a lake where I can fish all day long."

"Fishing? Boring," Tommy groaned.

"You think, huh? Well, what's your big idea?"

Tommy was sitting back, his weight resting on his palms behind him. "That's easy. I'm never going to work again. No more bullshit 'do this' and 'do that.' No more waking up at the same time every morning to do the same damn thing every day. I'm just going to be, you know. Just be."

Talia heard Reuben muttering again, and could only imagine what he was saying under his breath.

"I know what I'm going to do," Marlie chimed in. "First, I'm going to see what kind of exposure being on this show gets me in the entertainment industry."

Talia took in the tiny triangles of cloth barely covering Marlie's chest and decided that the twenty-year-old didn't have to worry about being underexposed.

"Then I'm going to hire a manager because really the only way to get an agent in Hollywood is to have a quality manager. And I'll need a publicist. I mean, a publicist can make all the difference in a career. Oh, and, of course, implants."

"Of course," Talia concurred tongue-in-cheek and watched every man's head turn as if pulled by some natural force in the direction of Marlie's breasts.

"I think you look good now," Tommy said in what Talia assumed was an attempt to lay the groundwork for a seduction. He was going to have to get behind Dino though, who it seemed had already laid a claim.

"Oh, I know. But in Hollywood bigger is really better. For boobs, anyway."

Talia had to swallow a chuckle. Then she glanced at

Nancy who was currently checking out her own significant chest, probably thinking that being bigger had
never gotten her anywhere. And Talia resisted the in-
stinctive urge to check out her own two handfuls to see
how they measured up. Not that she had to look. It
seemed Reuben already had his eyes on them. She met
his blatant stare with a scowl, but he wasn't intimidated
in the least. He did, however, mouth the word *perfect*.

Ridiculously flustered and needing a distraction, she
turned to the housewife. "What about you, Nancy?
What would you do with a million dollars?"

"I don't know. I mean, of course I would pay for my
children's education." Her voice broke on the word *children,* but she quickly recovered. "I'm sorry. I guess I've
been a little emotional."

A little? Again, Talia had to bite back words and instead listened to what the woman was saying.

"It's just that my husband leaving me for
that…girl…really shook me up. I came here because I
wanted to prove to him and to my kids and to myself
that I wasn't some boring old housewife. Maybe if I
win, I'll have a makeover and get myself a younger boy-
friend. That would show him." She laughed at the idea,
but there was a definite twinkle in her eyes.

"See, now I'm going to be predictable," Sam explained. "I came here because my therapist said it would
be good for me. I guess I'm having what you call a midlife crisis. So if I win, I want what all fortysomething
guys going through a midlife crisis want…a cherry-red
Porsche so I can get a hot young girlfriend."

There was a smattering of chuckles, then the group

grew quiet and looked to Reuben who was sitting next to Sam. A moment passed where Talia thought he would stick to his strategy and say nothing about himself. She was about to speak up when he blurted out his intentions for the money.

"I'm going to buy a bar."

That was it. No other explanation forthcoming, but he'd played along and Talia figured that counted for something. He was at least making a small effort to be a part of the group. She wasn't sure why, but she thought that was important.

"Your turn, Talia," Iris instructed.

"My dad…" She hesitated, deciding that it wasn't really fair to share her father's screwup with strangers, and modified her story. "He likes to hunt for treasure. You know…sunken ships. It costs money for equipment and information. I would help him do that. Other than that, the money is going to help me bide my time until I get a job."

"What do you do?" Nancy inquired.

Talia could feel Reuben sit up straighter, knowing he was going to get an answer to the question he'd asked her earlier. Since she'd defied him merely to be difficult, she didn't see the harm in answering Nancy.

"I'm an accountant."

"Bullshit," Reuben erupted.

She turned sharply toward him. "I am. I have my degree in accounting. I still have to take my CPA exams, though."

"If you're an accountant, sugar, then I'm a priest. And trust me when I tell you I ain't no priest."

"She can be an accountant if she wants to be," Tommy snapped, more to buck Reuben than to support Talia, she knew.

Reuben's eyes didn't leave her face when he said, "Whatever." He stood and addressed the group. "Game's over. I suggest we try to get some sleep."

Talia stood, too, and considered pursuing him for an answer as to why he was so adamant that she couldn't be an accountant. Just because she was on a reality show didn't mean she didn't have a serious life with a very serious career waiting for her back home. Exactly what she'd planned from the moment she'd finished her last dive. Her father's predicament was only postponing it.

But by the time she made her way to the pseudo-bed, Reuben was already stretched out at the edge of the primitive futon, using his backpack as a headrest. His arms were crossed over his chest, his eyes were closed. He was clearly done talking for the night.

Everyone else made their way onto the mat, also, people shifting and struggling to get comfortable, using their T-shirts and packs as cushions and blankets. Talia stared down at the small space left to her and considered how bad the sand mites really could be.

Then Reuben's eyes opened, peering through the darkness directly at her. He uncrossed his arms and patted the space next to him in a blatant invitation.

Lying down with bugs or a snake?

It was definitely a tough call. But she rationalized her decision with the knowledge that she had no fear of snakes. At least one she was pretty sure wouldn't bite her in front of the group.

Stepping over his body, Talia settled down between him and Gus and heard what could only be described as a sigh of deep satisfaction. It hadn't come from Gus.

Bastard.

Chapter 3

She was warm. Toasty warm. So comfortable that it
forced her from a sound sleep because her subcon-
scious knew that she wasn't supposed to be quite this
comfortable.

Why?

That's right, she was on an island. Camping. Outside.
Her back should be stiff, her limbs cold from exposure despite the moderate temperature. Instead she was…mmm.

Talia opened her eyes and found herself staring into
the face of a sleeping Reuben. He had one hand under
his cheek, the other wrapped snuggly around her waist.
Her shirt-covered hands were tucked up between them,
gently resting on his chest. And one of his legs was
draped casually over her thigh, while her leg had slipped
in between his.

Against her back she felt nothing and when she turned her head to glance over her shoulder, she could see Gus on his side, facing Iris. Except that he wasn't covering Iris like a candy wrapper. No, only Talia and Reuben were tucked together like a couple used to sleeping together.

She pushed against his chest gently to create some space, but the instant she did his grip tightened.

"Closer," he muttered, pulling her toward him more tightly.

She felt his strong frame pressed against her body from her toes to her shoulders and willfully denied the tingle throughout her body as a result of his morning erection pressed into her belly.

Okay, the tingle was getting a little too hot to ignore. Not good.

Fortunately, another tingling sensation, the feeling that she was being watched—a far worse sensation— brought her immediately to the present. Turning her head and raising it a little bit, she spotted the camera staring at her. It looked like an alien Peeping Tom with arms and legs and one eye.

"Hmm," Reuben growled, then moved his hips in a suggestive invitation against hers.

"Okay, that does it. Show's over." With a firm thump against his chest, Talia sent an unsuspecting Reuben rolling off the makeshift mattress onto the sand.

His eyes popped open. "Hey!"

But he quieted immediately once he saw the camera. Then, as if realizing what had just happened, and the state he was currently in, he had at least enough shame to blush slightly.

"Joe, you might want to keep that camera pointed away from me. I understand this is supposed to be a family show."

Talia watched Joe's shoulders shake, then he moved on to his next target, Iris, who was up and had a troubled expression on her face. It was barely dawn—far too early for the bad news Iris was about to impart. Talia wasn't sure what could have gone wrong between the time they had fallen asleep and the time they woke, but she needed to find out.

Her first concern, however, was her hands and making sure they had healed enough not to be a nuisance for the duration of her stay. Of course, if there was a problem she only had herself to blame.

In hindsight she could admit that she'd pushed herself deliberately to prove to Reuben that she could do it. It wasn't dissimilar to the response she'd always had whenever her diving coach had told her there was something she couldn't do. She was going to have to work on that. Accountants made sensible decisions, not stubborn ones.

She gingerly removed the cotton T-shirts from around her hands. Studying them, she saw a few patches of missing skin, but no bleeding and nothing so red that she was worried about infection.

Tossing the shirts at Reuben's face, she said, "Thanks for them. And for the record, I'm not playing the role of your stuffed teddy bear for the duration of this game."

Reuben pulled the shirts off his head and smirked. "Funny, my stuffed teddy bear never gave me a hard-on in the morning."

Since she knew he was baiting her, she did the only thing a respectable woman could do in this situation and ignored him. The goal of this adventure was very clear. Stay long enough to win enough cash to bail her father out and give herself a little breathing room to find a job. Period. Getting involved with the other players, in any way, should be the furthest thing from her mind.

Not that she was buying Reuben's crude attempt at seduction. It was no doubt nothing more than a strategy for him to win. He probably thought that by seducing her he could control her. That wasn't going to happen. He might be wielding his blatant sexual allure like some kind of sword, but she had no intention of being skewered. Not when she wasn't sure she even liked him.

Making her way over to Iris, she braced herself for whatever bad news the woman had to report. She got a pretty good indication when she saw that the bucket they had used to collect fresh water yesterday was empty.

"What happened?" Talia asked even as the others were sitting up, some looking in their direction, others going through their individual morning rituals.

"There's a hole in the bucket."

Talia took the metal bucket from the older woman's hand and stared down at the tiny but visible hole smack-dab in the center of the pail.

Dino and Joe were both at camp this morning filming, but Evan was missing.

"Hey, Joe," Talia said, calling him over. "Is this supposed to be some kind of warped challenge?"

The older man looked at the bucket, but shrugged his shoulders.

"Got me. Evan didn't say anything. He dropped us off early to film and took the boat back to work on getting the game set up for today."

"What are we going to do without water?" Iris wanted to know.

At this point, most of the group had been alerted to the fact that they had a problem. Talia wasn't convinced that this was the result of faulty equipment. It seemed too staged. Probably a gimmick to garner a reaction from the group. But why there was a hole in the bucket didn't matter as much as what they were going to do now. How were they going to carry and boil water?

"Let me see." Reuben sauntered over and took the pail from Talia. He frowned when he saw the hole. "It was full last night, right?"

"It was when we brought it back from the stream," Marlie added. "I remember. It was heavy."

"We must not have noticed the hole," Iris suggested. "It must have been dripping all night and gotten bigger."

"Oh man! What kind of bullshit supplies are they giving us?" Tommy howled. "I'm dying of thirst right now."

Nancy, the last to wake, joined the group. "Oh dear. I'm sort of thirsty, too."

"We can each go to the stream and drink from our hands if we have to," Gus stated calmly.

"But Evan said it needed to be boiled," Sam reminded the group. "He said there could be parasites."

"You won't care much about a few parasites when you're suffering from dehydration," Gus replied.

"Oh man!" Tommy wailed. "No way. They've got to give us another bucket. Hey you." Tommy charged toward Dino who had been dutifully capturing everyone's reaction. The cameraman took a step back and stumbled slightly, but still kept filming. "You need to talk to someone. Get us another bucket."

Reuben captured the younger man's upper arm, halting his progress before he forced Dino into the lagoon. "Look, we can fix this until they get us a replacement. We just need to stop up the hole with something. I'm thinking maybe some rubber from the sole of one of our sneakers."

Marlie gasped. "Ew gross. I'm not drinking anything from anyone's shoe unless it's champagne and the shoe in question is Prada."

Reuben glanced over at Talia with an expression that suggested she find a way to shut the girl up.

"Hey," Talia replied directly to him cheekily. "A girl's got to have standards."

"Let me see what I can do with the bucket," Gus said. "I'm pretty good with stuff like this."

"Fine. Then I'll see what I can do about getting us something to eat."

Talia headed for the lagoon and tilted her head back to check the sky. They had no clock, but judging by the soft light that illuminated the beach, Talia figured the sun had been up for just an hour. The island birds were cawing to one another inland, and a few hopped along the beach in search of a morning snack. The water of the lagoon was perfectly still, and she decided now would be the best time to fish.

Easing her way into the water so as to cause the least amount of ripple as possible, she found a spot where she was up to her knees just a few feet from the shore. Then carefully, she lowered her hands into the water and waited.

"What do you think you're doing?"

Reuben's sharp question had her abruptly lifting her head, but she managed to keep her body still.

"I'm fishing," she whispered back.

"Why are you whispering?"

She didn't bother to answer, but instead shook her head and concentrated on the shapes moving past her legs. A silver fish came to examine her fingers.

A little farther, just a little farther to the right and...
Splash!

Snapping her hands together, she trapped the fish by the tail and in a single motion tossed it to where Reuben was standing. Instinctively he backed off and let the small fish drop to the sand to flop around.

Talia smiled at his horrified reaction. "You're not going to last very long if you're afraid of fish."

He grimaced. "I'm not afraid. You just took me by surprise. I didn't think you could catch fish with your hands."

"Small ones," she said quietly. "Why don't you find a stick we can impale them on?"

"Screw that. I want to see what you're doing."

He started to enter the water, when Talia held her hand up in a motion to stop. "Easy. If you cause a disturbance in the water, the fish will bolt. Keep your movements slow and graceful."

"Graceful," he muttered as he made his way to her. The water was a little deeper, just over his knees. She could see him studying the area, probably for the first time really seeing it. The lagoon was surrounded by the island. On one side there was the white sand beach that led to the thick growth beyond. But the rest of it was a volcanic rock formation, covered in green life that rose from the water maybe thirty or forty feet high. A thin stream of water ran off the rock's edge in an endless falls.

"That will be good to clean off under," he said using his chin to point.

Talia followed his gaze, but shook her head. "I don't think you could stand under it. It looks like the surface drops severely a few feet that way." She showed him. "See how dark the water is underneath it. Who knows how deep it goes?"

"What do we do now?"

"What makes you think I'm going to teach you my tricks?"

"Because right now there are too many mouths to feed for one person to handle. That silver fish you tagged isn't more than a mouthful. And I can tell right off the bat that you're too soft to keep what you catch all to yourself."

That was true. It wasn't in her nature to eat while others went hungry. Then again, how many people could do something like that? She thought of Tommy's blue backpack and decided probably more people than she realized. Survival could be a ruthless game.

"Dip your hands into the water, slowly. Then you just wait for a fish to swim by and… Gotcha!" She tossed another one onto the sand and smiled, infinitely pleased with herself. In her mind, she whispered a silent thank-you to her mother for passing on her tricks. She was thrilled that she hadn't forgotten them.

"Shit," he muttered, watching the beach where the fish flopped about until finally settling. Their activities caught the attention of Gus and he wandered over.

"Nice catch," he called to them. "I think I got the bucket sealed. It's holding water. Iris and Marlie set off to get some fresh water to boil."

"We're going to try and get a small fish for everyone," Talia said softly, but loud enough for Gus to hear. Understanding how he could help, he went in search of something to collect the catch and Talia went back to work.

A few feet to her right, Reuben was staring at the water with fierce concentration. Then he snapped his hands together and sent an armful of water sailing through the air.

"Damn it."

"This is all about patience. And stillness," Talia told him. "You've got to be like driftwood, a part of the scenery. Then you wait until the fish comes to you and…there!"

Fish number three hit the sand.

"You're a freak, you know that?" He put his hands back in the water and waited.

Talia did the same, but bristled a little at his description. "I'm not a freak. I just happen to know a little something about fishing."

"And you're not afraid of sharks. And you swim like a fish and you can start fires with your bare hands."

"Gus helped," she mumbled.

"All I'm saying is you're not like any accountant I've ever met."

"But I am an accountant," she insisted.

He shrugged. "If that's what you want to tell yourself."

"What the hell does that mean?"

"Got it!" His hands were coming out of the water and she could see that he had a fish, but he didn't throw it far enough to reach the sand. He huffed with frustration, and clenched his jaw so tightly that she imagined his temper would get the better of him and he would give up. Most men hated it when a woman could do anything better than they could. She knew that from growing up on a boat with men around.

But he just shook it off and dipped his hands back in the water and waited.

For a second she found herself wondering how deep Reuben went. She suspected pretty deep, like the lagoon, which unfortunately only made him more attractive.

He lifted his head and caught her staring at him.

His teeth flashed against the contrast of his brown skin and Talia scolded herself for being affected by that smile. "See something you like, sugar? Say the word and we can take a long walk away from the group. You and me for an hour…or two."

"In your dreams."

"Honey, in my dreams we're talking about four or five hours. No physical limitations to hold me back there."

Shaking her head in an attempt to cleanse the image of the two of them naked and entwined taking shape behind her eyes, Talia tried to redirect the conversation. "So…that's strange about the bucket, isn't it?" she said quietly.

"Yeah," he replied sarcastically. "Real strange."

"You don't think it was just shoddy equipment." It was a statement rather than a question.

"I think it was another stunt."

"How can you be sure?"

"The hole was made purposefully. It was obvious. No rust, no seam splitting, and it was dead center. Someone put a hole in the bucket on purpose. Evan, I'm guessing. Just to see how we would react."

"That's a harsh test," Talia stated. "Drinking water is serious business on an island. And if someone had panicked and tried to drink directly from the stream they might have gotten really sick."

"I'm sure Dino or Joe would have stopped us before it got that far. No doubt they probably had a back-up pail tucked away in the woods somewhere just in case. But Gus was on top of it."

"He seems to know what he's doing."

"He's ex-military. My guess is army or naval intelligence."

That took Talia by surprise. "How could you possibly know that? Did he tell you?"

Nobody had been as closemouthed as Reuben during the trip out to the island, but no one had revealed much about his or her day job, either. At least not in a public forum. It was entirely possible that Gus and

Reuben had formed some sort of alliance without any-one knowing. She wasn't sure why, but it bothered her to know that maybe someone else knew more about the man fishing with her than she did.

"No, he didn't tell me. But trust me, I know. I have a sense about these things."

"A sense?"

"Yeah."

"Want to tell me where that sense comes from?"

He paused for a moment, and met her eyes as if searching for something. She imagined he didn't find it because he shook his head at her request.

Deciding to ignore him and his sense, she went back to focusing on what was important. After almost an hour in the water, Talia had snagged four more fish and Reuben had pulled in two. Gus had used a palm leaf to gather them up and the camp applauded their morning success while Joe continued to film.

Iris was able to cook the fish on a stick. Each fish was only worth a few bites, but only Marlie had the nerve to complain that she was still hungry.

Almost on cue, the sound of an engine could be heard and the boat careened around the crest of the island into the inlet. Evan, naturally, was at the helm. He beached it, then joined everyone by the fire.

"Well, it seems everyone survived the first night. And based on those fish bones, it looks like you were able to eat a little this morning."

"A very little," Marlie said, pouting. As the smallest in the group, she'd gotten the smallest fish, and it was clear she wasn't happy about it.

"Joe let me know about the bucket. That definitely wasn't planned. The next time one of us heads back to the yacht we'll get you a replacement for that. But for now you all seemed to have managed."

"Yeah," Tommy chortled. "Good thing Gus's feet don't smell."

"Right," Evan drawled. "Today will be our first contest. Like I said yesterday, you're competing as teams. For the team that wins, each of you will be able to choose one item off your wish lists. For the other team, you'll be making a decision as to whether or not one of you should leave. Keep in mind nobody *has* to go home. But the longer people continue in the game, the longer the eventual winner will have to endure. If everyone is ready, get your shoes on, and get in the boat. We're going to another cove on the south side of the island that we have set up."

Talia thought about the list that she'd made out. A fishing spear, a sleeping bag, a waterproof poncho, blankets and some luxury items like a toothbrush, soap and shampoo that would help to make life bearable on a tropical island for an indefinite period of time.

Then she considered the group and wondered what Nancy might have on her list. Probably a picture of her kids, which would serve absolutely no practical purpose, but would no doubt make for great television. And Marlie was probably salivating over a chance to win some nail polish.

It was evident that winning whatever game Evan had laid out was critical if only to ensure that she was better equipped to help feed the group. If they did win, the spear would be her first pick. With it she could catch larger, meatier fish from the inlet.

Stepping into her sneakers, which were still a little damp from yesterday, Talia ignored the discomfort and headed for the boat with her mind made up to win. Technically, she and Reuben had finished last in the race to the island, but she had no doubt who the strongest team was. Granted, the other team had three men, but hopefully she and Reuben could make up for whatever disadvantages Iris and Nancy would bring.

The trip around the island was surprisingly long. Having the scope of it now, Talia could see the forest that blanketed the heart of it was deep and peaked with varying different spears of rock. Leftovers from a volcanic belch.

"Did you survey the whole island?" she asked Evan, who was once again at the helm of the boat, carelessly steering it over the water.

Both Joe and Dino were along for the ride, making it a tight fit—especially with their equipment. But neither had their cameras out and at the ready, no doubt saving their batteries for what was to come. Everyone else was gazing at the island, or at the water on the lookout for Nancy's shark. Talia didn't have the heart to tell them that if they did see a shark, it was unlikely to be the same one they had had the close encounter with yesterday. No doubt the idea of more than one shark in the ocean would be alarming for Nancy.

She'd already gotten queasy over the fish this morning.

Then again, everyone had made faces of varying degrees as they skewered the fish and cooked them whole. Marlie and Nancy had been on the verge of passing it up, but Reuben had set them both straight. Fish would be breakfast, lunch and dinner for the duration of their stay. Any fruits or nuts they found in the forest would only serve as a compliment to the protein and nutrition offered by the sea's bounty. If they didn't eat, they would pass out and he wasn't picking anyone up.

Eventually they ate. Nancy had gone so far as to politely thank the cook.

"Sorry," Evan shouted back with his hand wrapped around his ear to let her know he hadn't caught her question.

"The island. Did you survey the center of it?"

"Absolutely. We know everything there is to know about this little slice of heaven. We wouldn't have picked it, if it wasn't perfect for the producers' needs."

The producers needed ratings. She doubted much else mattered. She also doubted Evan. If he'd been to the center of the island, she'd eat…anything, actually. She was still pretty hungry.

He navigated the boat around a natural jetty into another cove that wasn't too dissimilar from where they had made camp. It scooped into an inlet that wound its way into yet another larger lagoon. Only here the water was much bluer and deeper in color, which meant an ocean floor full of holes and craters formed from ancient volcanic activity.

The course for the upcoming challenge loomed in front of them. Parallel buoys strung together with rope to bobbing two-foot-square rafts painted in green and red marked spots throughout the lagoon. The set-up made no sense at the moment.

Evan cut the engine and the boat meandered the last few yards to the shore. Without having to be told, everyone poured out of the boat into the knee-deep water and made their way to the beach, where two canoes sat on the sand. Farther back, two ladders, in the same red and green colors, were pushed against a high incline along a rock cliff. They gathered and watched as Joe barked some orders to Dino. He didn't seem to understand them at first, but quickly got in sync, hefted the camera on his shoulder and headed for the red ladder.

Everyone watched as he climbed it. Some to see if he would drop the camera, some just to see where he was going. Talia was curious to know if the ladder would hold. In keeping with the island theme, the thing was made out of bamboo and was no doubt straining under the weight of Dino and his camera.

"Don't worry everyone," Evan told the group as heads that had automatically tilted up to follow Dino's ascent turned their attention back to the host. "The ladders are secured to the cliff face with hooks and rope. Now, here is how this is going to work. You all see the buoys, the two canoes and the two ladders that lead to the cliff peak. There are two paths up there—one that winds down to the lagoon, the other that drops off over this inlet. The test is simple. One member of each team will climb the ladder to the peak. Once there, he or she will have a choice to take the low road or to jump off the cliff into this lagoon."

Someone gasped behind her, but Talia couldn't be

sure who it was. "And you're sure that the water is deep enough here?"

Evan kept his smile firmly in place, but Talia could sense he was becoming annoyed with her endless questions. Tough. She wasn't taking any chances.

"Yes, of course. This has been tested thoroughly by professional stunt people. Now while this is happening another teammate will take the canoe out onto the water. Your goal will be to pick up each of your team members—the one coming off the cliff and the two others waiting out on the rafts. As you can see, if your teammate can make the jump, the distance the person will have to paddle is much less than taking the low road.

"Once you have all your teammates, the first group to have everyone across the finish line behind my shoulder will win. And you all know what's at stake if you win. One item off your must-have list, which could make the difference in this game. Is everyone clear?"

Consensually, they nodded.

"Then teams get together and pick who will be doing what. You have five minutes and then the game begins."

Talia and Reuben huddled together while Nancy and Iris already seemed to know their roles. They were each heading for the rafts in the water.

"I'll jump," Reuben said immediately.

"I'll jump," Talia countered. "You're stronger. You'll be able to paddle faster."

"Yeah, but I don't want to have to paddle all the way into the lagoon."

"I'll jump."

He craned his head up to see where Dino was positioned on the edge of the cliff. "That's at least thirty feet."

"Yep. Trust me. Get the canoe close, but not too close. I don't want to smack into you."

He smirked and she could tell he doubted her, but he would soon find out. "If we win this, what are you picking off your list?"

"A fishing spear," she told him, somehow understanding that he was asking because he didn't want to select duplicate items.

He nodded. "Good. Then I'll go with blankets. Tonight we can snuggle."

She didn't give him the satisfaction of making a lame retort. Instead she just walked over to get ready for the race. The other team had picked Tommy as their jumper. He was hopping up and down on the balls of his feet trying to look like an athlete getting ready for a serious competition.

Talia had been in enough competitions in her life to know that half of every athlete's performance was mental.

"I see you don't have your backpack with you, Tommy. Did you leave it back at camp?"

Immediately, his attention was focused on her rather than the race. He was glaring at her beneath the cover of his hand that he used to shade his eyes from the sun.

"What about it?"

"Nothing. I'm just hoping it's safe, that's all."

"All right, Gus and Reuben you're going to be rowing," Evan declared. "Talia and Tommy will be jumping. Iris, Nancy, Sam and Marlie are making their way to the rafts. Once everyone is in position, I'll say go."

He paused and Joe signaled up to Dino. Talia heard the senior cameraman curse something under his breath, frustrated apparently with Dino for not picking up his signals quickly enough. Finally Dino was in position and Joe was in the middle of the beach ready to film the climb, as well as what was happening in the water.

Talia watched as Iris struggled to climb up on the farthest green raft, leaving the one closer to the beach for Nancy. Evan raised his hand in the air, catching Talia's attention.

"Ready…" Next to her she heard Tommy scrambling for the red ladder. Once a cheater, she thought.

"Go."

She sprang into action and started to climb. Tommy was three rungs ahead of her and moving faster. She was taking her time, making sure that her foot hit each rung and that her weight was pushing the ladder against the incline. Secured or not, the wrong kind of move could pull the rungs from the rock and plunge the ladder, with whatever body happened to be attached, to the beach.

Talia checked her distance. She was about halfway up, but Tommy was near the top. She was about to quicken her pace when she heard a creaking noise from his ladder. Eye-level with where the ladder was secured, she could see that the ropes holding the bamboo poles to the drilled rings were loose and hanging in two pieces. She didn't have to know when Tommy took his next step, because she could see the ladder tilt, separating from the cliff to stand almost vertically.

"Tommy," she called up to him. "Lean forward. Now!"

"Huh?"

By looking over his shoulder, he shifted his weight the opposite way she needed him to and instantly he'd gone from ladder-climber to stilt-walker.

"Whoa!" he cried out, but fortunately pitched forward. The ladder hit with a smack against the rock face. For a moment, they were both still, realizing that a slightly different shift could have sent him on a deadly thirty-foot drop. The second Talia caught her breath she was reaching for the rope. If she could secure just one side of the ladder, he was close enough to the top and aware now of the situation to make the rest of the climb.

"Hold still until I'm done." Talia was hanging precariously off her ladder, listening as the strain from her position pulled at the fastenings. Needing a few more inches, she reached out even farther, wrapping her leg around one of the poles to secure herself as she stretched. She pulled the dangling rope through the ring that was drilled into the rock and tied it as tightly as she could.

"Okay. But go easy."

Tommy's eyes were pinned on what she was doing. Then he checked her expression and must have determined that she had a face he could trust.

Once again he started climbing and, ignoring her warning, was moving even faster. That's when it occurred to her that this was still a competition and she was going to have to do her own climbing if she was going to claim that fishing spear.

With him so far ahead of her, her only hope at this point was that he would get freaked out by the jump and take the low road. Given his ability to maintain his cool on the ladder, that might not be the case. Tommy might want to spend his life doing nothing, but he had no problem doing that as quickly and recklessly as he could.

She saw him reach the top of the cliff. Saw Dino back up to give him space to decide which path he was going to take. Immediately, he went for the cliff. Talia forced her legs to move faster. Driving her now was the sheer need to win.

How could she have forgotten how competitive she was?

Just as she reached the top and caught her breath, she spotted Tommy near the edge looking over it to the black water below.

"No way, man—that's crazy." He shook his head. "No one is making that jump." Their eyes met and the kid actually had the nerve to laugh. "Forget it! You're never going to do it."

Clearly confident in his assessment of her capabilities, he bolted past her toward the path that would take him to the lagoon. Talia could see Gus starting to row for him and she could see Reuben behind him getting his paddle ready to do the same.

"So little faith." She stepped up to the cliff, surveyed her landing spots, then counted back five steps.

One, two, three, hop, hop…. Over.

She was falling through the air and it was perfect. Her body arched, her eyes searched for and found the markers she'd picked out on the other side of the lagoon. On cue, she tilted her chest out, then turned her body over and grabbed her wrists, flattening her palms horizontally upon entry.

The plunge was a familiar pain as her skin slapped at the water before it could penetrate, but, oh, so worth it. Not trusting the environment to be completely smooth like the pools she was used to, Talia shallowed her body quickly, using her arms both to act as brakes and to turn her toward the surface. When her head bobbed up, the canoe was in front of her eyes and Reuben was wearing that familiar smirk.

"Nice," he noted as he reached out his hand to pull her into the boat. Talia could see Tommy still swimming out to the center of the lagoon and Gus furiously rowing for him. She picked up one of the paddles and seamlessly they began to cut through the water.

"So I've just got to ask one question," Reuben called as they made their way to the raft where Iris was waiting to be picked up.

"What's that?"

"How's the hand?"

Talia smiled. "Guess I gave away my secret."

"I would have recognized that swan dive anywhere." He paused for a second. "It's beautiful."

She wasn't sure why—many people she'd met had commented on it—but the idea that he'd seen her dive and had appreciated it made her feel slightly sentimental. Maybe because he was such a hard-ass. If he could recognize the beauty in her sport, that told her something about him. More than he'd ever revealed with words.

Iris was still laughing as she carefully made her way off the raft and into the boat. Reuben was there to give her a hand, while Talia kept her paddle in the water to hold the small boat still.

"That showed him," she snorted as soon as her soft bottom plopped on the seat. "If you could have seen Tommy staring at you. I only wish I had a better view of his expression. Maybe that cameraman fellow will show us the video."

The old woman continued to chuckle as Talia and Reuben got back to work, stroking on a direct course for Nancy, who was furiously waving her arms as if they would miss her round body on a green raft in the middle of the water.

They pulled alongside and this time Reuben didn't so much give her a hand as he bodily lifted her off the raft and into the canoe. She made a squeaky sound but quieted when she realized she was safe.

"No sharks this time," she announced in a way that was probably supposed to be a joke, but sounded far too serious for anyone to laugh.

Moving efficiently through the water, on their way to the beach and the finish line, Talia glanced over her shoulder to check on the status of the other team. They'd already picked up Marlie and now were trying to get a nervous-looking Sam into the boat. Like Nancy, he'd forgone the life jacket for this event, but even from a distance she could see it was a mistake. His fear of falling was making the transition from the raft to the boat that much harder.

Talia's paddle hit the sand in the shallow water and she focused her attention forward again. Reuben was hopping out and pulling the canoe on to the shore. Both Nancy and Iris were able to step out onto the sand. Talia stepped into the shallow water even as her team sprinted toward the finish line that Evan had traced in the sand.

"Move it, sugar," Reuben called to her.

But her eyes were still on the red team. Sam was in the boat, but he was standing, trying to use his outstretched arms to balance himself. It wasn't going to work.

"Son of a bitch," she muttered.

Moving before it actually happened, Talia was already knee-deep in the water when she saw Sam topple over—even as Gus reached out to catch him—and his head made contact with the raft. More worried about the prospect of blood in the water than she was about the concussion he might have suffered, she quickly dove forward and began to swim out to them.

"What the hell!"

It was Reuben shouting to her, but she ignored him. The only one she knew would be of any use in the situation was Gus and if Sam went under the surface he was going to need help. She pushed her way through the water, kicking with an extra burst to get there as fast as she could. Then she sensed something large coming up behind her. For a moment she tightened, but then felt the tremors of a swimmer stroking next to her, coming even, then passing her—a feeling she wasn't used to at all.

When she lifted her face, she saw Reuben's red swim trunks plunging deep, letting her know that Sam was indeed underneath the surface. Tommy and Marlie were still in the boat searching for signs of life. Talia couldn't see Gus, which meant he must be under, as well.

"Do you see anything?"

Tommy shook his head. "He hit his head on the raft. I tried to hold him up."

"Where did he go under?"

Tommy pointed to the raft and with a dolphinlike move she arched her body and dove. She saw a blurry Gus straight ahead. He was rising up with empty arms. Then she turned a little to the left and saw Reuben trying to pull a lifeless Sam along. She kicked over and grabbed one arm, and the two of them got his head above water quickly. Gus had gotten back into the boat, and he and Tommy worked together to lift Sam into it. As soon as Sam's midsection hit the edge of the canoe, he threw up the salt water that was in his lungs.

Marlie screeched, but Talia breathed a sigh of relief because the next sound she heard was Sam coughing, sputtering, then gasping for breath.

Together she and Reuben exchanged a satisfied nod.

"You two climb in," Gus told them.

"There's not enough room. We'll swim back. Is he coherent?"

Sam's head was in Marlie's lap, his legs sprawled over the side.

"His eyes are open. But he's got a major lump on his head," she reported. "Are you okay?" she shouted, apparently under the impression that a bump on the head could cause deafness.

"My head hurts," Sam mumbled, lifting his hand to the bump.

"That's a good sign," Talia told Gus, who was taking his cue from them. "He's breathing. He's coherent.

We'll have to watch for signs of a concussion, but he should be fine. Get him to the beach."

Gus and Tommy each took a paddle and began to make their way back to shore. Once they were off, Talia started to breaststroke her way back. Again Reuben swam up next to her.

"You're fast," she noted.

"You have no idea."

"I didn't mean your moves," she snorted. "I meant your stroke."

He flashed her a rakish grin. "Honey, I can stroke it fast or slow. Whatever you prefer."

"You're a pig."

He laughed again. "You have no idea."

They swam the rest of the way in silence and pulled themselves up to the beach. As soon as they did, they saw Tommy jumping up and waving his arms.

"This counts. This totally counts," he told Evan.

All four members of the red team had made it beyond the finish line first.

Evan glanced over at Reuben and Talia, who were still laboring to catch their breath after rescuing a red team member. Judging by his expression, he had enough sense to be worried about how Reuben would react. Talia was sort of waiting for it herself.

"You've got to be fucking kidding me." Reuben set his hands on his hips, glaring at both Tommy and Evan, but it seemed that he didn't know who to fight first.

Gus, clearly irritated with the young man, tried to intervene. "This isn't right. They won."

"You said the first team across the line. That's us."

"I did say that," Evan said grimly. He shrugged his shoulders in a manner to suggest that he didn't see another way out. "Red team wins."

"Yes!" Tommy shouted.

Then Evan walked over to where Joe was filming and whispered something into his ear. Immediately, Joe shifted the camera to Reuben.

Reuben flipped the camera the bird.

"That's going to need to be edited," Talia quipped.

"Be glad we don't have our mics on or I would really be giving them something to edit."

"Let it go," she said. She was tempted to run a hand over his bare arm in a soothing gesture, but didn't because she doubted it would soothe him, and she was very much afraid she would like the feel of his skin under her hands.

Best not to go there.

"Yeah, I'll let it go. I know whose fault this is."

"Tommy's," Talia stated, sensing they were in agreement.

"Nope. Yours. If you'd stayed on the beach I would have gotten Sam. But no, you've got to be Miss Tess Trueheart, get your damn nose in everything. Next time stay out of it."

After that blistering attack, he stormed off, turning his back on her before he could see that she was now flipping him the bird.

Joe lowered the shoulder camera and shook his head, clearly annoyed that he was going to lose some of that footage.

"Yeah," she told him as she walked by. "You're going to have to edit that one, too."

Chapter 4

Purposefully, almost resentfully on the green team's part, each faction sat on separate sides of the fire. Sam still had a lump the size of a golf ball on his head and hadn't said much since the incident.

"I don't know. Maybe we should take him to, like, a doctor or something," Marlie suggested as Sam continued to stare blankly at the fire.

"Evan said that anyone who leaves the show is automatically out," Tommy reminded everyone.

Talia couldn't tell by his tone if Tommy was trying to encourage Sam to stay or hoping that he would go, leaving them with one less contestant. The game was about attrition, but it didn't seem fair that an injury should take someone out.

Realizing that he was the topic of conversation, Sam

seemed to come to attention. He blinked his eyes a few times. "I'm fine," he stated adamantly, even as he raised his hand once more to check the lump.

Talia considered the idea that maybe they shouldn't be giving Sam a choice to stay or go—rather that they should be using the emergency walkie-talkie to call for help. Her concerns deepened when Sam appeared almost surprised by the air mattress that Evan brought to him as the first item from his necessity list.

At first Talia and everyone else merely attributed his sudden haziness to the headache. Since the fall he'd said little. And when he did say something it was to apologize for being so clumsy. But a few hours later and he didn't seem to be coming around. On the positive side, his pupils weren't dilated and he showed no signs of nausea to indicate a concussion. She supposed that without a sufficient medical reason, it would be awfully harsh to eject him from the game if that wasn't what he wanted.

The mattress, which he and a few others had spent all day blowing up, probably wasn't the most practical item for survival, but at least he would sleep better than everyone else tonight. Then again, without the collective warmth of the group's body heat, maybe not. Clouds were rolling in, hiding and revealing the moon in spurts and the wind had picked up. It was still tropically warm, but without shelter or blankets, it would make for an uncomfortable evening.

Marlie, unsurprisingly, had a different set of priorities for her necessity item and had chosen a comb. Tommy had opted for food. Not something to catch food, and the rules of the game wouldn't allow for a long-term supply, so it was just a single food item. He'd stated that every item on his list was a food item. This time it was a single packet of Pop-Tarts. He'd eaten it in seconds and hadn't offered to share.

Typically, Gus was the only sensible one in the group. He'd gone with a fishing pole. It could be useful in the lagoon, but it wouldn't be as efficient as the spear Talia would have chosen. He'd caught a single fish since the challenge and, although he'd offered to share, there wasn't enough meat on the poor fish to make a dent in their hunger.

Tommy was the only one not going hungry tonight.

"Look at that. A freakin' comb," Reuben muttered as he sat down next to Talia. They watched as Marlie ran the thick comb through her long blond hair. A hundred times, fifty each side. Talia knew because she had counted.

She said nothing in response to his exacerbation, choosing instead to dismiss him. Then for good measure she scooted a few inches away, but that was probably overkill.

"What?" he prompted, following her scoot with one of his own until his hip bumped hers.

Distracted by the touch of his skin and irritated because it had distracted her, she got up and headed for the water. Away from the blazing fire, it was chilly, but she figured a little cool air might work to soothe her boiling temper.

And if she were honest, it would settle her libido, too.

Then she felt him step up behind her, not touching,

but close enough that she could just sense him, and she knew she was kidding herself. Her libido wasn't going anywhere.

It was all so strange. She couldn't remember a time when any man had ever affected her so quickly and so completely as this one did. It was as if once she'd gotten a whiff of him, he'd taken root under her skin. Still not ready to give in to her crazy body's demand, though, she stepped forward and away from him until her toes touched the water. Peeking down, she was grateful to see there wasn't any steam coming off them.

"What?"

There was no point in replying and the silent routine had always worked to irritate her dad whenever she was annoyed with him. Which, given his often impractical nature, was quite often.

Reuben apparently was as easy to frustrate as her father.

"Oh, come on," he wailed. "You're not pissed off about what I said earlier."

Still no reply.

"You know I'm right."

That had her reacting. "Right? You basically told me to behave like a little lady and let the big strong man do all the rescuing."

He considered her statement, then nodded. "That about sums it up."

"So you're not only a pig, but a chauvinistic one, at that. You know what's sad? It's just so predictable." She smiled in a way that offered no humor but showed a lot of teeth. Hers maybe weren't as white as his, but they would make an impact in the dark. "I'm no one's little lady."

"No, you're the big bad Olympic diver. I remember thinking anyone who would voluntarily jump off a ten-meter platform into a pool of water was either suicidal or lacking in fear. And people who aren't afraid make me nervous. Fear is what keeps people from doing stupid stuff."

"Like antagonizing a shark?" she snapped.

"Honey, make no mistake. I was scared spitless."

It surprised her that he would admit it. But instead of weakening him, which it could have, it only made him more real. Damn it. It was becoming harder and harder to resist the asshole when the man beneath it was turning out to be a good guy.

"I wasn't trying to be anyone's hero," Talia qualified. "I didn't think with Sam. I saw him go under. I did what I had to do."

"And what about the ladder?"

This time she turned around. In the fading light she could barely make out his irises, but what she could see was pinned on her. It was the first time he had mentioned anything about the ladder. Given everyone's positioning, she hadn't thought that anyone else saw what had happened. Evan, who had the best vantage point, certainly hadn't said anything.

"You saw that?"

"Sugar, when it comes to you I don't miss much. What happened up there?" he wanted to know.

"The rope came untied so the ladder wasn't secure," she answered simply.

But it wasn't that simple. Something about it had been bugging her all day, but between losing the competition and worrying about Sam's condition, she hadn't worked out what.

"All I saw was the ladder pull away from the cliff face suddenly. Then I saw you holding on to both ladders. Considering it was Tommy up there with you, I wasn't sure if you were trying to save him or push him off."

She smiled tentatively. "It was a close call."

Reuben turned back to the fire where the group was now singing camp songs led by former Brownie troop leader, Nancy. Talia could see that he was scowling but she didn't think it had anything to do with Nancy's singing.

"What? What's bothering you?" She was hoping that whatever he said might help her pinpoint what was bothering her about it, too.

"What condition was the rope in? Could you see? Were the ends frayed or unraveled looking?"

In her mind she saw the two metal clasps that had been drilled into the rock on either side of the ladder and the two ropes hanging from both of them. That's what had been bugging her!

"Yes. They were. The ends were…fuzzy, uneven. Not like the tie had simply come undone, but that it had been cut. What does that mean?"

He shrugged. "Somebody put a hole in the bucket. Somebody cut the ropes. I thought maybe the show people were playing with us. Now, I'm not so sure."

Talia refused to consider the conclusion he was alluding to. "You don't think one of us—"

"A million dollars is a lot of money. The sooner people get knocked out, the sooner someone is going to collect."

"No," she refuted. "I don't buy it. This is a game! This is TV. These people have all been screened by producers. Besides, no one had an opportunity to cut the ropes while we were on the beach. They were fastened halfway up the ladder."

"That beach was just on the other side of this inlet. A strong swimmer could have made it there and back this morning."

"You, me, Iris and possibly Gus are the only ones who fit that description." The point that it couldn't have been either one of them, since each knew where the other one was every minute of that morning didn't have to be said. "You think Iris is out to hurt people so she can nab her over-fifty condo? Or Gus for a log cabin? It's ludicrous."

"You don't know how well these people can swim. It could all be an act. Sam's accident could have been just a way to distract us."

"You really are paranoid."

"Observant. Cautious. You should be, too. Or is that beyond your skills as an *accountant*?"

Just the way he said the word had her clicking her teeth together in annoyance. "Why do you continue to harp on that? It's just a job."

He didn't answer; instead, he pointed to the water where a beam of light broke through the black sky and water, and the sound of a motor could be heard over the crackling fire in the background. Talia and Reuben made their way back to the group to get ready for the night's events ahead.

The boat pulled up close to the shore. Evan hopped out, followed by Joe and Dino. After Evan had dropped off the prizes earlier, he had indicated that the next time he came it would be to "take" something.

It was time for the first castoff.

"A few things before we start this," he began and pointed his fingers in the direction of Sam still sitting on his mattress. "Sam, are you all right to continue?"

The group grew quiet and all eyes focused on Sam.

He squirmed a little under the pressure, but eventually managed to spit out, "I…uh…yes, I'm okay."

"Excellent," Evan noted. "Now before I have you put on your microphones, I do want to share some news from mainland Hawaii that the yacht captain told me about via the radio before we started over here. First let me say, there is absolutely nothing to worry about. We just want everyone to keep their eyes open while they're on the island. It seems there was a break-in at some Hollywood star's home in Waikiki. She was shooting a film on the island and staying at the bungalow for the duration of the shoot. Anyway, she was killed and the person made off with several million dollars of her jewelry."

"And you're telling us this because—" Gus prompted.

"Which actress?" Marlie wanted to know. "I mean millions in jewelry, we're talking somebody big, right? J. Lo big."

"Carney Mellon."

There were a few gasps from the group, most noticeably from Marlie. "Carney? Really? She's dead. But she had her own show on network TV and everything. She won an Emmy and she was in that big action movie last year."

Nancy squinted her eyes. "I don't know her. Which one was that?"

"Uh, duh. Everybody knows her. *Along Came a Killer.* It was a huge breakout film for her. She's been courting the A-list ever since. The movie that she was filming in Waikiki was supposed to have been even bigger. I tried to get on the set as an extra the day before we were supposed to report to the marina, but they already had enough blondes. I can't believe she's dead."

Tommy scoffed. "Guess her killer came along."

Talia was mostly sure that he didn't mean to sound as crass and thoughtless as he did. Then she noted the backpack that was still on his shoulders and had been since they had returned from the challenge. It was a blatant reminder of his character, or lack thereof.

"You still haven't told us why we're supposed to care about a dead actress and some missing jewelry," Reuben pointed out to the host.

There were no easy smiles from Evan this time. "The police department in Waikiki has this theory that the killer escaped on one of the ships leaving out of the marina closest to the actress's home. There were a bunch of private vessels that set sail during the time frame when they believe she was killed. Plus, two cruise ships. And...our yacht. The police radioed all the vessels with the warning to keep a lookout for stowaways, but really I think they're just taking every precaution."

"Wait," Nancy interrupted him. "I want to be sure I understand. Are you saying that there could be a killer back on the yacht?"

"No," Evan assured her. "The crew has checked the boat from top to bottom, helm to stern, and there are no stowaways."

"And there wouldn't be if the killer left the yacht and headed for land," Gus supplied, vocalizing what everyone was thinking and at the same time making it clear why Evan was telling them this in the first place.

"It's a very remote possibility," Evan admitted. "Please, you all have to understand if we thought that any of you were in real danger, we would get you off this island and back on the yacht as soon as possible. But the truth is this is all just conjecture and suspicion."

Silence descended on the group and an underlying tension crackled among them as loudly as twigs crackling in the campfire.

"Of course, you all have the option to back out now if you want. Just say the word."

No one did.

"Okay then, if everyone could mic up," Evan announced. "We didn't want to get any of that on film. But this part is for real."

For real.

There was an oxymoron if Talia had ever heard one. She was still digesting the news of the missing murderer and the implications of what that meant in light of everything that had already happened to them, but it didn't seem to fit. If there was a killer hiding out, what possible gain could come from putting a hole in a pail or sabotaging a race? In this instance, she had to have faith that the events in Hawaii were far removed from what was happening on the island.

They all took their time to hook up the small units to their clothes. Once that was done, they waited for the host to set the dramatic stage for what was to come.

"Well, we all know what happens next. In future events we'll do this as a group, but tonight this only impacts one team. Green, you know who you are. Reuben, Talia, Nancy and Iris. You raced a good race, maybe even a winning one. But a technicality beat you in the end."

"A techni— What the fu—" Reuben started to interrupt, but Evan continued to talk over him.

"Now it's your turn to decide who is the strongest. Who is the weakest. Who wants to stay, who wants to go. You'll pick the person you feel is the strongest member of the team, then that person, and that person alone, will choose who should go."

"I suppose I should volunteer to go," Nancy offered timidly. "I mean it's obvious I'm the weakest link and I would hate for Talia to be put in a position to give me the boot. She's been so nice."

Talia could see Reuben's eyebrows arch slightly at the mention of her being the one to get the nod as the strongest team member, but he said nothing. There was no question he was physically stronger, even in the water. But she'd made the dive during the event, and she'd brought more fish to the fire that morning. Those factors, plus Nancy and Iris simply liked her better—no shock there—weighed heavily in her favor.

However, Nancy was right. The last thing Talia wanted to do was start kicking people off the island. Unless this was an attempt from Nancy to get back to the yacht while still saving some face. Maybe in her mind it seemed more honorable to declare herself the weakest link, rather than admit she suddenly was afraid of a possible killer on the island. Still, the name of the game was to get down to one. The quicker they did it, regardless of the reason, the faster it would end.

"Plus, I was the last-minute replacement," Nancy continued. "Makes me sort of the odd woman out. Yes, I definitely think I should be the one to leave." With that she stood up.

Shockingly however, Iris intervened. The older woman stood on legs that Talia could see weren't as steady as they had been up until this point.

"Sit down. You're not going anywhere. I am. Talia would have to pick you and, truth is, I think this experience is doing you some good. You need a little toughening up and this place can do that. Not to mention it's a ratty thing that happened for us to have to make this choice. And personally, I can't live with rats." She shot a pointed glance at Tommy and he had the grace to turn his head.

"Are you sure?" Talia asked.

"Absolutely. The deal is we get at least some money for each day we're here right?" Iris looked to the host. Slowly, Evan nodded as if unsure how much he should reveal. "Yes. Basically a small stipend for agreeing to be on the show. But nothing close to the million-dollar prize."

"I don't need a million dollars. Just enough money for a deposit on my luxury condo. Besides, I'm cold and hungry. I turn into a bitch when I'm cold and hungry and I would hate for you all to see that side of me."

This had a few members of the group chuckling, including Reuben.

"This means I go back to the ship, right?" she asked Evan.

"Absolutely. A warm bed, fine cuisine and a beverage of your choice."

"Now that's what I'm talking about." Iris gathered up her sack and slung it over her shoulder as Joe followed her every movement and Dino scanned the reactions of the group.

Purposefully, she stopped in front of Talia and Reuben, and pointed her finger in Reuben's face. "You don't let anything bad happen to her."

"No, ma'am," he responded instinctively.

"And you," she said now pointing at Talia, but her eyes still on Reuben. "You kick his butt. I have a feeling he needs it."

"Yes, ma'am," Talia replied. With that everyone got up to wave her off as she climbed into the motorboat. Joe and Dino dropped their cameras and everyone else unhooked their microphones.

"Okay, everyone," Evan said as he prepared to depart, "sleep tight. I'll be back tomorrow morning with another event."

He piloted the boat, Dino, Joe and Iris out of the inlet and once again the night turned black.

"I can't believe she volunteered to go," Tommy stated. "What a wimp. She was probably afraid of the big bad killer hiding out on the island somewhere."

Gus stood and got in the younger man's face. "That woman is about ten of you, son, so I would shut it if I were you. None of us is worried about some mystery stowaway killer, but we're all worried about how long we can last on this island. She got what she needed and got off. I say, good for her."

"Hear, hear," Talia chimed in. "Iris was a class act."

"And a very nice woman," Nancy added. "Since she left to give me another chance I feel like I should chip in more. I'll be the one to get the water from now on. I know where to go."

Tired and no doubt concerned, although no one voiced their fears, they pulled the sleeping mat as close to the fire as possible. Marlie actually had the nerve to complain about the cold, to which Reuben responded, but wasn't she happy that she had perfectly combed hair?

Without Iris or Sam, the space on the bed opened up, which made huddling together more awkward than it had been the previous night. It was one thing to be pushed up against someone's body when you had no choice, it was another when you did.

Reuben took the end position and, like he had the night before, pushed his body as close to Talia as he could. Instinctively, she tensed and was mad at herself that she had. He was only being practical.

"Don't be stupid," he growled in her ear. "It's about warmth."

"I know that," she hissed even as she felt his arms wrap around her from behind, and subsequently felt a slow burn develop down low in the pit of her stomach.

"Besides when I finally get around to doing you—and frankly, sugar, I think that's going to happen sooner than later—it's not going to be in front of an audience. I'm sort of bashful that way."

She plowed her elbow back into his stomach as punishment and took satisfaction from the *ooof* sound he emitted. But he only held her tighter.

"Oh, yeah," he whispered against her neck. "Definitely sooner. And it's going to be so good." She felt his lips press against the spot beneath her ear, but before she could reject the embrace, he was backing off.

She hated him, she decided. She hated him, but she was attracted to him. She hated him, but she wanted him. And that was the worst part of all. Cursing her female stupidity for falling for the natural alpha male in the group, Talia slept that night and dreamed of wolves.

Day three on the island began with rain.

Not a gentle spring rain, not even a steady winter rain, this was a deluge. It woke them in the predawn hours when it started to pour. Not that it had been easy to tell what time it was, considering the heavy cloud cover overhead.

Because of the rain, the planned game for that day was postponed and the group had little to do but huddle together and feel sorry for themselves. Joe and Dino didn't bother with filming much other than to catch bits of the competitors' discomfort. Instead, for most of the day Dino sniffed after Marlie who did her best to keep him at bay. And Joe spent his time chatting with anyone who would listen to him brag about his first grandchild.

Gus and Reuben worked to move some of the still-burning logs from the fire into the deeper part of the forest, hoping that the canopy of foliage would be enough to protect the flames from the downpour. The rest of the group sat around, drenched and freezing, watching as the fire slowly drowned.

Sleep had been all but impossible that night and as the new day began in much the same way as the last day had ended, cracks in people's determination to stick it out began to show.

"What are we going to do?" Marlie cried. "We can't live without the fire. We need to boil the water. One day fine, but two? What will we drink?"

Talia tipped her head back and opened her mouth, controlling the surge of rainwater into her throat, then swallowed. A simple demonstration that drinking wasn't an issue. The younger girl only cried harder.

Maybe this was a good thing, Talia decided. Exposed to difficult elements, Marlie might decide to quit sooner rather than later, bringing Talia that much closer to being the final contestant. Sam wasn't looking so strong, either. He was practically holding his body together with his arms. The bump on his head was smaller, and after a day of doing nothing but resting he seemed more focused today, but he looked especially miserable.

"I didn't think it would be this hard," he said when he caught Talia assessing him. "I wanted to do something challenging. My father, he was a holocaust survivor. He was starved, beaten, but he survived. My therapist says I'm not happy because I've never had to prove myself like he did."

Talia wasn't sure how Sam's therapist made the leap from holocaust survivor to reality game-show contestant, but she kept quiet. Poor Sam had had a rough time of it already, and by the looks of things he was starting to figure out that he wasn't going to be able to prove himself the way he'd hoped.

"This sucks!" Tommy shouted over the sound of the pounding rain. It was raining so hard now that the drops actually stung when they hit skin. Gus and Reuben, who had gone to check on the fire they had tried to salvage the day before, emerged from the woods shaking their heads doubtfully.

"It's still smoking," Reuben told the group. "But I don't know that it will last if it continues to rain like this."

"Even if it stays hot enough we can use it to make a new fire," Talia suggested.

"We're going to need to get lucky," Gus said ominously.

"We're not going to be able to fish again today, either," Talia told Reuben. "Maybe Gus can use the pole, but the water is too choppy with the rain to try and grab the little ones. I'm thinking of going looking for some coconut or fruits that we might be able to eat."

"I'll go with you."

"I can do this alone," she told him.

"Why do that when I'm willing to keep you company?"

"Just company, huh?" she asked skeptically.

He moved in closer and his hand reached out to wrap around her waist. After a few nights of sleeping with him, she quickly had grown accustomed to the feel of him touching her. And if she were honest with herself, had grown to like it, as well.

"Are you ready for more?" he asked seductively.

"I don't know what you're talking about," she lied.

"Yes, you do. And you'll let me know. But for now I'm not letting you go off by yourself."

The seducer was suddenly replaced by the hard-ass. Reading in his face what she guessed was going to be a ridiculous show of stubbornness, Talia acquiesced. "Fine. Do you know what you're looking for?"

"No."

"Then you'll carry."

Before they could take off though, once again the sound of a motor greeted the camp. The boat carrying the usual suspects pulled up to shore, and Evan and crew, all properly attired in blue windbreakers with hoods and boots, jumped out. This time they had covered the cameras with plastic. Dino and Joe both focused immediately on Nancy, Marlie and Sam, who were clearly the most uncomfortable.

"Come to film our misery again, huh?" Gus asked the host.

Evan just shrugged his shoulders in a hapless gesture to indicate a job was a job. "We still can't hold the challenge and I thought maybe after another day of this someone would be ready to break. Crucial that we get that on camera."

"Any word from the mainland about the murderer?" Reuben wanted to know.

"Nothing," Evan reported. "Like I said that night, me telling you was just a precaution. I'm sure we're hundreds of miles away from the killer."

"Let's go," Talia urged Reuben, tugging on his wrist. "Before one of them decides they need to follow us."

He didn't need any further encouraging. Taking her hand, they both deliberately left their microphones behind and trotted off into the thick foliage. Once underneath the canopy of palms, the rain wasn't as heavy, although it continued to pound down.

"This worries me a little."

Reuben stopped and turned to see her looking up at the dark sky. "What?"

"The weather pattern. It doesn't feel like a typical short storm. The clouds are not a sudden dark, but a gathering-storm dark. The wind is really picking up, too. And listen, the birds are quiet. Mynahs, especially, are loud. If they're bunkering down, there's a reason for it. And it is cyclone season."

"Cyclone? Isn't that the big wave?"

"No, that's a tsunami," she corrected him. "A cyclone is basically a hurricane in the Pacific or a typhoon off Asia. They call them willies down here. We don't hear about them in the States unless they're catastrophic. I'm not saying one is on the way, just that we need to be alert. When we get back we should have Evan check with the ship to see if they're hearing any news regarding the weather."

"Killers…killer storms… I'll tell you, this game isn't as fun as I thought it was going to be."

He followed her for a time, stepping where she stepped, his eyes pinned to the ground the way hers were. It amused her slightly when she recalled that he had no idea what he was searching for.

"Find anything?"

He lifted his head then grimaced. "Very cute. No, I haven't. Will you tell me what the hell I'm supposed to be looking for?"

She smiled. "If we're lucky there should be some papaya trees. Coconuts are great but without a machete, they're hard to get open. If we're really lucky we'll find an avocado tree. They'll grow too high for us to pick the fruit, so we'll have to make do with whatever has dropped but hasn't rotted yet."

He nodded and again turned his eyes to the ground. She supposed that meant he knew what an avocado looked like.

"Tell me, how do you know all this stuff? About the birds, the trees, the weather?"

"My mom was Australian. We spent a lot of time vacationing and camping on the islands off the coast of New Zealand and Australia. And my mother was always trying to teach me something. While my dad liked to play, she liked to work."

"Did she teach you how to dive?"

"No, that was my dad. He loves the water more than

anything. I was swimming before I could talk. Diving before I could walk. My mother added the work ethic. From her I understood that to gain something you had to sacrifice something else. And if you wanted something badly enough, then hard work was the way to get there."

"She should meet Tommy."

Talia chuckled. "She definitely would not have understood him. She passed away when I was young, but everything she taught me has stayed with me. I think she would have liked my job choice, too. She would have thought it was sensible."

"Okay."

"Then you have my father…. He works because he has to but prefers to dream about adventure and excitement. Add a little bit of the dream to hard work and you have—"

"An Olympian," Reuben finished.

Funny, she'd never thought about it that way before, but he was right. It took more than just hard work to be an Olympian. A person had to dream big for that to happen. Possibly for the first time, she understood that her father was just as responsible for her silver medal as her mother was.

"I guess so."

"Explain to me again how you go from being an Olympian to an accountant."

"Why do you keep picking on that?" More importantly, why did it continue to bother her so much?

"It's just a stretch, that's all. You don't seem the accountant type."

"Well, I am," she stated adamantly. "Very much the accountant type. I love numbers and counting and all of it." She loved the predictability of it. The day-in, day-out normalcy of the work. If she'd found some of her classes a bit stifling, then that was just the price she'd had to pay to get what she wanted. As her mother had taught her. It was all about sacrifice.

"Okay, okay."

She stopped searching as she saw something slither down a tree by his shoulder. "Watch behind you. There's a snake."

"Holy shit!" Instantly he turned, then screamed and tried to backpedal a few steps only to trip over a short plant and land on his butt.

Shaking her head, Talia walked over to the tree where the snake's head was bobbing, licking the air for a taste of dinner. Carefully, she wrapped her hand around the head, pinning the mouth shut, although she doubted it would bite, and pulled it from around the trunk. At about four feet in length, its tail barely touched the ground.

"It's a harmless brown tree snake. See the eyes? They're round, which means it's not poisonous."

He stood, but retreated even farther. "I don't care if it's a fucking vegetarian. Get it the hell away from me!"

With a casual flick of the wrist she sent the snake flying into the bushes and watched as it slithered underneath the rotting palm leaves. "You're afraid of fish. You're afraid of snakes. Mind telling me why you thought you could hack it on a tropical island?"

"I'm not afraid of fish," he retorted. "And I don't see

a lot of snakes where I'm from." He was once again walking behind her, stepping where she stepped. She could see he also was working hard to control his shudders.

"And where is that?"

He was the only one of the group who hadn't said where he was from. Part of the silent mysterious strategy, she knew, but they were quickly getting to the point where they both realized it was only a matter of time before they caved in to their needs and desires.

Before she even contemplated having sex with him, she wanted to know more about him, a whole lot more, but she would start with where he lived.

"It's a different kind of jungle. With different kinds of snakes."

"You said you were a city boy. New York?"

"Philly."

It fit, she thought. The attitude, the edge. "And something tells me you're from a dangerous part of town."

He smiled. "Dangerous is relative, sweetheart. There are bad people wherever you go. Even on a deserted island in the South Pacific."

Talia tensed. "That's not funny. You're not taking that stuff Evan said about a killer on the loose seriously, are you?"

"The bucket. The ladder," he reminded her.

"Originally, you thought it might be one of us sabotaging the game."

"Originally I didn't know that there could be another explanation. If this person is on this island somewhere, he or she has only one thought in his mind."

"What's that?"

"How to get off."

"You're scaring me. You can't believe there is some fugitive hiding out here just waiting for an opportunity to take off."

"I'm not trying to scare you, sugar, I'm pointing out the facts. Evan said we're not that far from the coast of Australia. On a full tank of gas one of the motorboats could get you there. From there it's just a plane hop to any Australian city, the Outback, anywhere.... All things considered, it's not a bad escape plan. It's what I would do."

The rain started to pick up, the clatter of the drops on the leaves heavier. It was just the two of them, she realized. No mics, no one around to hear her if she screamed. It hadn't occurred to her for a second to be wary of going alone with him. No, that wasn't true. She *was* concerned about fending off an amorous pass, even more concerned that she wouldn't even try. She'd believed that her virtue might be at risk—but not her life.

Talia took a step away from him. "You sound a lot like someone who understands the criminal mind."

"I do understand it."

She met his hard eyes dead-on, but as much as she thought she should be afraid, it occurred to her that she wasn't. She didn't know this man at all. He'd said nothing significant about himself or his past, but for whatever reason, she was certain he wouldn't hurt her.

That's when it came to her. Some of the comments he'd made, his sense about Gus, his observation about the bucket. She once accused him of being a pig. She was right.

She laughed at herself for not seeing it immediately.

"I don't believe it…. You're a cop."

Chapter 5

Adamantly, Reuben shook his head.

"No." Then he added, "I was a cop. Totally different."

No, it wasn't. She'd known enough cops—mostly through her father and his run-ins with con artists—to know that once one, always one. It was as though they were born to it. Much the way she'd been born to the water.

"Did you quit?" It would have surprised her if the answer was yes. For all his faults, and there were many, she didn't think being a quitter was one of them.

"I got shot. I was on leave for a while…then, I don't know. Lost my taste for it, I guess. It was always something I was supposed to be. My mom was Irish, her dad was a cop, his dad was a cop. Then she met my dad. He was Puerto Rican. My grandfather would have shot him off the porch the first day he picked up my mother for a date if it hadn't been for one thing."

Talia smiled. "He was a cop, too."

"And Catholic. Very important. So they married and had sons and we're all blue. One vice, one narc, one street and I was homicide."

"How did you get shot?"

"Like most cops do. By being stupid. A neighbor knocked on my door, complaining about a domestic dispute going on in the house next to her. I thought I could calm things down. I didn't even consider calling for backup and instead took one in the stomach."

It made perfect sense that he would have arrogantly thought he had the ability to calm down a volatile situation by himself.

"And now you're faster than anything I've ever seen in the water and you want to buy a bar. Talk about your stretches. That's a pretty big leap."

He turned away from her and studied the ground while he talked. "I did a lot of swimming with the rehab. I was on comp pay so I had a lot of time on my hands and ended up getting into it. Next thing I'm doing a couple of Iron Man races just to show everyone how tough I really was. No bullet in the gut was going to stop me.

"Then it came time for me to decide if I was going to go back. I decided I wanted to try something else. I wanted to be something else. But if you want to change your life you need money, right? Big money. Quick money. Some guy I was competing against in one of the state's Iron Man races told me he was signing up for this

game show. He gave me an application. I made it. He
didn't. Stupid luck."

"You think deep down inside you're really a bartender?"

He sighed. "I have a vision of this place. Some hole-
in-the-wall dive somewhere, anywhere, it doesn't matter. The same guys come in every night to pass the time.
Maybe I'll serve nachos or fries or something. But the
drinks will be cold, the snacks will be fresh and there
will be a dartboard."

"Absolutely. No hole-in-the-wall dive would be
caught without one. But you didn't answer my question."

His teeth gleamed. "No. I wasn't born a bartender. I
think I was born a cop, but that doesn't mean I don't get
to choose. Just like you're choosing to be an accountant. If that's not a departure, I don't know what is."

"Why do you always come back to that? Why do you
even care what I do for a living?"

"Because at least I know what I'm walking away
from. I don't think you do."

"You don't even know me," she scoffed.

"Not for a long time, no. But there's something between us. From the minute you stepped on that yacht.
I saw you walking up the plank, with your blond hair
and your long legs and your determined eyes. I thought,
she's the one. She's trouble. Just like me. Like met like.
You and me. I'm not romantic. But I know lust at first
sight and I had it with you and you had it with me. Bad."

She retreated a step and shook her head, denying everything he said despite its veracity. "That is one healthy
ego you've got."

"That is true, but I'm not wrong." He moved closer, invading her space, daring her to hold her ground, which, of course, she was forced to do. "Yeah, it was there. You know it, too. But a minute later I watched you shut it down. And you've been fighting it ever since. I'm thinking maybe you don't like my brown skin."

Instantly, she negated his comment. "I have brown skin," she muttered as his lips descended, almost touching, then withdrawing at the last second.

"Yes, you do. Your skin was made for the sun. It soaks it up like a sponge." His hands slid down her bare arms, lifting them as if to inspect them. He placed a soft kiss inside her elbow and she felt the stubble from his unshaven cheek. Then he rested both of her arms on his shoulders. Immediately, she pulled them back, but he caught her hands before she could escape completely.

"So if it isn't my skin then it has to be something else. Something that made you so wary. Something maybe you didn't want to see in me."

He tugged her forward and this time his lips came so close that he kissed her. It was a tentative kiss, the kind that tested for a response. The kind she had been expecting since…the first time they'd laid eyes on each other.

Damn it, she hated that he was right.

But she couldn't focus on that, not while his lips were playing with hers. They were softer than expected. Less demanding, more exploratory. She could tell that he was waiting for her to react. So was she, for that matter. Never could she remember being so conflicted.

One thing was for certain. She wanted him. Just as

he'd said. Deep down. It seemed as if a part of her had recognized a part of him on sight. But she didn't believe in any of that. She didn't believe in the destiny that her father so often spoke of or the fate that her mother had said was taking her to her next stage of existence. Talia rejected all of that in favor of things that made sense. Diving made sense to her. Numbers did, too.

This ridiculous attraction to Reuben…didn't.

He wasn't anything that she imagined she wanted from a man. A chauvinistic, arrogant drifter who called all women "sugar" and "sweetheart" and who couldn't understand what it meant to wear a business suit if it bit him in the ass, was absolutely not the type of man she wanted, or needed, in her life. Certainly not in her near future.

But the question she kept coming back to was…did it matter? In this time and in this place, could she have him without any consequences? Some inner sense was telling her that she couldn't. He was a book of matches and playing with him might get her burned.

"Tell me you're ready," he demanded.

"I don't know…"

"Yes, you do," he murmured. "Why are you still fighting? It's not my lips. You like those."

He slipped his tongue into her mouth and it was everything she could do to hold back a moan that would have made him think she was tasting ice cream for the first time. That would have been giving him too much and this wasn't that kind of game.

If she was going to engage him, then it would have to be a battle. One that she couldn't surrender to him.

That would be too easy. And she had no plans to retreat, either. If she was going to end this, she had to stop him from advancing.

His tongue slipped between her lips again, lingered, and ice cream had a new flavor for her. Her muscles tensed even as her body was pushing her to move closer, to let him go deeper.

Reuben pulled away, his tongue stroking her lips for a time until all contact between them was lost.

"I think you fight me because you know we're a lot alike," he whispered. "I think you're afraid to be that person, which I don't get because you're not afraid of anything else. I also think you know that the two of us are going to end up alone on this island together and I bet you can't wait until that happens. But we don't have to wait, sugar."

Talia didn't realize she was moving, so she wasn't sure how it happened but suddenly, she felt the roughness of tree bark against her body, the trunk curving almost perfectly to the arch of her spine. His hands dropped to her jean shorts, his fingers on the button-fly and, without any effort, the shorts slid to the wet ground leaving her wearing the blue bikini she'd worn for four days. His hand wrapped around her neck. Her eyes met his and she saw that even in this simple touch he was testing her, assessing her reaction, wanting to know if she was going to flinch.

But the butterflies in her belly had nothing to do with fear. He was right. In a way she was just like him. Enough that she knew him. He wasn't going to hurt her. Not physically.

Not unless she wanted him to.

"You're a lot like the shark," she told him. "An animal in the wild."

His hand dipped from her throat to her collarbone to her breast. "Wild. It's how I feel now. I don't normally fuck like this."

"No? How then?"

"Quick, fast, slow, easy, whatever her mood, never my mood."

"What's your mood?" She wanted to know as his head dipped and his lips fell to the space between her breasts.

His head lifted and again their gazes clashed. She tried to read into his black stare, then decided she didn't need to. She knew what he wanted. She knew what she wanted. She was so ready for it, as she'd never been before, that she gasped before she ordered, "Do it."

Talia continued to meet his gaze rather than look down at where he wanted to join their bodies. She closed her eyes and let herself feel. First his lips on the crest of her breast. Then his fingers slipping into the waistband of her bikini bottoms, searching where she was wet and entirely too sensitive.

"I can't." It wasn't a weak feminine protest, but a warning. "I'm too close."

It was a plea for him to move faster, a caution that she couldn't take the time to linger as she felt her knees buckle. The desire to have him inside her body began to build to the point where she knew she would lose it if he didn't. And she didn't want to come before he did. It was senseless, but it was all the control she had and she wanted to keep it.

He raised his head enough to give her his mouth, his tongue. But she wanted more. She wanted all of him. If she was going to do this, then there was no holding back. Not for him or for her. Her fingernails bit into his shoulders.

"You don't want to play?" he asked as his body pinned her to the tree, his sex digging through his shorts into her bare belly, insisting on its pleasure. "'Cause it feels like you want to play."

She lowered her hands to his waist and tugged at the material until she felt the spring of his sex once it was free. Her fingers clasped his firm erection, and she marveled at the heat that it generated.

"No games. Not in this."

"Okay. I don't have anything with me. But I'm safe. You need to know that."

She wasn't on anything, either. But for whatever reason, she decided it didn't matter. What was happening between them was too primal for anything to interfere. Rather than answer, she simply bobbed her head.

She saw the movement before she felt the impact. The sudden dip of his knees, the abrupt feeling of bareness as her bottoms were stripped from her body. Then the dominating thrust. In concert, her body was filled by something large and hot and welcome.

Again her mind tried to rebel against the illogical. She'd never jumped into a relationship in her life. She'd never felt the need for sex like some urgent hunger that was making her progressively weaker. Diving always had assuaged that need. The agile movements. The physical impact that was both pleasure and pain. The sheer joy of cutting through water like a sharp knife, tense and alert, only to float weightlessly to the top.

That's where she was now. On the edge of the platform. Falling into a dive.

Using the tree at her back, she braced herself and lifted her legs to wrap around his waist, giving him more access, by her very will forcing him to go deeper. He was thick and long and his movements were urgent and rough and almost a little out of control. There was a fullness with each penetration that would have hurt if he hadn't felt so perfect.

She squeezed her internal muscles around his hardness and his hand reached for her breast to squeeze the handful of flesh, in retaliation, she imagined. Revenge had never felt so good. Not to be beaten, she clasped her muscles around his penis even more, her body becoming a perfect physical machine as it clung to him, absorbed him.

Talia heard him cry out. Felt the last desperate push. She reached for that moment of pure pleasure while he was reaching for something inside of her. And the world fell away as it did when she was diving. Beyond the severe bliss there was peace in the form of a warm, liquid feeling that pulsed just under her skin.

"Holy shit."

At least that's what she thought he muttered against her shoulder as he tried to inhale. The rain fell harder, cooling them off like a refreshing shower. He pushed her legs away until they were touching the ground and then she felt him leave her body.

It took every ounce of discipline she had not to

whimper her disappointment. Fortunately for her, she had a great deal of it.

But why? Why should it matter if he knew that she'd been physically devastated by what happened? That she was happy because of it? The questions pierced her brain like thin needles and wouldn't let her wallow in the wake of pure bodily pleasure the way she deserved.

The answer was obvious. The reality, or nonreality as the case may be, was that they were still playing a large-scale game and each was on his or her own side. And none of that, she recognized, had anything to do with the television show.

Reuben braced his hand on the trunk over her head. She heard him huffing, felt the slight pressure of his chest as it touched hers in staccato movements.

"What the hell was that?" he growled.

"I'm pretty sure it was sex," she answered. That wasn't what he meant. But it was easier to be flippant now that the intensity was over.

"No, it wasn't." His voice was hoarse in her ear as his mouth moved in to capture her earlobe. "You know what that was?"

"Huh?" It required far too much strength to ask. Her hands, almost weak, helplessly reached out to stroke his smooth chest, his ripped abdomen. He'd been wearing a T-shirt, but at some point during the sexual fray he must have removed it.

Only four days on the island and already he was losing some of the extra weight that she knew he'd purposefully gained before the show. What would he look like by the time the game ended? What type of creature? What type of animal was he fast becoming?

"I said, you know what that was?"

She didn't want to know.

"Mating," he told her.

She pulled her wandering mind back from the fanciful image of wolves and lions and panthers and opened her eyes. His black eyes were clear and sharp.

"No," she croaked out. The feeble rejection only incited him.

"Yes," he nodded. In a flash the severe expression was gone, replaced by something far more needy. And frighteningly possessive.

"Again."

The word barely penetrated before he was removing her arms from around his neck, holding them to the side as he moved in to reclaim her mouth. Like an elixir, his kiss gave her strength. Once more she was feeling her body move from pleasurable lassitude to urgent need.

Briefly, she struggled against his hold, but he wouldn't release her. A primitive noise escaped her throat in protest. She wasn't fighting to get away. She was fighting to get closer. She wanted to dig her hands into his scalp and bring him deeper and farther into her body in every way possible.

He was like a fever she'd never experienced before. And she didn't want the cure.

Out of respect for her protest, she imagined, rather than any intention of leaving her, Reuben released her mouth to focus on her face. His hands still circled her wrists to prevent any escape, but there would be no attempt.

For a moment he studied her. Then, satisfied, he nodded. She hated that whatever expression she wore was so easy for him to read, but there was no help for it. He turned her, then placed her hands on the tree.

Her back to him, she craned her neck to look over her shoulder. His eyes were lowered to half mast, his hands were gripping her bare hips. She saw what she had only felt before. His erection was thick and hard and so full of life. She wanted to touch it, tease it, drive him insane, but that would have to be for another time.

"Ready?" he murmured.

As though there was a choice, she wondered hazily. Her head fell forward in a heavy nod partly in response, but mostly because she feared she didn't have the strength to hold it up when every ounce of blood she had seemed to be flowing in the opposite direction.

This time the impact of his penetration was less a jolt and more a familiar comfort. Like an old lover she'd gone too long without. This time his strokes were smooth and easy and fluid. Rather than push into her, he pulled her to him. Rather than rush to an end, he lingered. The steady beat of the rain, the harshness of their breaths, the slap of thighs, all of it swirled around them, her senses desperately trying to absorb the sensation.

One of his hands left her hip and trailed up her back urging her to arch her spine. When she did, she was rewarded with a deeper surge, a more complete claiming.

"That's it, sugar," he rumbled as his hand circled to her bare tummy and pushed aside the piece of nylon that still covered her breasts. At first he cupped her, then his agile fingers played with her impossibly tight nipples.

"Not sugar. Say my name," she cried weakly. Her body started to tense around him. The onslaught of sweet pain was on its way, but she wanted him to know who she was first, whose body he was inside. She needed to know that he knew her.

"I've got you, Talia," he assured her even as his thrusts grew more pronounced. "I know who you are and you know who I am. Don't you? Don't you?" With each question he pushed a little harder, pounded a little deeper.

"Y-yes," she stuttered right before she tumbled over the edge.

If she had turned her head, she would have seen a feral smile that was both triumphant and appeased. Then he was falling over her, hugging her to his chest like the teddy bear she once promised him she would not be. She cried out again as the pleasure rocked her body and claimed her muscles. She practically shouted from the sheer joy of feeling and being alive.

"Ahhhhh!"

The bloodcurdling sound broke through the haze of Talia's release. Behind her she felt Reuben's body tighten as if preparing for an attack. Abruptly, he left her body and reached to the ground to pull up his shorts.

"What was that?" she whispered. All of the sudden she felt naked where before she had felt natural. Quickly, she moved the bikini top back into position to conceal breasts that were still full and nipples that were still hard.

"Probably Marlie," he said. Bending down he scooped up her bottoms and shorts and handed them to her. "Probably a snake or a bug or some shit like that."

"Oh my God! Help me!"

"That doesn't sound like a reaction to a snake." Her bottoms snug around her hips, she pulled up the shorts and fastened them, then started to jog in the direction of the noise.

"You always have to be Pollyanna," Reuben grumbled behind her.

"It sounded like Nancy," Talia replied, ignoring the comment. "She didn't sound like that when she saw the shark. Something is wrong."

"Don't worry. I'm sure the cameras will catch it all. If we miss what's going on, we'll be able to see it on TV in a few months."

But Talia was done listening to his protests. There was a quality to the sound of the screech that had her hair standing on end, the pitch signaling real trouble. Talia's unease intensified so much that, before she realized what she was doing, she was leaping over bushes in her path, using loose vines to keep her balance and stomping whatever was underfoot.

"Jeez, slow down will you?"

The sound of foliage falling under his sneaker-covered feet met her ears, letting her know that he was still close behind. But that was the only sound she heard. What had happened to stop the screaming?

"This way," she called, pointing in the direction she intended to move. Turning to her right she saw a break in the woods. The bend in the trunks of the palm trees, the steady incline as she ran and the crashing sound of water told her that she was approaching the area surrounding lagoon.

Breaking through the brush, she spotted Nancy ten feet below the ledge, kneeling on the sand near the edge of the water. Her hands covered her face as she sobbed into them.

"What? What's wrong?"

The housewife craned her head upward and stared at Talia as if she was unsure of her identity. Tears streaked through the dirt on Nancy's face and snot ran out of her nose.

She shook her head communicating her inability to answer and merely leaned back.

Talia had no problem understanding what had made Nancy scream. On the ground next to her a man's body sprawled, his arms stretched lifelessly in front of him, his head submerged in the shallow water of the lagoon. She recognized the khaki shirt, the blue windbreaker and the Mets ball cap that Joe had been wearing when he'd gotten off the boat that morning.

What she didn't recognize was the small pocket-knife sticking out of his back.

Behind her a noise signaled that Reuben was approaching. She felt him come up beside her, but she didn't know what to say. She'd never seen a dead body.

He lurched forward, but she reached out to grab his arm before he could leap over the edge down to the beach.

"It's too steep to jump" was all she needed to say to stop him. Then she added, "It's too late anyway."

"What the fuck?"

It was crude, but it summed up her thoughts succinctly.

"Hey, what's going on?" Tommy burst through bushes in front of them, his backpack still slung over his shoulders. He stopped short when he saw Talia's face, then followed her gaze to the beach below. "What the hell? Is that Joe? What's he doing, man?"

"I heard screaming." Gus came jogging from the same direction that Talia and Reuben had come from. A few seconds later, Sam appeared from a thicket of trees just beyond where Tommy had emerged.

Silence pervaded the group as each newcomer assimilated to the scene.

"Okay, what am I missing?" Dino asked as he, too, joined them puffing hard from his trek through the forest. Apparently, he'd been following Sam, or possibly Tommy, since he'd come from that general direction and his camera was still mounted on his shoulder. "If it was something good, you guys are going to have to do it over. Evan will kill me if—" Like the rest of them, he stopped talking as soon as he saw what they were staring at. "Joe! Oh shit! Joe. Someone's got to help him."

"It's too late," Reuben told everyone. "But let's get his face out of the water."

Reuben climbed down the rock, using the bushes and vines to steady him until he was close enough to the sand that he could jump. Everyone followed, one after the other, until they were gathered around a still sobbing Nancy and a still dead Joe.

"Is this a party and nobody invited me?" Marlie

called as she strolled down the stretch of beach from the direction of camp. Her smile was bright and a little smug. Stumbling behind her was a surprisingly sandy and disheveled-looking host. That they had been together in some fashion was obvious.

Not that Talia could throw stones. She and Reuben had been in the middle of mind-blowing sex when Joe had been getting stabbed in the back. Guilt descended on her like a heavy blanket. What if he had shouted for help but she hadn't heard over her own cries? It was horrible to contemplate that while she was feeling the most intense pleasure she'd ever known, Joe had been feeling the most intense pain.

"Let's get back to the beach. Think our way through this."

"Oh my God," Marlie cried, pointing to the body that Reuben was now tugging onto the sand. The cameraman's face was nicked from the bites of tiny fish. "Is he seriously dead?"

"Seriously," Talia confirmed.

Wrapping an arm around Nancy's shaking shoulders, she encouraged the woman to her feet. Nancy wobbled briefly, but managed to stay standing. They fell into a single line to make their way back to camp, leaving Reuben behind with the body.

Everything was soaking wet from the rain, and the fire continued to elicit puffs of smoke as the deluge tried to crush the life out of it. As soon as Nancy saw Sam's mattress, she dropped onto it, as if her feet couldn't carry her one more step.

Talia shifted her attention back to Reuben, who was

squatting on his haunches, apparently studying the body.

A homicide cop. That's what he'd told her he was. At the time, the description had meant nothing to her, just another type of cop. Now it could mean everything.

"Everyone should stay put," she told them, not that anyone was listening. Each person was quietly trying to come to grips with what had happened. The next issue would be to ask why. But before that, they needed more information.

Reluctant, but knowing she was the only one who would go, Talia walked over to Reuben, who was searching the body. No, not the body. Joe.

Joe, who had been a veteran cameraman. Joe, who had made fun of Evan's teeth when he wasn't around. Joe, who had a new grandchild and still carried a picture of his ex-wife in his wallet. She knew because he'd shown her.

"I don't understand," she began to say. "I mean, I get…it has to be the killer, right? The stowaway. From Hawaii. He must have been on our boat the whole time and somehow made it to the island."

Reuben glanced up at her, his countenance neutral. "Maybe. It's a long swim."

"Two miles, Evan said. But that's doable."

"Yep."

"What? What are you not saying?"

"Come here."

He made a motion with his hand, and she walked around the body and crouched next to him. He pointed to the bloodstain on the front of Joe's shirt right under where his heart would be. Then to the blood on the sand under his body. "Whoever did this, stabbed him from the front first. Then the back and pushed him down so that his head was underwater."

"How do you know? That he was stabbed in front first."

"Even though the knife was lodged in his back, there's more blood on the front of him. Plus, we didn't hear anything."

"We were sort of involved at the time."

He grabbed her chin and forced her to meet his eyes. The guilt she felt must have been thick in her voice.

"Stop it," he ordered abruptly. "We weren't doing anything wrong."

"How can you say that? We were going at each other like two animals and all that time Joe was dying. He needed our help."

"We couldn't know that," Reuben reminded her. "Listen to me, there is no way we could have anticipated this. No one expects death. Trust me. I've been called to enough murder scenes, talked to enough family members and loved ones to know that."

"It's just that he was older and so defenseless. It doesn't seem right. I know that sounds ridiculous. That I'm expecting fairness from a killer."

"It doesn't seem ridiculous to me at all. In fact it seems like exactly something you would say."

Her lips turned. "You make me nervous when you're nice to me."

"Trust me, I make myself nervous, too. I only made the point about the noise because a stab wound in the back does not kill someone right away. He could have shouted for help. But you puncture an artery to the heart, the vic is usually dead in seconds."

"Why does it matter?" As far as Talia could see Joe was still dead.

He opened his mouth, then closed it. "Nothing. No point. Not now, anyway. All we need to do is get off the island and back to the yacht. We'll send someone back for the body and work this out once we're all on dry land."

That made sense to her. Together they stood and started toward camp.

"Son of a bitch!" This time the shouting was coming from Tommy, who was standing near the motorboat.

He was calling furiously for everyone to come see something. Clearly agitated, he looked as if he were removing tufts of hair from his head. Evan was the first to join him, and his expression did not bode well. Talia saw the host say something to the group, but she couldn't hear what it was. The fact that they were all racing to the boat and pointing at it told her everything she needed to know.

"There's a problem with the boat," she surmised.

"Yep," Reuben uttered.

Talia turned to him, reaching for his arm and forcing him to focus on her rather than the group. "Why don't you sound surprised?"

"Because I'm not," he answered enigmatically.

"I don't understand," she growled, frustrated with his half answers. "What does this mean?"

"For now…it means we're trapped."

Chapter 6

Together Reuben and Talia sprinted to the boat. Evan was hovering over the top of the outboard motor, examining the exposed guts of the engine.

"I tried to start it and nothing," Tommy explained.

"Why?" Reuben wondered.

The younger man looked confused for a moment, clearly not anticipating the question. "I…uh…we've got to get out of here. Right? I mean, someone is dead. I was going to get the boat ready."

Talia studied Reuben's expression, but his face and his thoughts were closed to her. All she could say for certain was that he wasn't telling her everything.

"I don't know anything about engines other than how to start them," Evan mumbled, then looked toward Dino. "You?"

"I don't know boats," the portly cameraman declared. "I know cameras. Give me a broken one and I can fix it. This…? It's out of my league."

"Let me take a look," Talia offered.

"There's a shock," Reuben snapped. "Sharks, snakes and engines. You are a hell of a woman."

Talia sneered at him because she knew he was being sarcastic, but then her gaze fell to the body that was sprawled out on the beach only fifty yards away. Joe was dead and Reuben was making snide comments. It didn't seem right. Then again, as a homicide cop, the death of a stranger was all in a day's work. She was glad it wasn't hers. He could make all the comments he wanted about her chosen profession. She'd take accounting any day.

"I grew up on a boat. I know something about inboard engines. I don't know how different this might be, but the basic functionality should be the same." She stepped around Evan and glanced down at the pieces and wires intricately woven together to form the combustible engine.

"Can you see anything?" Gus asked.

"Yeah, because we have to get off this island," Tommy added. "I'm not hanging around with some wacko killer on the loose."

Nancy looked at Sam and Gus who were behind her. "You mean we don't think what happened to Joe was an accident? That he just fell?"

"On a knife?" Tommy cried. "Get real, lady."

Sam patted the fragile woman on the shoulder. "It's going to be fine. We'll all get off and they'll find out who did this."

Talia could feel the weight of everyone's gaze on her.

"Well?" Evan urged. "Do you see the problem?"

"Yep," she answered, adopting Reuben's trademark less-is-more policy. Their gazes met and it was disconcerting to know that she didn't have to say anything for him to get the point.

"Can you fix it?" Gus wanted to know.

"Look. I'll help Talia," Reuben announced to the group. "I know something about engines, too. Why don't you all go pack up your stuff? That way when we're ready to go, we'll be set."

"Why should we leave you two down here?" Tommy wanted to know, his tone and his expression both clearly suspicious. "What if you just take the boat?"

"Talia didn't leave Nancy to the shark. She didn't leave Sam underwater. She's not going to take the boat," Reuben responded with clenched teeth. "Be grateful, because if it was me, I would leave your ass here in a second. Now do something useful and help Nancy back up the beach."

This time the younger man didn't flinch, but took one of Nancy's hands to lead her to the camp. Evan took her other arm to lend support.

As soon as it was just the two of them, Talia pointed to the engine. "See that?"

Reuben waited a beat, then answered. "No."

"You don't really know anything about engines, do you?"

"I know they run on gas."

She shook her head in mild disgust. "The spark plug is missing."

He winced slightly with embarrassment. "Uh…can you fix that?"

"Sure," she muttered dryly. "Did you happen to pack an extra spark plug in your bag?"

"Oh. I see. There's a piece missing."

"A small but very important piece, yes. No spark, no fire, no engine. Someone deliberately tampered with the boat. Someone who doesn't want us to leave."

Reuben took a second to consider that, then said, "Or someone who wants to use the boat for himself and needs to wait for the right time."

"And this person killed Joe because...?"

"Because Joe either caught him in the act. Or maybe caught something on tape."

Talia huffed with disgust over what seemed to be a senseless killing. "If he had time to take the plug, why didn't he just take the boat right then?"

Reuben shrugged. "Who knows? If it's the perp from Hawaii, then he's got some pretty big rocks somewhere. Maybe he didn't have them on him at the time, maybe he hid them somewhere. But he sees the boat, no one around, figures he can tamper with it now then wait until the time is right to make his escape."

His theory was sound. And her plan for what to do next was simple. "Fine. Then we let him have it. We all go into the woods or make our way to the other side of the island, let him come out of hiding and take the boat. Then we find a different way to get back to the yacht. Evan said he checks in every day. If they don't hear from us in two, I assume they'll send someone to check on us."

"Not going to be that easy, sweetheart."

"Oh, yes, it can. I get that you're a cop—"

"Was a cop," he clarified.

"Exactly. There is absolutely no need for us to play hero here and try to catch this guy. I'm sorry about Joe. I am. But I say let this person go and let the FBI or whoever does this sort of thing go after him."

Reuben's lips turned up slightly at her tirade. "Sugar, you've been playing hero since the moment you stepped on this island. Check that, you haven't been playing. But don't worry. I'm not so dedicated that I would try to track down a killer without any kind of weapon or backup. All I'm saying is that us hiding out in the woods and waiting for our guy to come get this boat isn't going to work."

"Why not?"

He shook his head, evidently reluctant to say what he needed to say. "He…or she…stabbed Joe from the front, facing him. No shouting, no screaming. Joe knew who this person was. Get it?"

Realization soaked into her brain, followed by real fear. She practically could feel the blood drain from her face.

"Yeah," he said in response to her sudden paleness. "You get it. The killer is one of us."

She dropped to her knees before her legs could give out beneath her. Horror and sickness rumbled in her stomach, making her gag on the emotions.

"I'm going to be ill," she warned him.

Reuben squatted next to her, his mouth at her ear. "No, you're not."

His assurance pissed her off. "How do you know?"

"Because you're not an accountant. Some suit would

be puking up her guts right about now. I'm sure when we tell them about the boat, Nancy is a goner. But you're going to hang tough because that's what you need to do."

Talia wasn't sure if she simply had needed a second for her stomach to settle or if his speech worked, but she sat on her haunches and ran her hand through her cropped hair. There had to be more possibilities, more scenarios than the one Reuben had suggested.

"What if this person was one of the crew? A waiter or…"

But he was already shaking his head. "It's unlikely. We stuck together on that boat, Joe and Dino included. And given the story Evan laid out last night, I have to think Joe would have been suspicious of a crew member popping out of the woods. None of us were that far away, either. Hell, Nancy, Marlie and Evan were somewhere on the beach. If Joe had spotted a stranger, he would have called out and someone would have heard."

There had to be another answer. Her gaze drifted up the beach to the cast of characters that she had known for a little less than a week but felt bound to in some inexplicable way. Was one of them a murderer? It didn't seem possible.

"Wait a minute. We all had to submit pictures, videos. Nancy was a last-minute replacement, but even she would have gone through the same application process. Everyone on that yacht should have been immediately recognized. Are you suggesting that someone who was about to go on a reality show just happened to kill an actress along the way and steal all of her jewelry?"

"Good point," he conceded. "Evan!" The host, who was kneeling in front of Marlie, lifted his head at the sound of his name. He trotted toward the boat as both Reuben and Talia stood to question him.

"Did you fix the boat?" Evan asked.

"No." Talia closed the casing on the engine. "It's missing a part."

"Missing? But that doesn't make sense. None of this makes sense."

"No, it doesn't," Talia agreed. A sudden idea had her reaching for his arm. "What about the radio? You can call the yacht and get them to come pick us up."

Evan blanched. "The radio is back at the camp. It's on the other side of the island. We've only traveled by boat. I'm not sure I would know how to find it over land."

A hiss escaped through Reuben's teeth, but he quickly got over his disappointment. "Listen, you've been part of this show from the beginning, right?"

"Not really. At first they went after the guy from *Fear Factor,* but he pulled out. Something about an all-senior citizen *Fear* show... I don't know."

"But you studied everyone's application," Talia insisted, willing it to be true. "You knew who we were before we got on the boat."

His face said it all. "What was I supposed to study? I drop you all off on the island, introduce a few games, make it all sound scary and dramatic and let the camera guys and editors do their thing."

Reuben put his hands on his hips. "Nice to find someone who takes his work seriously."

"That's not fair," Evan retorted. "I'm a great host. I

work out two hours a day to stay in shape and I really practice those introductions. So I didn't look through a bunch of folders—what difference does that make anyway? Right now there is a killer on this island. I think we should be concentrating on that."

Unfortunately, that's exactly what Talia was concentrating on. Looking at the group, she could no longer see them as what she had thought they were: a former military man, a housewife, a wanna-be actress, a marketing executive and…a cheater.

"Tommy's backpack." The words escaped her mouth unconsciously.

Reuben swung his head sharply in the direction of the youngest cast member.

"He had the backpack on his shoulders when he found us with Nancy. He's had it with him since he came aboard. The only time he left it was when he knew no one would be at camp."

Maybe it was paranoia setting in, the kind that made everybody else the enemy. But Talia only knew of two people for certain who couldn't have killed Joe. Herself and Reuben. Tommy didn't strike her as the kind of person who would have the internal strength or even the conviction to kill someone, but she sure as hell wanted to know what was in that stupid knapsack.

"I'm going to ask him to empty it."

She took a step forward before she felt Reuben's hand on her upper arm, holding her back. "You do this and you're going to open a big can of worms. Right now nobody knows they're a suspect. We should leave it that way."

Talia started to shake her head, letting him know that she didn't care what he thought because she wanted answers. But possibly unveiling a murderer deserved a second consideration. "We're going to have to tell them about the boat. You don't think Gus is going to figure out what that means?"

"As far as we know, Gus did it and will wisely keep his mouth shut."

"Not Gus." He couldn't be the one. Every instinct she had told her so.

"Why?" Reuben pressed. "Because he's a nice guy?"

"He does have military experience," Evan chimed in. "That would mean he knows how to use a knife, right? How to stab someone in the perfect place to kill them?"

"You've watched too many Rambo movies." Reuben dismissed Evan and forced Talia to look at him. "If we go after Tommy and he's got nothing more in that backpack than beef jerky, accusations are going to fly. At you and me, too."

"We know we didn't do it."

"You think he did?"

"No," she choked out. "I don't think *anyone* did it. But Joe is lying over there on the sand. Unless the producers of this ridiculous show have found some way to fake a man's death so that his heart doesn't beat and he doesn't breathe in order to pull off some dramatic TV stunt, then somebody *did* kill him. I want to know if that person is standing twenty feet from us with a spark plug in his backpack."

"It's not a stunt," Evan interrupted. "I would have known. They would have told me."

"Okay. Then let me." Reuben moved ahead of her and she had to jog to keep pace with his purposeful stride. "Tommy!"

Collectively, the group turned their heads in Reuben's direction. They had formed a circle, no doubt trying to offer each other support. Marlie and Nancy broke away leaving Tommy exposed.

"What's up? Did you fix that boat, man? This shit is getting weird."

"It's about to get weirder. Let me see what's in your bag." Instantly, Tommy reached for the bag that was at his feet, but Reuben was quicker and managed to snatch one of the shoulder straps.

"Let him have the bag, Tommy," Talia said in what she hoped was a calm and reassuring tone. Not that it would matter if he was the killer.

"No way. It's mine. Let go."

Evidently seeing no choice, Reuben raised his free hand and brought it down in a sharp blow against the younger man's upper arm. Instantly Tommy's hand went limp and he dropped the strap.

Without wasting time, Reuben unzipped the bag and emptied the contents onto the sand. An extra shirt, another bathing suit, a toothbrush and five granola bars stared at the group.

"That's food. He cheated." Nancy reached for one of the sinful granola bars in question. "Peanut butter."

"Whatever," Tommy said, sneering. "I came to win. And...I'm hypoglycemic, okay? I need to eat or I get weak."

Reuben looked over his shoulder at Talia as if asking, what next? She didn't know. She'd suspected Tommy of cheating before, but she wasn't sure if the fact that she was right meant he wasn't guilty of something more sinister.

"Someone removed the engine's spark plug. We can't use the boat to get off the island or to get to the other side where the radio is to call for help."

There was a small gasp. It might have been from Sam.

"And you thought I took it?" Tommy accused her. "Why me? Why would I want… Oh man! Oh man! You think I killed Joe? No way. That is sick."

Reuben's head tilted forward and he took in a large breath. She knew he was ready to tell them everything, but she thought that they might take it better coming from her. Not that the news one of them was a killer would be easy to swallow. But they would hear it better from her.

"Reuben is—" She stopped herself and looked at him knowing that she was making a bold move by revealing his past. But maybe having a professional investigator on the island would both alleviate the fears of the innocent and intimidate the guilty one. "He is…was…a cop. After looking at Joe's body he thinks Joe was stabbed in front first. The fact that we were all nearby but didn't hear any screams could mean that he was killed by someone he knew."

This time it was Dino who released a muted groan. "That's so wrong. He was a good man. He never would have hurt anyone."

"No," Gus challenged her. "This doesn't make sense."

"I know," she admitted. "But the truth is none of us knows if we are who we say we are. Evan didn't study our applications so he had no idea what we looked like. It's a good bet he didn't even know our names."

"Hey, this is not fair, blaming me. So I didn't study. I didn't kill anyone."

No one said anything.

"It's possible that the murderer heard about the show and the private yacht leaving the marina at a convenient time for him…or her…and replaced one of us," Talia finished saying.

"That's a lot of assumptions," Gus argued. "We're leaping to conclusions without any hard evidence. We don't even know if we're talking about the same person who killed that actress in Hawaii. It could just as easily have been some kind of dispute. Maybe Dino had it out for Joe and wanted him dead."

"*What?* Why me? Joe was a friend. More than a friend, he was a mentor. I didn't kill him." Dino ran his hand over his bald head, obviously upset.

"Look," Gus told him. "I'm not trying to accuse you. I'm trying to point out that anything is possible."

"Yeah," Tommy blurted. He took a few steps in Reuben's direction, his chest puffed. "Anything is possible. You say you're a cop. What if that's bullshit? What if you know how Joe died because you're the one who killed him?"

"He didn't kill him." Talia wrapped her arms around her stomach. She hated the idea that she needed to share their intimacy, but everyone had to know. "He was with me when Joe was killed."

"They probably were doing it in the woods." Tommy sneered at her briefly, then turned his focus back to Reuben. "He's been hot for her since the game began and she's been advertising it like a—"

"You do not want to finish that sentence," Reuben warned the younger man.

"Why? You going to stop me?"

"I'm going to beat the crap out of you," Reuben promised.

"Awfully violent there, Ruby. Can't you all see it's possible? The two of them did Joe…then they did each other."

Reuben's reflex was instant. He swung a right hook and followed it with a powerful uppercut. Tommy was sprawled out on the sand before anyone realized that a fight had broken out. Apparently not done, Reuben reached down and grabbed the kid by his T-shirt to haul him to his feet for another round.

"This isn't helping," Sam pointed out.

Talia agreed. "Let him go, Reuben."

There was a tense moment when she doubted he was going to listen. "We need to formulate a plan. We don't have time for this."

Reason must have penetrated his rage. With a forceful shove, he pushed Tommy away. Instantly, Talia stepped between them to prevent any more swings. She faced Tommy and slapped him across the face.

"What the—"

"That's for your foul mouth and for cheating. Now, you're going to break those bars into even pieces and distribute them. Don't forget Evan and Dino have to eat, too. Other than that I think the best thing we can do right now is empty our backpacks. If a spark plug falls out…we'll deal with it. If not, then at least we'll have some peace of mind."

Nodding, everyone opened their packs. Talia retrieved hers and Reuben's. There were extra shoes, socks, underwear, suits and T-shirts. But no seven million dollars in stolen jewels and no spark plugs.

"Okay."

"What does this mean?" Nancy had bent down to shove her exposed underwear in her bag. "What are we going to do now?"

"We wait," Reuben answered. Talia tried to read past his blank expression, but he wasn't revealing anything. "It's our only option. Evan?"

"What are you going to blame me for now?" the sullen host asked.

"How long before the crew on the yacht gets worried and comes for us?"

He shrugged. "I don't know. I guess a day, maybe two."

"Two days!" Marlie cried. "We could all be dead by then."

"Not if we stick together," Talia insisted. "There are nine of us. If the killer is one of us, that means it's eight to one. As long as we keep everyone in sight, no one gets hurt."

"What about the drinking water?" Nancy wanted to know. "It was my job to collect it."

"You can take Tommy and Marlie with you."

"No way!" Marlie cried, reaching for Evan's arm. "I'm not going into the woods with him."

Tommy's face fell as he realized that her affections had shifted to the host. Dino, too, seemed annoyed by the sudden connection between the two. Apparently, Marlie wasn't steadfast in her affections.

"I'll go, too," Evan offered. "There will be four of us."

Talia lifted her head to the sky. In the midst of all the excitement, she hadn't realized that the rain had stopped. The sky was still overcast, in fact ominously gray, and the wind was gusting, but with a little luck, the heavy rain would hold off and they might be able to get the fire going again.

"Gus, Dino and Sam, you stay. Reuben and I will retrieve the log and hope it's still hot."

The three men nodded. Dino sat next to his camera, his gaze periodically drifting to the spot where Joe was. The other two started to remove the damp wood on top of the fire pit in search of pieces that would be dry enough to light.

Reuben led Talia into the island's canopy, where he and Gus had left the burning log. "You seriously think we're going to get that fire lit?"

"No," Talia replied truthfully. "But it will give us all something to do. Collect water, try to get the fire going again. We were supposed to bring back some food and never did. We can try looking again. Something. Someone is going to crack if we've got nothing to do but stare at each other for two days."

"Right."

She stopped in her tracks. "What about going across the island to Evan's camp to get the radio?"

"I thought of that, but we'd all have to go. Given Nancy's physical condition and the distance she'd have to climb, the trek could take more than two days. We're better off waiting."

"I hate waiting," Talia confessed. "When I was diving I was never one to stand long on the platform. Just get up there, know the dive and jump. The longer I stood, the more I thought about it and that was never good."

Reuben was lifting palm leaves searching for the log. "I know. I'm not a big fan of waiting, either, but right now that's our only choice."

They worked in silence for a few minutes, each of them lifting palms, trying to sniff out the smoke. "Don't you remember where you and Gus put it?" she finally asked.

"It's around here somewhere. Sorry, but every palm tree looks alike to me." Reuben stopped his search and waited for her to get closer. "Can we talk about what happened before?"

It wasn't difficult to know what he was referring to. "I would rather not."

"Why?"

That was an easy answer. "Uh…I think we have bigger things to worry about."

"We do. That's why I want to clear up what happened this afternoon."

Clear it up. More than likely dismiss it. What had happened between them had been hot—raging hot, inferno hot—but now that it was over all the reasons why it had been a bad idea came crashing back. This wasn't a man she was going to have a future with, so the best option was to forget it ever happened.

"There is nothing to clear up," she said casually even as she turned her back to him, lifting a leaf that she already had lifted. "It happened. It's over. Forgotten."

"Forgotten?" There was incredulousness in his tone. "Sugar, I don't know about you, but it is going to be a long time before I forget what it felt like to be inside you with your legs wrapped around me."

He'd done it on purpose, evoked an image that made her belly flop and her knees tremble. He wanted a reaction but she wasn't going to give it to him.

"Whatever. All I'm saying is that there is no need to rehash."

She heard the palms crunching under his feet as he stomped toward her. Tommy wasn't all wrong when he said that Reuben had a tendency toward violence. It always seemed to be just below the surface. But any time he touched her, he never inflicted pain. It spoke to his self-discipline and control.

"I don't want to *rehash* it," he spat. "I want to make it clear that it's not over."

His words were unexpected and, more than that, a little unsettling. She instantly felt the need to reject them.

"It is over. There's a dead body, a killer," she stammered, trying to clarify all the reasons why they should not be having this conversation.

"You don't have to tell me. Trust me, I get it. But when all of this gets settled, and we get off this forsaken island, you need to know that you and I have unfinished business."

"What if I don't want to finish it?"

His eyes grew wide and his nostrils flared slightly.

"What? Are you daring me? Sugar, I'm warning you right now that I've never backed away from a dare."

Talia tugged her arm out of his hold. "You know, it occurs to me that if we hadn't been together when Joe was killed, you would have been the first suspect on my list."

He smiled his typical smile that seemed more threatening than any scowl. "But you were with me," he said seductively. "You were with me, your tongue was in me, your arms were around me and I was so deep inside you I thought I would never find my way out again. You trusted me. You had to, to open yourself like that to me."

"I trust that you didn't kill Joe. That's all."

He laughed softly. "You don't even sound convincing."

He was right. And she hated that he was. From the beginning, she had surmised that he was going to be her competition. She had considered him a hard-ass. She'd known that she needed to be on guard mentally, physically and emotionally, because he tugged at something deep inside her. But she'd also come to know that he was more than the image he projected. His actions, almost in spite of his outrageous attitude, suggested that there was good underneath the sneer. A noble heart somewhere beneath the innuendos.

A hero in a villain's costume.

She didn't want to tell him that. So her only recourse was to say nothing.

His hands circled her waist. One hand gently stroking the skin exposed by the bikini. "It's okay," he whispered, pulling her closer. "It's okay to trust me. I swear I won't let you down."

There it was again. The emotional pull. She couldn't

fathom why he would take that approach with her. It was as if he wanted something more than just sex. And that terrified her.

"We're supposed to be looking for a log and some food."

Backing away he studied her body language and her neutral expression. "Fine. I'll find the log. You see if you can get some coconuts or whatever. Then we'll get off this island and we'll figure out who killed Joe. And when all of that is done, we'll talk again. Maybe I can come and visit you at the accounting firm."

With that he turned away, shuffling through bushes and foliage in search of the smoldering log. Talia, too, concentrated her energy on finding something edible. There was nothing to be gained by worrying about Reuben. Nothing she could do that would distract him from whatever stick he had in his craw at the moment. All her efforts needed to be on staying alive long enough to get off the island.

Because when she did, she was going to kill her father for getting her in this mess in the first place.

"What was that?"

Her thoughts must have tumbled out of her mouth because Reuben evidently had heard her.

"What's your father got to do with this?"

Everything. "Nothing." She turned over a large branch and saw the smoke billowing out. "I found your log and it looks like it's still hot."

Reuben bent down beside her and carefully extracted the hot stick from the shelter. "No flame, but the wood is still red."

"It won't matter much if we can't find dry wood," Talia reminded him.

"Way to think positively. Let's go."

"I still haven't found anything for anyone to eat."

"We've got the bars. They'll last us for a little while. I don't want to risk losing the fire completely."

It was a sound point. They made their way back to the beach only to be greeted by the sound of shouting. Talia reached the beach first as Reuben was still carefully balancing the log, sheltering it from the damp palms he brushed past.

"I wasn't doing anything," Gus shouted angrily, standing just feet away from Joe's body. His body language screamed defensive as he was cornered by Sam and Tommy. There was no surprise that Tommy was the snapping dog out in front. Dino, however, was watching over the body like a faithful dog protecting his master.

"What were you doing poking him? I know," Tommy answered "Hiding evidence. What's the matter? Were you afraid maybe Reuben would see something if he checked again?"

"You idiot, I was confirming what he found, that's all. And I was hoping to find something else. Something that might tell us why or who."

Talia once again put herself between two pissed-off men. One of these times she was going to get trapped in the cross fire. Reuben pulled on her arm, trying to tug her out of the way. But she dug her feet in the sand. Literally. Another hot-tempered male was not what this situation needed.

"What's going on?" She directed her question to Sam, who should have been the most reasonable of the group.

"I don't know. We were all on the beach, the girls and Evan went to get the water. We looked up and Gus was kneeling near the body. Tommy started shouting and we all ran over."

"I told you," Gus stated curtly. "I'm a former investigator."

"I thought you said you were in the army," Sam argued.

That was it, Talia decided. If Sam was suspicious, then it meant that paranoia was now in full blossom and it was starting to stink.

"I said I was military. And I was."

"Army intelligence?" Reuben asked.

"Naval," Gus told him. "I was N.I.S. for twenty-five years."

Reuben nodded slowly. "You should have told us."

"Ha! You never told anyone a damn thing."

"I meant after," Reuben corrected himself. "You should have told us after. I could have used your help."

"Help!" Tommy screeched. "A, how do we know he's telling the truth? B, how do we know you're who you say you are, Reuben? This whole thing is sick, man. I want off this island."

He stomped away in the direction of the boat, but there was nowhere to go once he got there. Unless…

"Unless he's got the plug in his shorts," Reuben whispered in Talia's ear, finishing her thought. How *did* he do that? But as they watched, Tommy merely kicked wet sand at the hull, then plopped himself down on the beach.

"I didn't say anything because it's been a while," Gus finally admitted. "A long while since I've done this kind of work. I didn't want to say anything and give any kind of misinformation. When everyone backed away I thought I could take a look. That's all."

"We have to believe you." Dino shrugged his shoulders and shook his head. "We don't have a choice. None of us does."

"I'm going to see about the fire. Gus, I could use your help." Reuben walked off and Gus followed. With nothing left to contribute, Sam joined the other two. But Dino clearly didn't want to leave his post.

Walking as respectfully as she knew how around the corpse, Talia rubbed the stout man's back.

"My mother used to do that. When I was upset, she would rub my back," Dino explained.

"Mine, too."

"I was fired from my last job," he confessed. "Not because of anything serious or anything like that. Anyway, I was broke and I didn't know how I was going to get the airfare to get back home. Then Joe finds me and he says, 'I got this great opportunity for you.' From the beginning I felt like I owed him. I wanted to do a good job. Now he's dead and I was off filming snakes for effect…. I could have been helping him. I could have saved him."

"There was nothing you could have done," she murmured only because that was what she had to say. Because she had to believe he was innocent, that somehow they were all innocent.

"Let's get back to the group and hope they get a fire started. With our wet clothes it's going to get chilly if this wind keeps blowing."

Dino let out a huff. "You know this wind, it hasn't stopped at all. It just keeps getting louder and faster. Is it always like this on these islands?"

No, not always. But it was when there was a storm approaching.

Talia stood and tilted her head to the sky. She tried to remember everything her mother had taught her about willies and what she could do to keep the group safe without proper shelter.

It didn't seem fair that this should happen, that they should be faced with one more challenge that was out of their control to prevent. Somebody had killed Joe and no one had been able to stop that. Now nature was throwing something else at them.

No, it didn't seem fair at all. They still were weathering the storm of Joe's death. She didn't have a whole lot of faith that they could handle another one on top of it.

Chapter 7

"The wind is picking up." Futilely, Talia pushed the hair from her face only to have another burst of wind blow it back in her eyes.

"Huh?" Reuben shouted. He was on his knees by the pile of smoldering logs that had once been their campfire. Gus was beside him with his hands cupped over the barely lit ember. The two practically were willing the ember to turn into a flame, but the damp wood and wind were making it almost impossible.

"I said the wind is picking up. The gusts are stronger. We may need to forget the fire and think about shelter inland where the trees can offer more protection."

"But what about the water?" Nancy and her party had returned from their trip with a bucket of water that was slowly leaking from the center hole that clearly had been intentional. It was the killer's first attempt to get off the island. If there was no water, Evan would have had to call for another boat to bring a new bucket, or sent someone to the yacht. Either way, an opportunity for escape.

"We've got bigger problems if we have a serious storm coming."

"But if there is a storm, isn't that good? Won't the yacht have to come and get us?" Everyone in the group turned in Marlie's direction, no doubt shocked at the logic in that statement.

Then simultaneously everyone turned their expectant gazes on Evan. "Is it true?" Tommy persisted. "Will the ship come get us?"

Silence reigned. The wind gusted. But Evan had no answer.

Talia's mouth dropped. "I don't understand. If there was a problem—a storm or a hurricane on radar—they would have had to make provisions for that. Possibly even expected it. This is the season for those kinds of storms in the South Pacific."

He didn't shift his feet or avert his eyes, but his tense face, tight shoulders, the way his hands gripped either side of his hips told its own story. "Of course the producers wouldn't let anything really bad happen. That's what they told me when I took this job. 'Evan,' they said, 'we're not going to let anything really bad happen.'"

"Define *really bad*," Talia insisted.

"Well, it *is* a show about endurance. The audience would have wanted to see how you all handled adversity. That includes the weather."

"Does it include murder?" Reuben snarled.

"I don't think so," Evan replied lamely. Then came the hand wringing and the eye aversion. Gone was the fake smile, the fake dialogue, the fake man. In the place of the host was simply another person afraid for his life.

"I don't know how bad it has to get. Yes, they said they would keep me informed if there was a serious storm approaching. Only, I've lost communication. So does that mean the yacht is moving toward the island or this isn't a serious storm...? I don't know. Not without a radio, which I don't have. I was told to expect bad weather. I was told it would create a dramatic backdrop. No offense. But this is pretty freakin' dramatic."

"Absolutely. What I'm really hoping is that this is all going to translate into an Emmy," Reuben stated dryly. "After all, reality shows have their own category now."

"Oh my God, are you serious? Do you think we could win an Emmy?"

Obviously, Marlie didn't hear the sarcasm in Reuben's comment.

"Our priority is shelter," Talia informed the group.

"What about water?" Nancy was getting a little obsessed with the water.

"What about food?" Without his illegal cache, Tommy was finally understanding hunger pangs. The granola bars already had been broken up and eaten. Half of a protein bar wasn't nearly enough to compensate for two days without food.

"What about the killer?" Sam's question stopped the group from moving.

Talia, however, saw the situation differently. "A killer

might take us out one at a time. This storm, if it's bad
enough, could kill us all. That means for right now we
focus on it. We stay together. We find some decent protection, then we'll worry about how we're going to get
off the island."

She waited for anyone to protest, but no one did.

"Okay, nature girl," Reuben prompted. "What do we
have to do to stay safe?"

"Evan, you said that people from the show surveyed
the island. Can you remember any mention of caves?
This island is all volcanic rock—there should be a number of holes and caves along the peak for us to wait out
the storm in."

His eyes grew wide with excitement. "There is.
There's the cave that we're using to store your necessity
items, batteries for the cameras and all of our supplies.
But I've gotten there from our camp on the other side of
the island. From here, I don't know how we would get
to it. It's pretty far inland and high up on the hill."

"Too risky," Gus suggested. "Especially if the yacht
is on its way to pick us up. We need to be here, where
they expect us to be, if that happens."

"I agree." Talia glanced around the beach, her eyes
centering on the boat. "There might be something in
that we can use."

Evan fidgeted. "Uh…I don't know if that's allowed—"

"The game is over," she said cutting him off. "Offi-
cially. And let me tell you I'm not going to have nice
things to say to the producers about this experience
when I get back."

"Ditto," Tommy muttered.

Reuben was moving toward the boat and Talia followed. Beneath the control panel was a storage cabinet. Reuben already had it opened and was tossing out life preservers. Then a first-aid kit. Then he pulled out a thin blue tarp.

"To cover the boat," Talia answered when she saw his quizzical expression.

"It doesn't look very sturdy."

"The material's strong and it will help against the rain. Anything else?"

"No." He rolled up the tarp and hopped out. "What are you thinking?"

"I'm thinking we take this just inside the woods, let the trees buffer the wind, then use the tarp as a tent."

"Nine people are not going to be able to squeeze into one tent."

"I know."

Both of their eyes continued to scan the beach searching for ideas.

"What about the air mattress," he suggested. "It's plastic. If we cut that open, two maybe three people could fit under that."

"Yeah, but how are we going to cut…" The pocketknife that so grotesquely stuck out of Joe's back flashed behind her eyes. Judging from Reuben's grim expression, that was exactly what he was thinking of using.

"But don't we need to keep it as evidence? For prints and stuff."

"It's not going to come down to that. As soon as we get back on the yacht and can confirm everyone's identity we'll know who our murderer is. Prints aren't going to make a difference and we need the knife."

The thought of pulling it out of Joe's body shook her to her core. "I can't do it."

Reuben dropped the tarp and pulled her close to him. He reached out and cupped the back of her neck, kneading the muscles strongly. The release of tension that she hadn't even realized was there was sweet enough almost to make her cry.

"Hey, I wouldn't ask you. Stop trying to do it all."

"They're counting on me," she whispered. "I know more about this—camping and survival—and I have to…" Her throat tightened up on her and her voice cracked, so she stopped talking. For a second she considered putting her head on his shoulder and letting the tears that she'd been holding back since she'd seen Joe's body flow.

That was something she'd never been able to do with her father. When her mother had died and all Talia had wanted to do was wail and curse against the forces that had taken her away, she hadn't been able to because that was what he had been doing. She, the child, had been the one to hold both of them together. She had pulled her father back from the edge of a depression so deep she'd feared he might never recover. She had been the strong one.

Sometimes being the strong one could be so exhausting.

"Come here." Reuben tried to pull her closer against his body. It was an extremely tempting offer to let him shoulder the burden, to let him take on her fears, to let him have the burden for everyone else. But she resisted. Reuben couldn't do it alone any more than she could. Together, though, they might be able to pull through this.

"No, I'm okay. I don't want them to think—" She didn't have to finish that sentence. He would understand. If she was going to take the lead, the group needed to have faith in her. They needed to believe that she could do what needed to be done to protect them until help came. Seeing her cry and cling to Reuben wouldn't give them the reassurance. "You go get the…the thing. I'll see if I can find a cluster of trees not too far from the beach."

They went their separate ways. Unable to stop herself, she looked over her shoulder and followed Reuben's purposeful stride toward Joe's body. His shoulders were wide, his hips narrow. Too long on the island and eventually he would be too lean. But no matter how much weight he lost, Talia doubted it would ever subtract from the raw power he seemed to exude.

Tommy approached Reuben and started buzzing around him like a fly, no doubt questioning why he was returning to the body. Reuben simply ignored Tommy. Nothing was going to stop Reuben from the gruesome task.

He certainly wasn't an easy man, she decided. And she still doubted that they had a chance for a future that went beyond the island. But for now she was grateful that he was here.

A gust of wind blew so hard that it knocked her off her feet. Laughing at herself for being taken off guard, she picked herself up, brushed off the sand and got to the task at hand. He'd left the tarp on the beach so she carried it to the group.

"We can use this to make a tent. We need to find an area just inside the woods that will work for protection, but will still allow us to keep a lookout for the yacht."

"What's he doing?" Marlie asked, eyes pinned on Reuben as he crouched beside Joe's body.

"He's doing what he has to do. Now let's go. The more of us searching the better, but everyone stays in eye contact with one another. Got it?"

In unison they nodded. Gus held onto Nancy's arm as he helped her over the bushes. The cloud cover changed from a dark, ominous gray to a light gray to a hint of sun, then back to the dark, almost bluish hue of gray that spoke of something serious.

Diligently they worked together, finding a cluster of five palm trees that seemed to spring from one trunk. "What do you think?" Gus asked her.

Talia lifted her head to watch the movement of the leaves. They swayed and the trees tilted dramatically, but the wind wasn't strong enough to bend them severely. Not yet anyway.

"I think it will be bad if the wind gets stronger."

"That's an understatement." Reuben joined them, using the knife to cut the elastic strip from the edge of the boat cover. Tugging the strip out of the seam, they had a means of tying the tarp to tree trunks.

Everyone seemed to be waiting for her decision. It was a tough call, but they hadn't found anything better and she feared time was running out. "It's our best bet."

"We're not going to fit everyone underneath this," Reuben warned her.

"I know. And I'm not crazy about splitting up, but we don't have a choice. We could probably squeeze five of us. Each of these trunks is thick enough to block out whatever might come flying at us, too. I suppose if the tree starts to topple over we'll feel it."

"There's a bonus," Tommy barked sarcastically.

"We're doing our best," she stated calmly.

"Yeah, right. You said five, what are the four left supposed to do?"

The air mattress had already been cut open and pulled flat. It didn't cover nearly as much area as the tarp did. They were going to need to find another tree split into sections and hope that the plastic would serve as protection from the rain. But there was no way it would do that for four people.

"This isn't going to work. At best we get three people under this." Sam was merely putting into words what everyone already knew.

"Then we'll squeeze six under the tarp," Talia told them confidently. "It will be tight, but it will be fine. We'll keep warm that way. Let's see if we can find another tree like this nearby."

They spread out to search, always ensuring they could see at least two other members. Reuben and Gus stayed behind to secure the first shelter. The good news was that the wind hadn't gotten any stronger. The bad news was that it hadn't lessened, either. If the rain started again, they would have a harder time of it. What light they had was dimming as day's end fast approached.

Talia spotted an area that could serve as another shelter and made her way through some heavy foliage to check it out. Three trees sprang up from the ground like triplets. The trunks were curved, no doubt having battled many tropical storms throughout their lives, and anyone sitting in that curve would feel protected. With the plastic sheet serving as a lean-to, it just might work.

She was about fifty yards away from the other site. It wasn't the best idea to have the second shelter be so far away, but they didn't have much choice. She had climbed a significant incline to reach this point and could look down to see a hint of the blue tarp against the green backdrop.

Talia was about to call to the others when she saw Sam coming up the hill. Sam, but no one else.

Sam's falling could have been a way to distract us.

Reuben had suggested as much when they both still thought the accidents had more to do with strategy than with stolen jewelry and a dead actress. Suddenly, suspicion had her stomach clenching as questions raced through her mind.

Sam wasn't a good swimmer. Even with a life jacket he'd had a hard time reaching the island. Would someone really come on a reality show that was set on an island if he couldn't swim? What if he wasn't who he said he was? What if his dazed look when Evan had given him the mattress had nothing to do with the bump on his head, but had everything to do with the fact that he had no idea what was on his list because he hadn't been the one to create it.

"Did you find something?" he called to her. "I hope

so. It's getting dark and I've been feeling drops. I think it's going to rain again soon."

He was struggling a little with the climb, but still moving forward. Talia's heart was bumping inside her chest as she searched the woods for someone else and listened for voices that were close. But between the howling wind and the fading light, all she could see, all she could hear, was Sam.

Think, she told herself. What would be the point of getting her alone? If he was the killer, taking her out wouldn't help his cause, which everyone believed was to escape. Killing her would only confirm his identity. Small comfort considering she'd be dead. Still, it wasn't a logical move. Unless he was a sociopath and his ultimate goal was simply to kill anyone in his path.

"Stop!" He was no more than ten feet away from her when she finally found her voice. "What are you doing, Sam? You're not supposed to be out of sight of at least two other people. Those are the rules."

She had a hard time seeing his face, but he stood very still. If he took another step closer, she would run. Having witnessed his athletic ability firsthand, she was confident that she could outrace him.

"Oh my God. You think I—"

"Hello! Everyone, I'm up here," she shouted as loudly as she could. Only the wind answered and as Sam had predicted, the rain began to fall again, droplets snapping against broad palm leaves creating a cacophony of sound.

"Talia…I'm not going to hurt you."

Famous last words from a killer.

"I'm sorry, Sam. I truly am. But you need to stay where you are." She tried yelling again.

"Someone! Can anyone hear me? I'm up here!"

There was rustling behind Sam and she saw him turn around. To defend himself from whatever was coming, he put his hands in the air as if signaling immediate surrender.

"What the hell?" It was Reuben's clipped voice. He was angry. Talia didn't have to see his face to know it. Behind him came everyone else. Once they were assembled, the threat was over.

"Yo, buddy," Tommy confronted Sam. "What were you thinking? You know you're not supposed to go anywhere alone."

"For once I agree with Tommy," Reuben said. "Sam, you know the rules."

Sam continued to hold his hands in the air. "I wasn't thinking. I was looking for a tree and then I saw Talia. I thought that maybe she found something and I was just coming to see. I didn't realize there wasn't anyone behind me."

"Did he threaten you? Hurt you?"

"No. He didn't do anything. I'm sorry, Sam. I know this is crazy, but it is what it is right now. You understand?"

"I'm sorry. I…I wasn't thinking. I can't imagine that anyone might think that I could be a murderer. You have to know me, I guess. When I'm back home and I tell my friends about this, they'll really laugh because they know I couldn't hurt anyone. It doesn't seem so funny now, though."

"It's not," Reuben assured him. "We've got the first shelter secure. What did you find?"

Over her shoulder, she pointed to the triplets. "I think it might work. Three trees practically touching and the way they curve creates a pocket against the wind. Add the plastic—maybe use sticks to punch through it to secure the cover to the ground and the leftover elastic to tie it to the trees—and it should be safe and dry."

"Let's do it," Dino said. "We're running out of light."

Reuben handed him the plastic, what was left of the elastic strip and the pocketknife. "Keep the holes small. We don't want the plastic to tear."

"Got it. Hey, uh, Sam. Why don't you help me out?" It was a gesture from Dino to include Sam in the group again and it was the right move to make. Sam hadn't done anything, but by calling out, Talia had made him a prime suspect.

"Okay. Thanks."

Gus went to supervise, while Evan stayed back with Nancy and Marlie. Not surprisingly, Reuben made a beeline for Talia.

"Are you sure…?" he began to say.

"I'm okay. He didn't do or say anything. I looked up and saw that it was only the two of us and I panicked."

"That's not panicking, that's playing it smart, which is what you need to do. You have no idea he's not the killer."

Talia used her hands to rub some of the chill out of her bare arms, no easy task as they were getting soaked again. Reuben was wearing one of his extra T-shirts, having left one in the forest. He removed his shirt and pulled it over her head.

"I have my own," she protested.

"This is bigger. It will cover more. It's damp, but better than nothing. I have another one."

She couldn't say she was warmer, but something about being covered by his shirt had a comforting effect. Primitive, she knew, but true.

"I kept thinking about what you said earlier. How Sam might have fallen to distract us. Back then we thought it was about trying to win, but what if he did fall on purpose?"

"You mean as an attempt to get off the island?"

Talia nodded.

Reuben stared into the dark for a moment before speaking. "He didn't leave when he had the chance, but who knows what that might mean. Maybe they would have sent one of the crew to get him. It's possible he didn't think he had enough strength to throw one of those guys overboard. And the lump on his head was real. Too many ifs. It's a game of speculation."

"You're a detective. Isn't reasonable speculation what you do?"

"I *was* a detective. And yes, we did a lot of that. Lesson number one—to catch a killer you have to think like a killer. You have to understand why he did what he did and what he hoped to gain from it, be it money, the thrill, revenge, whatever. Once you understand what motivated him—it makes it easier to find him. But without knowing the details of what happened in Hawaii, we can't guess about motivation."

"But in this case it's simple, isn't it? He wanted money. He…or she…took the jewelry."

Reuben rubbed his chin with his hand and Talia heard the scratch of his beard. She'd felt that stubble on her body earlier that afternoon and the memory caused her to shiver a bit. She was grateful he couldn't see it.

"There are a lot of ways to steal money without having to kill for it," he finally said. "Look at me. I came on this stupid show knowing I was going to practically steal the million dollars from everyone."

His bravado was a ridiculous attempt to lighten the mood. It worked.

"You were *so* not going to win," she returned.

"Oh, I *so* was," he smiled. "Granted you would have put up a fight, but in the end the strongest would have survived. I would have kicked your ass."

"You wouldn't have had anything to eat. I would have stopped giving you my fish."

"Sugar, you're far too softhearted not to give food to someone who is hungry. I would have taken your fish and your body regularly. Both of which would have given me all the strength I needed."

She grimaced, figuring both statements were true. But she had absolutely no intention of letting him get away with it.

"Oh, yeah? In the end I would have put a snake on you while you were sleeping and when you woke up you would have cracked like a baby."

His smile quickly diminished. "Okay, that is not funny."

But it made her laugh.

"Hey, we're done. Come take a look."

Reuben and Talia turned at the sound of Dino's

voice, going to inspect what he and Sam had done. The plastic was rippling, but holding steady against the wind.

"I think it will stay," Sam stated confidently. "Now I guess we have to decide who goes where."

"I'm going wherever Evan is." Marlie linked her arm with Evan's.

"Uh…okay."

"You know, you sure changed your tune real quick," Tommy accused her.

"You can say that again," Dino muttered.

"What happened to us winning this game together?" Tommy wanted to know.

"That was, like, before someone died. There is no 'us' anymore. For all I know, you could be the killer. At least I've seen Evan on TV. I know who he is. And where he sleeps, I sleep."

"I don't mind where I sleep. It doesn't really matter anymore." Nancy was sitting on the ground, her chin on her knees and her arms wrapped around them. Her hair was blowing about her face but she made no effort to stop it. That she was on her last ounce of strength was evident.

"Nancy, you, me, Reuben, Evan, Marlie and Gus will take the tarp. Tommy, Sam and Dino will take the triplets."

Talia could see that Tommy was ready to protest, but he closed his mouth. No doubt he was more annoyed about being told what to do than caring about where he slept for the night. Fortunately he cut off his whining before it could start. It might just be possible that through all of this horror he was finally starting to grow up.

"Let's get settled. It's going to be a long night."

The three men stayed behind while the rest of the group carefully made their way down the hill to the tarp. The canvas struggled against the wind, but the thick bindings holding it to the trunks remained tight. One by one, they managed to take a position inside the crude tent. The way the trees were angled, three of them could sit, but the rest would have to lean against the trunks, with at least one person leaning on someone else.

After having made a quick trip to the beach for his backpack and another T-shirt, Reuben took one of the curved trunks and positioned Talia between his legs so that she was leaning against him. Evan did the same with Marlie, and Gus and Nancy were given the two remaining trees.

"My boys built a tree fort once, out in the backyard. Ronald, that was my husband, he stayed out there one night with them, but had to come inside eventually because the bugs were too much. They wanted me to stay outside with them, too, but I thought I couldn't possibly. I wasn't the type to sleep outside. Now here I am. It's a long way from home."

"I think your boys are going to be very proud of you, Nancy," Talia told her.

Reuben's arms squeezed gently in agreement with her gesture.

"I don't know about that," the older woman sighed. "I think they were disappointed more with me than with their father. After all, I was the one who lost him to that beautiful young thing. I got heavy and boring and she was tall and slim. She had money, too. She bought the boys all kinds of presents. She was everything I wasn't. I hated her. I hated her so much it made me sick. The worst part was my boys wanted me to be more like her. But I couldn't be."

An uncomfortable silence descended. The wind wailed and rain pattered against the tarp. No one knew what to say to Nancy.

"I thought if I came on the show maybe I could change. I could lose weight and learn how to be adventurous and win money so that I could shower my boys with presents. Then when I was so close and didn't get picked to be one of the eight finalists, I lost it a little bit. I was so mad that I just got on a plane and went to Hawaii anyway. I don't know why. I don't know what I thought was going to happen. That other lady dropped out, and the show called me. And I thought fate was working for me instead of against me. I really believed that life was going my way. But then everything went wrong and…I just want to go home."

Her voice cracked on the word *home,* and soon the sound of the storm was conjoined with the sound of Nancy sobbing. Neither of which was a pleasing sound.

"We're going to get you home, Nancy. You'll see. You'll have stories to tell your sons that will absolutely wow them. Remember the shark?" Talia had to get Nancy out of her funk. They couldn't listen to her crying all night.

"The shark," she whimpered. "That seems so long ago."

"Just a few days. Remember how you outswam it?"

"I did do that, didn't I?"

"Revisionist history," Reuben muttered in Talia's ear, to which she responded with a gentle elbow jab.

"All we need to do is stick together and we can get through this. Eventually, storm or no storm, the yacht will get us if they've been out of contact with us for too long."

At least that was the story Talia was sticking to. After everything that had happened, she could admit to herself that she would dearly love just a few hours of sleep. Forget Joe's murder, the earth-shattering impact of making love to Reuben was enough to exhaust her both mentally and physically.

Considering the tight squeeze of the shelter, she didn't see how sleep was going to be possible. Surprisingly, the body heat from Reuben at her back, as well as from everyone else, seemed to steam up the space under the tent.

A lazy warmth permeated her muscles and relaxed them. Added to that was Reuben's slow and steady breathing. In and out. In and out. She felt his chest lift and descend, taking hers along with it. Almost like rocking on a boat.

Leaning her head against his shoulder, her smooth cheek pressed against his rough one, she felt safe. It didn't matter if one of them within the tight confines of the shelter was a killer. He wouldn't let anyone hurt her.

She felt herself drifting off, felt herself becoming accustomed to the harsh sounds of the elements and the soft sounds of Reuben breathing, felt herself letting go.

It could have been an hour or five hours later, she had no idea, but at one point she found herself stirring. There was movement within the cluster of trees. Then a blast of wind hit her face as if someone had lifted the canvas.

Why?

Her fuzzy brain reached for an answer and then one came to her. Someone was leaving. That she should be alarmed by that didn't occur to her, but a sense of foreboding invaded her system causing her to rouse against the arms that held her in place.

"Nancy, what are you doing?" Reuben's harsh whisper came from behind her and she felt the hot breath on her ear.

"I have to go…to the bathroom… I have to."

"Stay close and make it quick."

Talia turned her face. "Hmm…a problem. I can go…"

"Shh," he soothed her as his arms loosened, repositioned around her waist and then tightened once more. "It's okay. Go back to sleep."

Soft lips brushed the underside of her jaw and once more she found herself at the mercy of his will. It was so easy to let him hold her. So easy to sink into the physical lethargy that had claimed her. For some reason she thought about her father and what he might think of Reuben. Smiling inwardly, she realized that was a nobrainer. Reuben wanted to open a bar. It was a sure bet that her father would love him.

Shifting slightly, she bent her knees to make sure she didn't sleep in a position that would leave her stiff the next morning and then felt him readjust his legs behind her so that they both had the support they needed. Before she could think about why she shouldn't be doing it, she fell once more into a mindless sleep.

Chapter 8

"Sugar, you got to move. My ass is numb."

They weren't the sweetest words a girl wanted to hear from the man she'd made love to the previous day, but they did wake her up. The wind was still blowing against the tarp, but the patter of rain had stopped. She had to believe that was a good sign, but the reality depended on the size of the storm. There could be pockets of relief only to have it surge again.

Pulling away from Reuben, Talia took a moment to acclimate herself to the morning. Island, storm…murder. Suddenly it was all coming back.

"I can't believe I slept," she said, grateful that she had. Her stomach was growling and her mouth was parched, but overall she felt refreshed.

"I actually think I did, too. For a while." Gingerly,

Reuben tried to twist his torso within the confines of their tree fort without disturbing anyone. He grimaced in pain, but seemed to loosen up quickly. Evan and Marlie were still pressed together. Both looked to be awake but drowsy. Evan had to be as uncomfortable as Reuben had been but wasn't willing to push Marlie aside.

"What time is it?" Before anyone could answer her, Marlie turned so that she was facing Evan, her arms around his shoulders and her cheek pressed against his.

"I'm not sure. Maybe morning?" Evan guessed. He seemed slightly sheepish about Marlie's easy embrace, but under the circumstances no one really had time to ponder the ethics of the show's host getting involved with one of the contestants.

Talia popped her face outside the shelter. A blast of wind smacked a wet leaf across her cheek. Once she was able to push it away she concluded that it soon would be dawn, given the hazy gray quality of the island.

"Definitely close to sunrise," she told the group.

"I didn't sleep," Nancy whimpered. "Not a wink. The wind kept howling. It was so loud. And then when I closed my eyes all I could see was Joe floating in the water. He was out there all night. On the beach just lying there."

"He's dead. It's not like he was cold," Reuben told her.

Nancy wasn't comforted by his answer. "I can't believe any of this is happening. This was supposed to be a game show. That's all. An adventure. And the wind won't stop howling and—"

Immediately, Talia reached across Gus and grabbed the woman's hands, forcing her to meet her steady gaze.

"Hey, calm down. It's going to be okay. We made it through one night. That means the boat will be here soon. If not today, then certainly by tomorrow when they don't hear from Evan. We'll be able to put all of this behind us and we'll find out exactly what happened to Joe."

"Speaking of the storm, what do you think?" Gus wondered. "It's not raining now. Is that good?"

"It could be."

Gus frowned. "That's not much of an answer. Are you saying we should be worried?"

Talia shook her head and worked hard to sound upbeat and confident. "Actually, no. I think we're okay. If this tent could hold together all night, then the winds aren't beyond fifty miles an hour. Probably just a tropical storm passing through. It could blow over by tonight."

It was a lie, of course. The winds could very well be a precursor of a more ominous storm. Without a Doppler radar, however, there was no way to know. Sensing that Nancy didn't need any more bad news, Talia's only choice was to play the optimist. It wouldn't hurt for Marlie and Evan to hear it, either. Gus and Reuben might guess that she was lying, but she counted on both of them to keep their cool and their mouths shut.

"Right. A tropical storm." Evan seemed to pick up at the news, latching on to the description as if calling it something other than a cyclone made it less dangerous. "They told me to expect them. Frequently. And that it was nothing to be too concerned with."

Marlie rolled over again, huffing and pouting to express her discomfort, and let her head fall back on his shoulder. "*They*," she repeated sarcastically. "Did *they* also say someone would die? That we would be trapped on the island with some psycho killer? You know, we should get something for this...like money. I'm suffering severe emotional angst right now."

"Oh, shut up." Reuben apparently wasn't sensitive to her emotional angst. "We're all in this together."

"Not all of us," she corrected him. "One of us is a killer. How do we know he won't strike again...like, whenever?"

"How do we know *he* is not a *she*?" Reuben said in retaliation, making it clear that the wanna-be starlet was not completely above suspicion. "Hollywood is a cutthroat place. A young actress wanting to make her mark might get an idea into her head to take out the competition. Take her life, take her jewelry and, bang, now she's the one on top. And didn't you mention that you had tried to get on the set as an extra? You knew who Carney was, knew where she worked. Maybe you didn't take getting rejected all that well."

The girl gasped in horror, then immediately looked to Evan to intervene in her defense.

"Uh...she couldn't have killed Joe, uh...we were...uh..."

"Enough," Talia cut in to stop them. She scowled at Reuben to let him know he wasn't helping the situation. Evan and Marlie had reached a screaming Nancy together and it had been obvious they hadn't been on the beach playing patty-cake. As obvious as she and Reuben must have been to everyone else.

"He started it."

The sensible and mature response she expected from someone of Marlie's intelligence. Talia struggled to hold on to her patience. "This gets us nothing. We need to hold it together for one more day. That's it. One more day and this is all over."

"Are we going to have to stay underneath this thing all day?" Nancy wanted to know. "And what about the others? Shouldn't we check on them?"

Talia met the expectant faces of the five people huddled so close together. It would be a seriously long day if they had to wait it out with no more than a few inches to maneuver.

"I think the best bet is to stay within the woods between the two shelters. Fishing won't be possible, but we can all look for avocados or coconuts on the ground. With the wind shaking the trees, there should be a lot more to pick from."

"I'll go check on the guys," Reuben said. "See how they made it through the night."

"And I'll head back to the beach to get the bucket. If it's still there, maybe we can make do with some of the water still clinging to the leaves." Gus lifted the tarp and stepped out.

Reuben was about to follow when from the other side the tarp was lifted. Dino's bald head popped up in the center of them, startling Nancy and causing Marlie to screech.

"Hey, have you seen Sam or Tommy? I woke up this morning and both of them were gone. I looked around but…I'm freaked, you know?"

Talia moved first, extracting herself from the tree tent to stand beside him. Without the shelter, the gusts were hitting hard, forcing her to widen her stance to brace herself. "What do you mean gone? Didn't they say where they were going?"

"No. I mean, I was sleeping. We were pretty sheltered by the trees, and the plastic kept the rain out. I guess I drifted off. I just got up and saw that they were both gone. I shouted, but I don't think anyone could hear me in this wind."

Reuben came up behind her. "We've got to go look for them. You come with us," he told Dino. "Gus will take Evan, Marlie and Nancy and head for the beach."

"Try to keep your faces covered if possible," Talia told them. "The wind will have the sand kicking up."

Everyone left the shelter, Marlie the most reluctant. For once Talia couldn't blame her because, as the tiniest of the group, she had the hardest time staying on her feet against the powerful blasts.

Gus had the two women each take a hand to form a chain as he led the way to the beach. Talia and Reuben followed Dino to the other shelter.

"Tommy!"

"Sam!"

Their calls remained unanswered. It wasn't until Reuben spotted blue among all the green that he grew hopeful. "Hey, over there."

They rounded a tree just in time to see Tommy pulling up his blue swimsuit trunks over his white bottom. He turned around and scowled at them. "What the hell! A man can't have a few minutes of privacy?"

Dino's shoulders slumped with evident relief. "I woke up and you were both gone. I didn't know what to think. I panicked."

"I woke up and Sam was gone. I figured he was doing his business and I needed to do mine. No big deal."

"Fine," Reuben snapped. "But I'll be happier when we find Sam."

Then they heard it. Through the wind and the rustle of trees, a high-pitched scream that could only come from a human in fear for her life.

"The beach." Talia started to sprint, hopping over fallen branches and bamboo shoots as she did. She tried to be careful and watch where her feet were landing, but more often recklessly pushing through the forest. She saw the water and white sand in front of her beyond a cluster of banyan trees, and made her to way on to the beach where, as she'd predicted, the sand became tiny bullets that showered her exposed body.

Ignoring the stinging pain, she searched right, then left, and saw the group at the water's edge. Nancy was pointing out into the inlet. The water was choppy, little whitecaps forming on tiny waves, but Talia easily picked out the bobbing form.

A sense of déjà vu washed over her as she headed for the body, diving forward into the water as soon as it became too difficult to walk. She didn't think about the current. She didn't consider that what she had seen floating hadn't been moving. She only knew that she needed to reach him as quickly as possible.

Sam.

Sam, who couldn't swim very well. Sam, who wasn't very athletic. Sam, who had come to this island to prove something to himself, and knew that he was failing the second he stepped off the boat.

Talia's hand came over her head to cup the water, but instead came into contact with the body. Lifting her head up, she worked her legs hard against the current to maintain her precarious position. Pulling on his T-shirt, she turned the body over and knew that any chance Sam might have had to be resuscitated passed about three or four hours ago.

His face was already bloated and had turned a sickly blue shade. And the fish had gotten to him. Chunks of skin were missing and they had already taken an eye. Fighting the nausea that threatened to weaken her, Talia rolled him facedown. When she pulled him onto the beach, she would need to make sure that his head was covered.

Turning around, she kept one hand on his shirt and used her other to stroke. Reuben was already in the water swimming to meet her. He pulled alongside and stared beyond her to the body she had in tow.

"Sam?"

Bobbing her head, she paddled past him. She couldn't speak or even think right now. About how this happened, or why, or even more importantly who. It was too overwhelming, too consuming for her mind to grasp. That's when she knew that maybe she, like Nancy, was coming to the end of her rope.

Maybe all the strength she had had been used up. Dealing with her father's dilemma, having to face the cameras again, having to put her shot at normalcy on hold. Coming to the island, fending off Reuben, rescuing Nancy, beating Tommy, trying to help Sam. Then Joe's death.

Now Sam's death.

It was too much. Her legs stopped churning and for a moment she slipped below the water, but her hand held tight to Sam's shirt. The gasses being expelled by his body served to keep him afloat, acting as a life preserver for her as long as she maintained her grip. The irony wasn't lost on her. But she couldn't reflect on it for long.

Regardless of what she was feeling, she needed to act. It was important that she get him out of the water. He would hate to be left in the water. She had no idea how she knew that, but she did. Before she could kick her legs to resurface, she felt Reuben beneath the water with her, his hand on the back of her bikini bottoms hauling her up with him.

Their heads broke free, and they stared at each other for a moment. She knew he was trying to see something in her eyes, in her expression. Or maybe he was trying to see into her thoughts. From the beginning it seemed that he'd been able to do so with relative ease.

"Tell me what you're thinking," he prompted.

Not this time, apparently. She supposed it was because she wasn't thinking. It was as if her brain had shut down, leaving only one command. She had to get Sam to the beach. That's all she wanted to do.

"We have to get him to the beach."

"Okay."

He moved and grabbed another handful of Sam's shirt, kicking and paddling with her. Soon their feet touched bottom and they dragged the body to shore, Reuben clearly taking on more of the physical load than she did.

This time no one raced up to see. Everyone stood back, huddled together, waiting for whatever came next. Gus had his arm around Nancy, probably trying to hold her together. But her sobbing was louder than the wind.

Reuben crouched and inspected the body. He winced when he saw the man's partially missing face and had to swallow a few times before he could look again. He studied Sam's neck, his chest, then climbed over him to investigate his back.

"No stab wounds," he announced.

"He'll be happy to know that."

Instantly, he fixed his sharp gaze on her. "Talk to me, sugar. What's going on inside there?" He tapped his head once to give her a reference.

But there was nothing to say. Out of the blue something occurred to her. "I hate it when you don't call me by my name. Do you even know my name? I think you said it once. When I made you, but other than that, you always call me *sugar* or *sweetheart,* which is strange because I'm not that sweet really." She was rambling. She knew it, but she couldn't seem to stop.

Reuben moved away from Sam and came to sit next to her. Talia had been resting on her knees. Quickly, effortlessly, he pulled her off her perch and into his lap then forced her head against his shoulder.

She wanted to fight him. But as she suspected earlier, she had used up all her strength. Like a character in a video game, her tank was on empty. If she didn't find some magical strength pellets soon, the game would be over.

"Talia Mooney, sexy as hell, powerful, Olympic platform diver, silver medalist, survival contestant…and accountant."

"Figures you'd save that for last."

"Because it's the last thing you are. Listen to me, babe. I know you must be at the edge, but I need you. We all need you. You're the only one who has a clue what she's doing on this island and if we have any chance of getting off alive, it's going to be because of you."

"Joe didn't make it. Sam didn't make it."

"No, they didn't. But the rest of us will."

"How do you know? How can you possibly say that?" Anger gave her energy to sit up so she could see him. "I lied about the storm. I have no idea if this is the beginning, the middle or the end. It could get worse, stronger. I don't know."

"I know that."

"We don't know if the boat is coming. We don't know if the conditions are worse where it is. The yacht could be underwater for all we know."

"It could be."

"And there is someone who is killing us. One at a time. Maybe that's the only way he thinks he can escape."

"Maybe."

His calm in the face of her fears was really pissing her off. So much she lifted her hand and punched his shoulder. Hard. She saw him grimace, but he said nothing.

"How can you be such a robot? Isn't any of this affecting you at all? If I didn't know better, I would say it was you. I would say you did it. Killed the actress, killed Joe, killed Sam. Someone like you could do it and not even blink."

His jaw tightened, but all he said was, "But you do know better."

Her head dropped forward and she caught her face in her hands. The anger was gone, leaving a gaping hole in her stomach where fear and fatigue and pain were swirling, vying for control.

"Talia, look at me."

She didn't want to. She'd had sex with him, reveled in the pleasure of it, and while she was sitting on his lap, while he was trying to comfort her, she'd called him a cold-blooded killer.

He put a finger under her chin and forced her face up. Instantly, she met his gaze, deciding that she didn't need to be pushed.

"I'm sorry."

"You don't have to apologize," he said. "But I do need you to get it together. Dig deep. Find whatever it is inside you that made you jump off thirty-foot platforms for fun."

She puffed out a small chuckle. "I'm worse than Nancy. Losing it like this."

"No. You just didn't realize how much energy you've

had to put out until now. I don't think I did, either. Trust me, all I want to do is take you somewhere deep into the interior of this island where we can hunker down until help comes and not have to do another blasted thing, but I know we can't. And I know you know we can't."

"We can't," she agreed. "They need us."

"They do. And I need you."

There it was. The magic pellet that seemed to revive her. Had it been just her, she might have been able to quit. But it was clear that Reuben wasn't giving up. And probably more than anything, the competitiveness inside her wouldn't let him get the best of her. If he was going to keep pushing, keep trying, keeping working to stay alive and keep everyone else alive, too, then she was going to be right there next to him.

Pushing herself off his lap, she managed to stand. A blast of wind shook her, but she held her ground. "We should get back to them."

Reuben stood and reached for her hand. Together they made their way to the group. The group minus one more now.

No one said anything. If there had been any doubt it was Sam in the water, the swim trunks gave him away.

"Dino and Tommy didn't see or hear anything," Gus told Reuben, evidently having already started the questioning process.

"He was gone when I got up to take a leak this morning, that's all I know," Tommy insisted.

"Was he…like Joe…stabbed?" Dino asked.

"No. There were no stab wounds. And I didn't see any bruising around his neck to indicate he'd been strangled. He drowned. That's all I can tell."

"Wait a minute," Tommy stopped them. "That could be good."

Everyone including Reuben was shocked at the horrific suggestion.

"I'm serious. What if he killed Joe? What if he was afraid that the yacht would come and he would be caught and so he decided to try and swim for it?"

"Whoever killed Joe took the spark plug from the engine," Talia reminded him. "If Sam was planning to escape, why swim? Why not put the spark plug back and take the motorboat?"

Tommy threw up his hands. "I don't know, maybe he lost it. Maybe it fucking fell out of his pocket. It's not like he would have been able to find it in the dark. So he loses the plug, realizes he's not going to fix the boat, knows that the game is over today, tomorrow at the latest, and decides he's got no choice."

"That could be true," Marlie stated. "It seems reasonable."

"No, not Sam. He was so sweet. He couldn't have killed Joe. I don't believe it. Not Sam." Once more Nancy started to sob.

In what was becoming a familiar habit for him, Gus circled her shoulder with his arm in an attempt to comfort her. "Hush Nancy, it's okay. We don't know anything at this point."

"We know who it couldn't be," Evan stated. "The six of us were all together all night."

"That's not true." Attention returned to Reuben. "Gus was gone at one point. So was Nancy for a time."

Immediately, Nancy stopped crying, her eyes almost miraculously dry. "I had to…you know…I had to…" She blushed rather than finish her sentence.

"I'm not accusing anyone. I'm simply putting it out there. We can't point fingers today any more than we could yesterday. As crazy as it seems given the number of people on this island, we're still in the dark about who the killer is."

"What happens next?"

There was a weariness in the question. Talia looked at Gus and, for the first time, saw his age. Like her, he was probably feeling the effects of lack of food, water, warm shelter and safety. But given his seniority, it wasn't a certainty that he had the wherewithal to keep going. He was tough, but it was hard to know how much tougher he needed to be. And for how long.

A tug on her hand distracted her and she looked down to find Reuben pulling her away from the group.

"Give us a few minutes," he asked them.

"What?" Tommy shouted, obviously annoyed at being left out of the process once again. "Why should we? Why do you two get to make all the decisions? You know no one is absolutely sure that one of you isn't the killer."

"Let them go," Gus snapped.

"I don't get why he's always the boss."

"You wouldn't," Gus muttered tiredly and plopped down onto the beach. The rest did the same.

Ignoring the debate behind him, Reuben pulled Talia

a few feet away and crossed his arms over his chest. "What do you think? About Tommy's idea."

"You're the detective."

"I'm asking you what you think."

Regretfully, because if it were true then it would mean that they were all out of danger at least temporarily, Talia shook her head.

"You saw him in the water. He wasn't that strong of a swimmer. I don't think you can fake something like that. The idea that he suddenly decided to swim all the way to the yacht in the middle of the night doesn't seem feasible. Besides, what was he going to do when he got there? It doesn't make sense."

"No, it doesn't seem to fit. On the other hand, he did have the accident, which could have been staged as a way to get off the island. Then he cornered you alone. He must have left Dino and Tommy at one point to be one-on-one with the killer. Those things add up, too. Maybe he wasn't thinking straight. He could have been in a panic and thought swimming was his only option."

"We both agreed that he had a chance to leave after he hit his head, but he didn't take it. And when it was just the two of us, he didn't do anything to me. I don't think we can relax our guard and assume the murderer is dead."

"I'm not talking about relaxing our guard. I'm talking about what happens next. If it wasn't Sam, and we both think it wasn't, then we've got a murderer on this island who has killed twice. Possibly to protect his identity, or because he got caught doing something, or worse…he likes the killing. He or she is taking one hell of a risk and I don't think he has any plans on stopping."

Dread had her swallowing another wave of nausea. "You think we're all in danger."

"I do. I don't think we can wait for the yacht to come get us. Not another day."

Ideas raced through Talia's head. "Well, we could make paddles, I suppose. All of us get in the motorboat and see if we can somehow meet the yacht on the way out."

He already was dismissing that idea. "Too slow. Too risky. If the wind and waves knock over the boat, we can't save everyone from drowning."

"What are you considering?"

"I swim for it."

This time Talia dismissed the idea. "Not possible. The water is too rough. Two miles in the open ocean—"

"It won't be that far if the boat is coming to pick us up."

"If the boat is coming, then we can wait."

He said nothing, but his frown deepened.

"The yacht could be farther away if the storm has it drifting off course," she countered. "Did you consider that?"

"Look, I've done the Iron Man. I've trained in the ocean, and swam a hell of a lot farther than two miles doing it. I can usually do it in an hour. Given the circumstances maybe two. That means I'm at the boat in two hours and I'm bringing it back maybe as soon as thirty or so minutes after that. Three hours instead of twenty-four, less if it's already on its way. I think it's worth the risk."

Three hours. It definitely was tempting. "Then I

should do it. I'm just as strong a swimmer and in case something else happens you could be here to stop it."

"It won't work. They need someone they can trust. Someone who they know is who she says she is. That's you."

"That's also Evan."

"But Evan can't hold them together. You can." Reuben reached for her shoulders, his eyes piercing hers. "You stay. I swim. This is over in three hours."

Talia's eyes drifted to the blur of whitecaps beyond the inlet. "Reuben, I don't think it's possible."

He followed her gaze and saw the white foam. "The waves aren't that high yet and two miles of swimming, without the biking and the running, is nothing more than a leisurely workout for me."

She scoffed at that. "Right. On no food and no water in the middle of a storm in shark-infested waters. Just another workout."

"Okay, not just another workout," he replied testily, clearly annoyed with her lack of faith. She was afraid. Afraid for all of them, but really afraid for him. "But, sugar, we're running out of options and time."

"I can't believe it has come to this." And she wasn't ready to let Reuben go quite yet. "What if we tried going for Evan's radio on the other side of the island? We could all go together and—"

"You saw the circumference when he took us to the beach for the challenge. With this group in tow we're talking days. My way is still quicker."

Gus got up from the circle and made his way over to them. "Let's have it. What's the option on the table?"

"I'm going to swim out and meet the yacht."

Talia watched Gus's face for a reaction. She was hoping for incredulousness, something that might convince Reuben that what he was considering was insane. But the old man merely squinted his eyes against the wind and sand and looked out to the water.

"How are you going to know where it is?"

"Good question," Talia pointed out. "If you take the wrong line you could end up in the middle of nowhere and then have no strength left to get back."

"Evan," Reuben called. "Do we know where the yacht is anchored?"

Evan stood brushing sand from his shorts, but stopped when he realized the wind was just blowing it back on again. "Due west. That's what the captain said anyway. Two miles due west."

"There's no sun. How are you going to know where west is?"

Reuben didn't answer Talia, but instead made his way to the motorboat. On the console above the starter was a compass built into the dashboard. Pushing down on one side of it, he was able to pop it out of its casing, then he returned to the group.

He held up the compass and turned toward the lagoon until the needle was pointing north. Then he pointed out to the ocean. "Due west."

Agitated, Talia kicked at the sand. "This is crazy. Tell him this is crazy, Gus."

"You're worried this might be something more than protecting a handful of jewelry," Gus stated.

"Yeah. I'm worried that by the time the yacht gets

here there won't be anyone left to pick up…except one. God knows what kind of story that person could tell," Reuben said.

"Can you make it?"

"I think."

"He thinks," Talia repeated sarcastically. "Very reassuring. What if you don't make it? What do we do then?"

"Then you wait for the boat like you were going to do anyway. You stick together and you don't let Gus out of your sight." Reuben looked up at the older man. "Not because I think—"

"I got it. Don't worry. We'll do everything we can to keep everyone safe."

The rest of the group must have sensed that something was happening. They circled around Reuben.

"So what's the big decision?" Tommy asked.

"I'm going for help."

"Oh, thank you," Nancy blurted out then seemed to catch herself. "I'm sorry I don't know…how?"

"I'm going to swim out to meet yacht and bring it back."

"Whoa. That's a long swim." Tommy's concern alone should have been a tip-off that this wasn't Reuben's brightest idea.

Then Marlie expressed disbelief in the only way she could. "You mean…like, swim…out there?" She pointed to the sea. "But what about the shark and everything?"

"Don't worry. He stands a much better chance of drowning than of being eaten."

Reuben glared at Talia, but she ignored him. Instead she walked away from him while everyone else peppered him with questions—how long it would take and when to expect him back.

But nobody told him he shouldn't do it.

She felt the spray of water from the inlet against her face, then felt the addition of heavy raindrops on her head. Looking up at the sky, she could see that the pale gray patch they'd been living under was being replaced swiftly by clouds that were thicker, darker and more menacing.

The faint hope that they had lived through the worst of the tropical storm was gone.

"Hey," Reuben called to her. "Walk me to the edge of the inlet over there."

She wanted to say no. She wanted to rail at him not to go. She wanted to cling to his arm and cry like a baby and tell him that she couldn't do this by herself. She needed him to keep her steady and strong.

What if she lost it again? What if she couldn't function anymore? And, heaven forbid, what if somebody else died because of it?

But he already was walking the narrow stretch of beach bordering the inlet before climbing the rocky surface that jutted out into the ocean. Taking a deep breath, knowing she had no real choice, she followed him, slipping occasionally on the wet rocks. He stopped at the edge and waited for her.

"You can do this, Talia. Just keep everyone calm for the next few hours."

That made her smile. "You're about to swim two miles in that and you're comforting me."

She stepped closer to him, wrapped her arms around his waist and squeezed. "Keep your pace even, your head above water and don't lose the compass."

"Exactly what any good coach would say."

"If you don't make it back, so help me I'll come out there after you."

He arched away so he could see her face, his expression stern. "No, you won't. I'm serious. You stay on dry land. If the boat doesn't come, then—"

"We'll go for the radio," she told him and hated that she had. She didn't want him to think that she was already planning for the contingency that he wouldn't make it.

"That's my girl," he said, grinning broadly. "Always thinking. Don't stop. And don't let appearances fool you. I told you I thought Gus was okay, but I don't know for sure. No one goes off alone at any time for any reason. Got it?"

"Got it."

He paused for a moment then cupped her cheek in his hand. "When I get back we still have some talking to do."

"Okay. We'll talk."

Then he smirked. "Don't get me wrong. I'm going to bang the hell out of you first. But right after that we're going to talk."

She smiled weakly at his attempt to lighten the mood with his trademark over-the-top bluntness. "You sure know how to keep a girl pining."

On a more serious note, he added, "I mean it, sugar. This isn't done. You and I both know it."

"I guess that is a pretty strong motivation to get there and back as fast as possible. Isn't it?"

"You're not kidding."

"Swim strong," she whispered.

"Be brave," he returned. He kissed her hard on the mouth. Their eyes held as he stepped away, until he turned and dove from the rocks into the water a few feet below.

She watched his head pop up, saw that his hand was still clutched around the glass compass. She stood there as he slowly, methodically began to cut through the water, stroke after steady stroke, heading due west until he was out of her view around the crest of the island.

For several minutes after, she continued to stare out to sea. It shouldn't hurt so much, she thought dazedly. She barely knew him. Had already decided that he was not a man she could have a future with despite their very potent physical attraction. Yet standing on that rock, she feared that if he didn't come back, her heart would be broken.

Silly.

"Talia!"

The shout pulled her attention back to the group. Tommy was jumping up and down waving his arms frantically. Evan and Dino were quickly herding the women back to the woods. What in the hell were they doing?

Gus was still on the beach, his hands cupped around his mouth. "Talia! Talia, watch out!"

What was going on? She could barely make out what he was saying, but then she made out the words *watch out.*

Watch out? Watch out for what?

The sound was like nothing she had ever heard. It came from the south. Louder than the wind. Louder than thunder. More like the rumble a train might make if a person were standing directly in the path of one.

She turned and saw it. A long, thin, solid blue twister spinning crazily on the water…and heading directly for her.

Chapter 9

The waterspout weaved and skipped on the choppy ocean in a twisted version of a samba dance. Left and right and back again, it made its way to Talia standing helplessly enthralled on the rocks. She took her eyes off it for a moment, searching west where she'd last seen Reuben in the water, but he was long gone and safer from the spout than she was presently.

Forcing herself out of her trance, she started to move, turning her back on the ferocious beast as she headed toward the beach. There the group, too, seemed paralyzed with fear. No longer were they running away, but instead were watching the awesome natural phenomenon approach the island with all the subtlety of…well, Reuben.

Twisters didn't warrant names. Just hurricanes. If she survived this, she made a mental note to talk to somebody in the weather biz about that. Something so large, so ominous, so brilliantly spectacular deserved to have a name assigned to it. If only so a person would know what to call it when it swept her up.

But in order to do that, she needed to survive first.

Craning over her shoulder, she tracked the progress the waterspout was making, watching it as it continued to whirl in a haphazard fashion with no clear direction. She felt her sneakers slipping on the wet rocks and worked to steady herself against the wind and the vibrations it was giving off even from more than a hundred feet away. It was as if she found herself shaking from the inside.

"Get it together," she breathed, doing everything she could to will the fear out of her so she could move faster. Turning her back once more on the monster, she started to move slowly over the rocks. Against the backdrop of the powerful twister, she could hear the faint cries from Nancy and Marlie.

Her instinct was to look up at them, to take her cue from them to see which direction she should move, but that would waste time. The first priority had to be getting off the rocks without incident.

Lifting one arm, she waved the group toward the woods, hoping they understood she wanted them off the beach. But a quick glance told her that they were still waiting for her.

"Go," she cried out. "Get off the beach."

The force of her warning sent her the slightest bit off balance and her foot slipped from under her. Her bare knee made impact with the rock and searing pain sliced through her leg to her thigh. Gritting her teeth against the sudden numbness, she regained her footing and continued to move. With each step she was getting closer to the sand.

One more step. One more.

It's just like a wet platform. Keep your balance or else you'll fall the ten meters before you can dive.

There! She jumped off the rocks and took the time to check behind her to gauge the position of the spout. It was so close now she couldn't see where the tip met the ocean, just the thick swell of water at least five feet across barreling toward the rocks she'd vacated. Now able to run at full speed, she waved her arms frantically at the group once more.

"Run! Into the woods as fast as you can! Run!"

This time, maybe because they were certain she was following them, they started to move. Tommy was the first to act and took off. Evan looked dumbstruck as Marlie tugged on his hand, trying to pull him behind her. When he failed to respond though, she quickly let it go in favor of Dino who had grabbed her other hand, dragging her into the forest beyond the beach.

Gus was struggling with Nancy, his hand wrapped around her elbow, shouting at her to move. But like a statue, or more literally, a woman scared into shock, she resisted his efforts to run. Out of breath by the time Talia reached them both, she couldn't speak. But with a firm grip she took Nancy's other elbow and, between her and Gus, they were able to pull her off her feet and drag her into the woods.

"No, leave me! I can't do this anymore. I can't."

There wasn't any time to argue, only time to drag. Her significant weight slowed them down, and for a second Talia considered the choice between leaving Nancy behind or survival, but intuitively she knew she could never let go.

After a few steps they made it past the first layer of trees that bordered the beach.

"How far?" Gus wanted to know.

"As far as we can go" was Talia's only answer.

Glancing over her shoulder, Talia could see the waterspout hit the rocks. The spray of water that it sent shooting out was intense, like the power of five fire hydrants bursting open at once. Then it veered to the left, eating up bamboo and palm trees along the inlet as it made the transformation from waterspout to tornado.

"Which way?"

She barely heard him over the vibrations of the swirling wind joined by the sound of trees being pulled from their sandy roots. Talia tried to see if there was a pattern in the movements, but it was moving too fast, approaching them too rapidly, to take the time to study its path.

"Left." It was a hunch. Nothing more.

Behind them the roar grew more intense. Then a high-pitched scream seemed to float over their heads and before her mind could comprehend what her eyes were seeing, a thick palm tree crashed a few feet in front of them. The impact forced them back a few steps.

Gus fell and, without his support, Nancy fell on top of him. Seeing no other option, Talia threw herself over the two of them, hoping that if the twister overtook them, death would be swift.

A torrential downfall of water poured over them. It became difficult to breath through the seawater. She covered Nancy and Gus's heads with her arms, felt Nancy shuddering beneath her and waited for some kind of impact.

Please, God. Let Reuben make it.

The absence of noise was what struck her first. There had been a screeching sound pulsing all around them. Then it was as if a switch had been flipped and everything was gone. Only silence was left.

Talia's first thought was that this was the beginning of death. But if that was the case, she doubted she would still be able to hear Nancy bawling.

"Please. I don't want to die. Please."

"Shh," she told the woman, trying to concentrate on what might have happened. Raising her head cautiously, Talia could see a thicket of trees in front of her still standing, although swaying dramatically against the heavy wind. Looking behind her, she could see a path of destruction a few feet wide where bushes, plants and trees had been torn up.

She could see what it had destroyed, but she could no longer see the destroyer.

Tentatively, she took a deep breath and lifted her body off Nancy's. "I think it's gone."

"How can you know?" the older woman cried. "It could come back. It could be waiting for us."

"It's a freak of nature, Nancy. It doesn't think. It doesn't plan. And it's typical for a waterspout to dissipate quickly once it hits land. At least I've always been told. Good to know my mother was right."

More certain of their relative safety, Talia stood and helped Nancy to her feet. Gus was a little slower getting up and instantly she crouched down beside him.

"Are you okay? Anything broken?"

He winced in evident agony as he reached for his back. But he shook his head as if to suggest he was okay.

"Nothing broke. This old body just can't take it like it used to."

"And you're weak from hunger and probably dehydrated," Talia added, lending him a hand to gain his feet. "Don't be so tough on that old body. It's held up pretty well, all things considered."

"I don't how much longer…" He let the rest of the sentence drop, not wanting to complain, but clearly knowing that he was swiftly approaching the limits of his endurance.

In this case, the name the producers had picked for the show was no joke. The idea that there would be only one contestant was suddenly taking on a whole new meaning.

"A little longer," Talia pleaded. "Hang in there. I'll think of something. I promise."

His head bobbed a few times as he tried to work his body into a straight line. It was a good bet that he wasn't going to be running anytime soon. Nancy was still sobbing uncontrollably, and aside from the annoyance factor, it was also speeding up her descent into dehydration.

"Nancy, you need to stop."

"I…ca-can't."

There was no point in trying to fight her on the issue.

Instead Talia needed to put her thoughts together. But it was hard to get beyond the ringing in her ears caused by the twister. Or maybe it was adrenaline causing the buzzing in her head. Or her own hunger and probable dehydration.

It was a tough call with so many choices.

"That's my girl. Always thinking."

Reuben's words came back to her and she used them to steady herself. That's what she needed to do. Concentrate on the steps, not the outcome. Like a dive. Don't think about going into the water until you've completed the somersault. Don't worry about the first somersault until you've cleared the platform.

Which all basically boiled down to: first things first. And that was simple.

"We need to find the others."

"They could be dead. They all could be dead."

Talia sighed and for a moment let her weariness overcome her civility. "Nancy, a little optimism right now wouldn't hurt. Just start shouting. Marlie! Evan! Dino! Tommy!"

"We're here!"

Talia heard the sound of feet tromping over bushes and saw Dino moving toward them with Marlie in tow.

"Oh. My. God. That was so scary." Marlie shook her head, her hand clutching Dino's, who was clearly replacing Evan as her new protector. "You saved my life, Dino. I could have died."

"I didn't…I didn't think. I acted…I didn't think," he stammered. His body was shaking, no doubt with the same fear and adrenaline they were all experiencing.

"Where are Evan and Tommy?"

"Who cares? Evan, like, just stood there."

Talia didn't have time to remind Marlie that not everyone on the island was here to look out for her. If she hadn't figured it out by now with everything that had happened to them, it was doubtful anything Talia said would make a dent. A shame really. So much beauty, so little substance.

"We can't separate," Gus reminded her.

She didn't want to tell him that they might be out of choices. "Tommy! Evan!"

For a moment there was still only wind, but Talia's ears seemed more attuned to the sound now. She could block it out and listen for other things. Like someone calling for help.

"Help me! He's…help!"

"This way." She didn't expect them to follow. Both Nancy and Gus were still shaken and as long as they stayed together, it wasn't an issue. Following the cry, Talia pushed through the battered undergrowth deeper into the woods until she came upon a frightening scene: the two men she was searching for, one on his back, the other standing over him with something in his hand. Something large and heavy.

"Help me. He's going to kill me."

Talia met Evan's gaze from where he lay on the forest floor, his leg seemingly pinned under a fallen palm tree.

"Chill. I'm not trying to kill you. I'm trying to help."

She closed the distance, but slowed when her mind processed the fact that Tommy was still holding on to the stick. She came up alongside him, watching him cautiously as she checked on Evan's condition.

"I was trying to get the tree off. It's not a thick one. I don't think his ankle is broken or anything. He's only stuck."

"Put the stick down, Tommy."

"I was going to use it for leverage. I was trying to help."

It could have been true. But in this world of doubt, death and distrust, it really didn't matter.

"Put the stick down." And because she was her father's daughter who believed that being polite could protect a person from the most ferocious loan sharks and sinister modern-day pirates, she added, "Please."

Tommy tossed the stick away with an angry flip of his wrist, smashing it against another fallen log.

"Fine. Whatever. You figure out how to get him out." Huffily, he stomped off, fortunately toward the spot she'd left everyone else so she didn't have to worry about where he was going.

Now she had to figure out how to get Evan free. Squatting, she studied the host's position. His right ankle was caught between the cracked trunk and the ground. She agreed with Tommy's assessment that the ankle didn't look broken, just pinned.

"Does it hurt?"

A break would have serious consequences for the group. If he couldn't walk or run from danger, it would leave them all vulnerable. And she knew she wouldn't leave Evan. With his handsome face and dramatic flare, he'd taken this job because he thought it could be a stepping stone to a better life. A better show probably. He was so woefully unprepared for it all going wrong that it was pathetic. If she had the energy, she might have actually felt sorry for him.

As an answer to her question, Evan shook his head. "I don't think it's broken. I can't feel anything, really. I was running and tripped. I turned over and the tree sort of crashed. It didn't seem real. I saw it falling, and thought that this was the end and then boom. Then I opened my eyes and I knew I wasn't dead. I tried to pull my foot out, but I couldn't. Tommy was there with this stick in his hand and this look on his face…. I thought, it's not fair, I survived the tree falling only to be smashed over the head."

"It's okay," she murmured, trying to appease him. She couldn't blame him for being suspicious of Tommy, not when she had felt the same way at the very start.

"I didn't know he was trying to help," Evan told her sheepishly. "It was the two of us. It's not supposed to be only two of us. And with that stick in his hand…I shouted for help."

"You did the right thing."

"I knew her," he said softly.

"Who?"

"The actress who was killed. Carney. I knew her. I didn't want to say because I thought you all would think it had to be me, and it wasn't me. I didn't hurt her. But…"

There was something in his tone that had Talia sitting on her haunches out of range of his free and perfectly healthy arms.

"But…" she said, encouraging him to finish his thoughts.

"But I guess I didn't like her. She was a lot like Marlie."

"You slept with Marlie."

"I had sex with Marlie—it's different. And only because—"

"Tell me."

"You know. Because I could."

Had that been Reuben's thought process? Nail the diver because he wanted to and because he could. If that was true, it hurt. It shouldn't have hurt, but it did. Talia swallowed the bitter retort that started and ended with *smug male bastard* and concentrated on what was important.

"So you slept with her. You knew her. Did you know her long before she died?"

"No. Could we talk about this after you get the trunk off of my leg? I think my foot is falling asleep."

No, she didn't think she could. In fact, she believed that before freeing him she wanted all the details.

"I can't believe you're saying this now." Disbelief coated her voice. "Everything that's happened and this is the first time I'm hearing this. You knew her."

His lip stuck out in a petulant pout. "I said I couldn't tell anyone before. You would have immediately suspected me because I was the only one who did."

"And you don't think I suspect you now?"

"But you know I didn't kill Joe. I was with Marlie on the beach when it happened. Last night I held her all night long so I couldn't have had anything to do with Sam's death, either. You know that."

A convenient alibi in both cases. "Marlie tossed Dino over for Tommy, Tommy over for you, you over for Dino. Marlie's ethics don't really scream trustworthy. How do I know you didn't guarantee her a shot on your next show to keep her quiet about what she knows?"

Evan stared at her dumbfounded. So dumbfounded it was clear to Talia that he'd had no idea she would question his story. Unfortunately, that reaction made it seem even more plausible.

"I want every detail you have about this actress."

"Details," he screeched. "I don't have any details. We hooked up back in L.A. once. We met at a reality TV award show. She was a presenter. The only details I can give you are about her breast size. And even that I don't remember that well. They were big. Perfect."

"Did you know she was in Hawaii?"

His guilty expression was answer enough.

Talia exhaled a puff of air. This was getting surreal. She had eliminated Evan from the list of suspects because she was certain that he was a known quantity. He was recognizable; he'd had an alibi in Marlie at the time of both murders; and the truth was, he didn't seem like the type. Not that any of them did.

Considering what she knew about him now, that seemed like a ridiculous reason not to consider him. Especially when lives were on the line. It was time to get serious.

"So you knew her," she said. "You knew she was in Hawaii. Did you see her there?"

"My ankle is starting to really hurt."

"Let me know when it gets too bad and I'll cut it off."

He gasped then quickly started talking. "Yes, I knew she was in Waikiki, and I guess I was thinking about hooking up with her again, but that's it. She's a major star. Being seen out with her means huge publicity. Only things got crazy with the show and I was trying to get caught up, and I never called her. That's the truth."

"Why should I believe you?" It was a question more for herself than for him.

"I didn't have to tell you that I knew her," he pointed out.

"Then why did you?"

He shook his head dazedly. "I don't know. I thought I was going to die. I thought Tommy was going to hit me with that stick. I started thinking about stuff, you know, about my life and everything. Then I started thinking maybe she felt the same way I did. Maybe it was Tommy who did it and she went through the same things I was going through. I thought about how I slept with her, even though I didn't know her. Hell, what I knew I didn't like. But she must have been really scared. I know because I was."

Great. The fake host with the cheesy smile suddenly decides to grow a conscience. She wasn't sure he was a good enough actor to pull off such a speech, and she didn't see that she had much of a choice but to believe him. The rain was still falling, the wind was still blowing and she couldn't leave him under a tree.

"I'm going to lift the trunk. When I say pull, you yank your foot out."

"Yank? Is it going to hurt?"

Talia moved around the trunk until she was even with his head, then she bent down getting her face as close to his as their several-day-old breath would allow. "I'm going to lift and you're going to yank. And I don't give a damn if all you pull away is a bloody stump so long as you can walk on it. You're scared? I'm scared more. But the difference is I'm dealing with it. Are you ready?"

Automatically, he nodded.

She stood and moved to the edge of the trunk. She wrapped her arms around the narrow part and tugged. It wasn't a thick tree and she knew she could create enough of a gap for him to get his pinned ankle out.

"Ready," she prompted. "One. Two…"

"Wait! I have to mentally prepare for this. It's okay though. I've been trained by the finest yoga instructors in Hollywood. "

Reuben, you bastard! You totally knew what you were doing when you decided to swim for it.

Reuben lifted his head out of the water and sucked in…more sea water. When he'd left the island he'd thought he could handle the choppiness. The swells hadn't been any higher than two feet. Nothing to worry about. Now it was worse. He couldn't consider how much worse it could get.

I'm going to die out here, he thought morosely. *Hell, I should have taken her up on her offer and let her swim.*

He took a moment to realize that even while he was confronting death he was still a smart-ass. No wonder he'd never gotten anyone to marry him.

Every one of his girlfriends had walked out on him with the parting words "you bastard" either echoing off the walls or hanging in the air. For the most part, he could have cared less. None of them had touched him emotionally. He wasn't even sure there was anything to be touched inside of him.

He'd been raised that way. By his parents, grandparents and many, many uncles. Be tough, be strong, don't let anyone see your weaknesses and, most importantly…be a good cop. He'd done all that. But after the bullet with his name on it had come too close for comfort, he'd started to think about things. He'd never thought he was the sort of person who would evaluate his life or his decisions. But being laid up in a hospital bed with time on his hands, he'd been left with little choice.

He finally had concluded that he was never going to find out what else he could be until he stopped being a cop. The physical training had helped him regain his strength, then gave him something to do with his time. It was during that phase of his recovery that he'd imagined his hole-in-the-wall bar. A place where people came to get away. Where everyone knew everyone else's business. Where the talk was free and the beer was reasonable.

His brothers told him he'd watched too many episodes of *Cheers*. It was entirely possible. He'd been a big fan. But he couldn't let the idea go. He wanted to see if this dream was more than some pie in the sky, if it was a chance at a new life. To make it a reality, he needed cash. Easy cash.

Go on a game show, smile for the camera, walk away with a million.

Like stealing candy from a baby. Except now he was in the middle of the South Pacific swimming to God only knew where, looking for a yacht that could be at the bottom of the ocean and fearing that at any second either a wave crashing over his head would drown him or a shark coming from the deep would eat him.

I should have stayed on the damn force. It was safer.

Just go, he told himself. *Stop thinking about what might happen and worry about what you can do. First, figure out where the hell you are.*

Working his legs hard in the water to keep his head above the crest of whitecaps, he lifted the hand wrapped around the compass and loosened his grip just enough to see which way the needle was pointing. The motion of the water made it difficult to keep steady and the salt stinging his eyes made it almost impossible to see.

Another blast of water smacked him in the face, but he shook it off and squinted to see the slim black needle. When he did see it, he realized he was too close to north, which meant he was drifting.

Shifting his body, Reuben focused on getting turned around. Once he was certain he faced west, he scanned ahead as far as the angry ocean would allow. Nothing. No boat. Just water. White foam on top of a black mass.

He wasn't going to make it. And that seriously pissed him off.

There was no way to determine how far he'd swum. It felt like days but reality was he'd probably been in the water for only an hour. He'd lost sight of the island not too long ago so maybe he was about a mile out.

Another mile to go. He could do that. For Talia. Methodically, he put his face in the water and started kicking and stroking as emotions and thoughts crowded his mind.

It occurred to him that in all his life he'd never done anything special for a woman other than his mother. Had never even considered it. Why bother when he knew someday all the women would walk? Then he'd landed on that damn yacht, took one look into Talia's sky-blue eyes with the twinkle she tried so hard to hide behind a serious facade, and he'd crumbled like a cookie.

There was more to it than lusting after her. He could admit that now since it was a good bet the fish weren't going to hold it against him. There was something about her that made every instinct in his body cry, "Yes." It didn't take his brain long to catch up, either, and when it did, it silently shouted, "Her, you idiot."

When he saw her dive off that cliff on the second day, his gut had leaped into his throat and stuck there. He'd told her to do it. Practically dared her to jump, but when her feet left solid ground he'd been scared in a way he'd never been before. That was until he saw her falling so perfectly, so effortlessly through the air.

It was like nothing he'd ever seen before.

No, that wasn't true. He'd seen it once before and had been just as affected.

Vividly he'd recalled watching the TV years ago, cheering as the gritty girl with the long, hot body climbed the steps again even when the whole world knew she was in agony. She'd won his respect.

The woman she'd grown into didn't disappoint, either. As a bonus, she was still ridiculously hot. He wondered if she even knew that about herself. Did she see the white in her hair that she'd gotten from the sun that so many women tried to achieve with chemicals? Did she understand what it did to a man to see that body in motion, turning walking into an art form? Did she know what her full mouth made a man think of?

He doubted it. She wasn't the type to spend a lot of time in front of the mirror. Far too action-oriented for that. He suspected that there hadn't been a slew of men in her life because, like him, he speculated that she didn't let people get close easily.

He'd practically had to kick the castle gate down, her fortress was that impenetrable. But he'd gotten inside and, man, was it worth it.

So he'd keep swimming, one arm over the next, legs steadily kicking because he had renewed determination. He needed to find the damn ship, bring it back to the island and collect her. Then they needed to talk about how the rest of their lives were going to work out.

He suspected she would be freaked by his very long-term intentions. But when a man found a woman that powerful, combined with all that elegance, who could see inside his head to know what he's thinking and give him everything that he demanded...he kept her.

Just a little farther, he told himself. *A little farther and you'll find what you're looking for. You'll make it back to her.*

* * *

Come back, Reuben. Please. This is getting out of hand.

Since Talia had no illusions that telepathy was a gift she possessed, she had little faith that he'd heard her. She'd gotten Evan from under the tree with nothing more than a thin scrape that he had screeched like baby about.

Currently, they were all huddled inside the cluster of trees that had served as shelter just the night before. It didn't seem possible, but the winds had gotten stronger in the past few hours.

Talia knew that the wind still hadn't peaked. The trees were still standing, although their swaying was more noticeable with each gust. The tarp was pretty much in shreds, leaving the group defenseless against the deluge of rain that pelted them.

In her mind, Talia counted the minutes Reuben had been gone. She didn't want to think about his absence in terms of hours because she would have to accept the inevitable that much sooner.

One hundred and seventy-five minutes. One hundred and seventy-six. One hundred and seventy-seven. Certainly not one hundred and eighty. That would mean he'd been gone three hours and that was too long.

At the one-hundred-and-eighty-minute mark she was going to have to reevaluate.

Given the conditions now, she had no hope of surviving this storm so close to the beach. The inlet was churning and the waves were overtaking the thin stretch of beach with each crash. The trees to the left and right of them were bent practically to the ground. Waiting here for help—if help was even coming—was getting risky.

"Evan," she said, jerking the man out of whatever daze he'd been in. He hadn't recovered from the sudden suspicion thrown his way once everyone had learned of his involvement with the dead actress. Apparently, being the perennial host, he was used to controlling the game, not being a part of it. But he was a big part of it now, and possibly their only chance at salvation. "Evan, snap out of it."

"What?" he answered sluggishly.

"You said there was a storage place in the interior of the island where you kept our necessity items, remember? You said it was a cave?"

"Huh?"

"Is it a cave?"

"Oh. A cave. Yes, it's a cave."

Talia studied the condition of the group. Most were shivering, all of them were hungry. Nancy, true to form, was sobbing softly.

One hundred and eighty minutes.

Sorry, Reuben.

"We've got to go."

Gus lifted his head. "What are you talking about?"

"We can't stay this close to the beach and we need something stronger than trees for shelter. If we move now, and move quickly, we should be able to get to the interior by nightfall. I know we can't make it all the way to the other side of the island to get the radio, but we should be able to reach the cave."

"But I told you I wouldn't know how to find my way from here," Evan whined. "I only know how to get to it from my camp."

"You said someone from the show surveyed the island. They would have drawn a map, an overhead shot of some kind. They would have given it to you."

"I guess, but—"

"Think about the map. I don't need precise directions, just the general location of cave. North? Northeast? Southeast?"

"Northeast. It's high up. Even from the east side of the island it's a climb, but it was the deepest cave they could find."

She nodded once. "Then we move northeast. I know what direction north is—we'll take it a few degrees to the right of that. If we make for the high ground, we stand a better chance of finding shelter along the way. If Evan can spot the actual cave, then we'll have the provisions we need to last us awhile. Eventually, this storm will blow over. When it does, we'll track to Evan and Dino's camp to get the radio."

"Awhile?" Dino questioned. "But Reuben said he was coming back with help. He said only a few hours."

"That was a few hours ago. You see what this storm is spawning. We have to protect ourselves. Don't worry," she tried to assure everyone. "If Reuben does make it to the yacht and they make it to the island, he'll know what I've done."

"How?" Marlie asked.

"He'll know. And he'll come get us. But we can't wait any longer."

"I can't," Nancy croaked, shaking her head, her arms wrapped so tightly around her waist she could have torn herself in half. "I can't walk in all of this. I'll never make it."

"You'll make it. Dino, Tommy, you stay as close to her as you can."

"I want to go with Dino," Marlie insisted.

"You're such a tease," Tommy snarled, leaning into Marlie's suddenly frightened face. "You don't care who you're with just as long as he's doing what you want."

"Hey, back off," Dino warned, reaching out to pull Tommy away. "Now is not the time to start fighting. Especially over a woman, okay. She's not worth it."

"Gus, I want to use the elastic holding the tarp to the trees to tie us together. Nobody gets left behind. We'll work as a unit."

Tommy, Gus and Dino went to work on the tarp, fighting the wind to get what they needed from it.

"Even if we have to fashion something together," Talia instructed as she could see where the elastic had snapped leaving only pieces of rope. "Just so I know that every person is connected to someone else."

"Leave me," Nancy begged. "Just leave me."

Marlie rubbed the older woman's arm. "You can do it, Nancy. And when we get to the cave there will be food."

The mere mention of food seemed to perk up the woman. "Really? Food?

"I had a jar of peanut butter on my list," Marlie told her.

"Peanut butter," Nancy whispered reverently. "I can try for peanut butter."

Talia considered mentioning that her life was also a pretty compelling reason to make the journey, but she was too busy looping the strap around her waist to bother. Everyone did their part to get hooked up behind her. Carefully, she left the cluster of trees and instantly felt the full impact of the wind.

She tilted her head against the spray of sea water and rain, and oriented herself to the direction she wanted to take them in. Her eyes focused on a peak that rose above the trees. It was definitely northeast and the most likely place to find some caves. "Is everyone ready?"

No one answered. No one needed to.

"Let's go."

Chapter 10

Okay, God. I swear if you let me live, I'll go to church every Sunday.

Reuben dropped one arm over the other and continued to kick his tired legs evenly, the way he was supposed to, and waited for the next wave to drag him up only to push him under. He could feel his body being pulled five, maybe six feet at a time as he crested the surges of water.

Up and down. Up and down. It was worse than being on a roller coaster. In fact, it was making him sick. He tried to lift his head to get his bearings but failed when all he could see was more water closing around him.

So Sundays aren't enough, huh? You drive a hard bargain. I swear if you let me live, I'll stop chasing women. I'll settle down. I'll get married…. No good, you know I'm already going to do that if I live. Okay, okay. If you let me live, I'll never take your name in vain.

This time when Reuben lifted his head, he was thrust to the top of another swell. For a second he thought he was hallucinating because he could have sworn he saw something large and white among the black water. Then the wave sent him down the ride, tumbling him a few times beneath the surface.

For precious seconds he lost his orientation and struggled to determine which way was up. But a force inside him, more powerful than his wasted muscles, had him righting himself and clawing to the surface.

Dimly he recalled that it had felt this way when he'd been shot. As he felt the blood seeping from his body threatening to take his soul, he'd fought like a cornered animal. He'd let his stubbornness kick in and willed himself to live beyond all reasonable odds.

He needed that stubbornness now.

This time, knowing what he was searching for, he rode the next wave using his legs and arms to keep his head above water. And once on top, he sure as hell could see.

It was a damn beautiful sight.

The yacht was also riding the waves precariously. But, bottom line, it was a lot bigger than him. Releasing the compass and using every last ounce of energy he had, he powered through the water, taking an angle that would put him directly in front of the small ship.

"Help!" he called out, but as soon as he did, his mouth filled with salt water. He decided it was pointless to call for help. No one was going to hear him. Someone was going to have to see him. He had one hope that the captain piloting the damn thing was on the deck, eyes pinned to the water determining how best to ride out the storm. If he spotted the strange shape among all the waves, Reuben had a chance.

Once he was closer to the yacht, Reuben tried again to lift his hands and wave them over his head, but he had only seconds before he drifted beneath the surface. He pushed himself up and tried again.

Come on, captain. See me. You went on and on about what great vision you had after you had the LASIK surgery. See me now.

But there was nothing. No horn to signal man overboard. No one racing to throw him a life preserver.

Come on, you bastard! I'm right here! Goddamn it! Uh-oh... That couldn't have helped.

"How much longer?"

Instantly, Talia flashed to a bad sitcom where the anxious kids in the back seat of the car continually pestered the driving parent. By the end of the show, the parent was tense, frazzled and curt. She was no better.

For the past hour she'd been telling them not too much longer. Of course it had been a lie as she knew they were at least two miles from the interior of the island. But fortunately for Dino, who was the one asking her this time, it was the truth.

The elevation was rising. They were at the base of the peak she'd been using to track their position. If she was right, she suspected that the cave was somewhere on this hill. It was the highest point on the island and it looked to be the only formation that could house a cave

of the necessary size. They had already passed two div-
ots in the rock that she'd briefly considered using as
temporary shelter, but the lure of food and water was
pushing her and, by default, the rest of the group, forward.

They had taken very short breaks when necessary,
but during the trek she adopted the mantra of her former coach—if you can go, go. A variation on don't
stop until you drop.

Either way she felt it was the best move. If she let
the group rest for too long, especially Nancy, they might
not want to get up again. Ever. As long as Nancy's feet
were moving underneath her, it was best to keep her that
way. And it couldn't be much longer. The damn hill
didn't go up that high.

Talia looked over her shoulder at Dino, who was
tied directly behind her. Nancy was behind him, Tommy
behind her, then Marlie, then Evan and finally Gus
bringing up the rear.

"How much longer?" Dino repeated as though she
hadn't heard him.

"We're getting closer."

"You said that a mile ago," he groaned, clearly not
satisfied with the answer.

"I know what I'm looking for. I'll let you know when
I find it."

"Do you think Reuben made it to the ship?"

She shook her head. "I don't want to talk about it."

She didn't want think about it, either. She couldn't
think about him and the condition he must be in while
taking care of the group. Mental distractions could drain

energy as much as physical ones. She needed to think only about moving forward and bringing them with her.

One foot in front of the other, she reminded herself. *Keep pushing your body against the wind. Keep your eyes open.*

A palm leaf smacked her in the face in defiance of her words. She clawed at the wet leaf, tossed it aside and focused on the swaying trees. The wind was definitely coming from the east. Now that they were on the west side of the hill, the rock was running interference for them. Luckily the rain had stopped temporarily. It was easier to move. If they could go just a little faster, they could cover more ground.

She heard a *woof* noise behind her and turned to see Gus dropping to his knees. Immediately, she scampered to him, everyone circling so as not to break the connections between them.

"Gus." She kneeled and waited while he took a minute to catch his breath. "I'm sorry. I've been pushing everyone too hard."

"You're trying to get us to the cave. I know that. I was doing okay, but they just fell out from underneath me."

He reached for his legs, identifying the traitors. He'd gone as far as he could. She knew that by the way he struggled to turn so he could sit and by the way he put his hands on his knees to stop them from shaking. The stubble on his chin was pure white and the deep lines on his face were more pronounced, making him look infinitely older than his sixty-some years. His T-shirt clung to his skin and along his arms were goose bumps.

"Okay, okay," she muttered to herself, thinking about plan B. "We just passed a small cave, where the rock created a V. It wouldn't have fit everyone, but there's more than enough room for you. We'll get you tucked in there. I'll get everyone else to the supply cave and then I'll come back for you. How does that sound?"

Weakly, he nodded.

She dropped the line from around her waist and did the same to Gus's.

"I need everyone to stay here. Just sit tight for a minute. Tommy, I need you to help me with Gus."

Tommy, who had been eerily quiet throughout the trip, dropped the elastic strip from around his waist and joined her. They got their bodies under Gus's arms and lifted him to his feet. He couldn't put all his weight on his legs, but it was enough for her and Tommy to manage.

Carefully she guided them through the tall grass and bushes that covered the lower part of the hill until she found the rock shape that signaled the opening she'd noted earlier. "Over there."

Using her body as a guide, she pulled them through a thicket of bamboo and stopped when she saw a dark hole.

"How afraid are you of bats, Gus?"

"Bats?" he asked, his face scrunching up as if he'd just tasted something bad.

"Oh man, bats? Gross."

"Shut up, Tommy." Recognizing she was out of patience, Talia took a deep breath and tried to calm herself. "Let me go first. It's a small cave. You might not need to worry."

She left Gus with Tommy and approached the cave. On her way she picked up a few loose sticks and fallen branches. Then she grabbed a large palm leaf and twisted them all together.

Dipping her head, she stepped into the shallow crevice. It was cool and the rock was wet but it was blessedly quiet and free from wind. There was a gap where Gus would be able to sit, and above, where his head would be, in the inky blackness of the cave, she saw the outlines of what she expected.

"I'm real sorry about this because you look rather comfortable up there, but I need this cave and I think it's too small to share."

Piercing eyes suddenly opened in the dark and sent her heart skipping inside her chest.

"No wonder you scare people. You're creepy as hell."

Crouching down and covering her eyes and head with her arm, she lifted the makeshift broom and swatted at the animals above. There was a flurry of wings and high-pitched screeching noises. She swatted again, fearing that they would attack and get caught up in her hair, but on the second swipe she made solid contact and sent them flying from the cave.

Outside she heard an "Oh shit" from Tommy and decided that was an understatement. Checking for any other critters that might give Gus a cardiac arrest and finding none, Talia deemed the cave safe.

She poked her head out and waved them both toward her. "It's fine now. Bring him over, Tommy."

Talia met them and once again wrapped Gus's arm around her shoulder to give him a boost.

"You're not afraid of bats?" Tommy asked, apparently doing his best not to be freaked out by what she'd done.

"Are you kidding? Who's not afraid of bats?"

Neither Gus nor Tommy said another word. All three of them couldn't fit inside, so Talia took Gus the rest of the way and got him situated. She removed Reuben's T-shirt and handed it to him. It was still damp, but once the rain had stopped, the wind had dried it significantly.

"It's not much, but you can tear it up and use it to cover your arms."

"I can't, it's all you have."

Talia glanced down at her bikini top and jean shorts. As soon as she'd removed the shirt, it had felt as if the temperature had dropped twenty degrees. She found herself strangely sentimental about ripping up the shirt that Reuben had given her. But among the supplies, she knew she had a rainproof poncho. Gus would be stuck here for an indeterminate time. It was the right call.

"Take it. Stay warm and dry and the next time you see me I'll have a handful of food. How does that sound?" Talia turned to leave when she felt Gus tug at her arm. She glanced back, surprised at the strength of his hold given his overall condition.

"Reuben wanted me to look out for you."

"I'll be okay."

"You have to be better than that. Keep your eyes open and be careful. Don't trust anyone."

She smiled as she slipped her arm free. "You sound like Reuben."

"Don't give up on him yet, either. He's got a pretty

good reason to make it back to this island. You should know if I were about a hundred years younger, I would have given him a run for his money."

Girlishly, Talia blushed at the comment and rolled her eyes to let him know she didn't take a word of it seriously. "Gus! You're flustering me."

He chuckled. "I don't think anything could fluster you. Just…hurry up…okay?"

"I will."

She left the cave and found Tommy waiting for her patiently outside.

"Is he going to be okay?"

"Until we get back, yes."

"I feel sort of bad leaving him."

The comment took her aback. It seemed so out of character for Tommy. Unsure of her ground, she tapped his back reassuringly. "He'll be fine. Let's go."

Once they rejoined the group, she could see everyone looking at her expectantly. It was a true demonstration of trust that they didn't question her decision to leave Gus behind and continue. If she wasn't in such a hurry, she might have taken a moment to be humbled by their faith in her.

"Gus is safe. I'll come back for him once I get you all settled."

"Sweetie, you left your shirt. You'll catch a chill." Another surprise. That Nancy had been able to focus on anything but her own misery was as uncharacteristic as Tommy worrying about someone other than himself. Talia imagined it was Nancy's mothering instinct overcoming her fear. Whatever it was, it finally dried up her tears, for which Talia was extremely grateful.

"I'm fine."

"Don't be ridiculous." Nancy surveyed the group and her gaze fell on Dino who was still wearing the blue windbreaker he'd been wearing since day one. "Dino, you should give her your jacket. Just until we get to the cave."

He paused only for a second before he nodded. "Of course. I'm sorry. I should have offered before."

He removed the windbreaker and handed it to her. Talia thought about passing once she saw that he was left with nothing but khaki shorts and a white, short-sleeved T-shirt, but the truth was she was damn cold and they needed her as sharp as possible for the remainder of the hike. "I have a poncho among my supplies, so just until we get to the cave."

"No problem."

"Do we need to get retied?" Marlie asked.

"No, I think we're okay from here." She bit her lip slightly when she said it. "It's really not that much farther."

In unison everyone groaned.

"Really. This time I mean it," she assured them.

But they only groaned more. After their mumbles of complaint diminished, Talia took the lead spot and started climbing higher. Minutes passed as they covered the terrain slowly but methodically. She stopped for a second when she spotted another large rock protruding from the side of the hill about twenty feet away.

"That's it!" Evan called out as he raced to her side.

"I remember that rock. That's where we came to get the necessity items."

He continued to run, pointing his finger wildly. Talia joined him at the entrance and let loose a sigh of relief. There was a mesh net over the cave. Proof that it was the natural bunker they had been looking for.

"What's the net for?" Dino wondered, breathing heavily as he joined them. Everyone, it seemed, had dug deep to find the will to sprint the remaining distance to the cave. Talia didn't blame them. After everything they had suffered, the idea of even a few meager supplies was as tempting as ambrosia.

"To keep out bats," Tommy answered. He exchanged a quick glance with Talia, then put his head down.

Evan reached up and found the catch that secured the net and they went inside. Piled back in the corner were four trunks of varying sizes. Talia noted the locks on the trunks and almost wept with frustration, doubting that Evan had the key. On closer inspection she saw that they were combination locks.

"Open them."

Kneeling down in front of the first one, Evan spun out the combination. The sound of the lock disengaging echoed in the cave as everyone held their breath. When he opened the lid, the group started to crush in, but Talia held them off.

"Sit tight," she said to stop them. "Let's figure out what we've got first."

Inside the trunk were neatly arranged compartments with names on them. The first name Talia saw was Sam's. The second was Reuben's. Knowing which would be better equipped, she reached for Reuben's.

"There's mine!" Marlie pushed past both Evan and Talia with more strength than Talia realized she possessed and reached for the box that had her name on it. She opened the plastic storage unit and squealed when she extracted a tube of toothpaste. "And look, a toothbrush and shampoo and nail polish."

Talia inspected the rest of the box and extracted the jar of peanut butter that Marlie had mentioned earlier.

"Hey, that's mine," she snapped.

"It's ours," Talia corrected her.

The girl shook her head as if forcibly slapped out of a daze. "Oh, yeah. I'm sorry. I was going to share. I want to share with everyone."

"You won't need to. I forgot about this." Evan stood back and showed Talia the second trunk. It was stacked with bottles of water, protein bars, blankets, slickers and, most importantly, another radio. "It was for emergencies."

"I would say this constitutes an emergency." Talia took the radio and snapped off the cover to check for batteries. They were in there.

"It should be set to the ship's channel," Evan told her.

Studying it, she found a switch at the top and snapped it on, but the only sound that greeted her was static.

"You push the orange button on the side to talk."

Talia handed the radio over to Evan. "You know what you're doing. See if you can get through to somebody. Tell me the combination and I'll open up the rest of these trunks."

Evan recited a series of numbers and both Dino and Tommy went to work on opening the containers. In the meantime, Nancy and Marlie were spreading blankets down on the floor of the cave to use as mats.

Dino extracted a yellow poncho from one of the units. "I think this is what you were looking for."

Talia nodded, but didn't immediately take it from him. Instead she was busy counting out the bars and the water to establish how much every one could have for the remainder of the day. Considering they had a radio and that any storm, even a cyclone, should blow over the island by tomorrow, Talia decided to ration for three days in the cave.

That meant two bars and two waters for everyone tonight. The peanut butter would be considered for emergency use only. Talia handed them out with instructions.

"You don't want to eat too fast. Your stomachs haven't had anything solid in them for a while. Take little bites. Chew slowly and wait a few minutes between each bite. You don't want get sick and lose the nutrition in these things. Same is true for the water. Tiny sips. Make it last."

Everyone nodded and went to work opening their first bar. Talia decided that for a second she, too, could sit. She was going to have to go back for Gus soon. She wanted to get him to this cave before dark and, based on the color of the sky just outside the opening, she only had a few hours left before nightfall.

Still, a little time to rest and a little food in her stomach hopefully would give her the energy she needed to get Gus up the hill. Taking her own advice and biting off a small piece, she chewed the tasteless bar and took note of everyone's activities. Nancy, Marlie and Tommy were wrapped in wool blankets, silently working on their meal. Dino sat across from them studying the bar as if trying to figure out what constituted a small bite. Finally, he gave up, took a bite and worked to slow his chewing process.

Evan, who was still fussing with the radio, stepped outside of the cave.

A quiver of fear raced down her spine and Talia immediately stood. That radio was their lifeline and if Evan was planning on making a run for it, he was going to have to outrace her.

"Step inside the cave, Evan," she ordered. When he hesitated, she barked, "Now!"

"But I can't hear anything. It's all static. I need some open space."

Those who were sitting looked at Evan, then at Talia. Her expression must have worried them because they instantly concluded what had her on edge.

"Give her the radio, man."

Tommy's threat might have been more menacing if he'd bothered to stand, but he didn't move. This was a standoff between Evan and Talia only.

Evan sulked, evidently frustrated. "We're not going to get reception in the cave."

"Fine. I'll take it with me when I go for Gus."

Again the group turned their heads toward one then the other as if watching a tennis match.

"This is still about Carney. Because I told you I knew her. But I swear I didn't hurt her. I couldn't hurt anyone."

"All I want is the radio."

The tension built. Talia considered making her move before Evan had a chance to bolt. Having never played professional football, she had no idea what kind of tackler she'd make, but the one thing she knew for certain was that she was not going to let the radio go under any circumstances.

He dropped his arms to his sides in defeat then walked inside the cave. Talia moved forward and took the radio out of his hand as carefully as she would a loaded gun.

"I would never hurt anyone," he repeated, his voice cracking a bit as he said it.

Talia could only shrug. "I'm sorry." The back of the radio had a belt clip. Lifting up Dino's blue windbreaker, she clipped the radio to her jean shorts, then covered it with the jacket to protect it from the elements.

Too geared up at this point to consider resting, she figured the best thing to do was get Gus now. As long as her adrenaline was flowing, it was important to use it because she knew once she crashed, it would be a long time before she recovered.

She shoved a bar in her back pocket. "I shouldn't be long."

"But wait," Dino said. "You can't go by yourself. Then it will be just you and Gus."

"If Gus is the killer, trust me, he's in no shape to be of any threat to me."

"I don't think you should go alone, either," Nancy added. "What if you fall and break something? It's too dangerous."

"I'll be careful."

"Who is going to go with her?" Nancy asked, clearly not satisfied with Talia's answer.

"I don't need anyone else. You're all settled. I'll move faster on my own."

Tommy shucked the blanket. "I'll go."

"You can't go," Evan declared. "What if you're the killer?"

"I'm not," he insisted.

"You were standing over me with a stick. You could have crushed my skull with it."

"I was using it for leverage, you ass."

"Talia didn't need any leverage," Evan pointed out. "She just lifted the tree."

"Yeah, well, Talia is a freakin' superhero, okay?" Tommy retorted. "What do you want me to tell you?"

"This is ridiculous," Dino interrupted. "I'll go."

"We'll both go," Tommy suggested.

"You can't both go," Marlie cried. "Then that leaves Nancy and me with Evan. And we wouldn't be strong enough to fight him off if he is the killer."

"But I'm not and you know it."

"I don't know what I know anymore. All I'm saying is that I'm not staying alone with one of you and just Nancy."

Nancy wrung her hands and shot Talia an apologetic glance. "I'm sorry, but I…I agree with Marlie. I don't trust anyone."

"*You* don't trust anyone?" Tommy snarled. "Well, what about you? All that damn crying and whimpering you've been doing. How do we know it's not some act?

Has it occurred to anyone else that Nancy was the one to find both bodies? She was all alone when she started screaming after Joe was killed. And she was on the beach when we realized Sam was in the water."

"That's crazy," she whispered. "What you're saying is crazy."

"You said your husband left you for a younger woman. Maybe that's why you did it. You got so pissed off at seeing pretty young things get ahead while you got fat and old. Then you saw that actress in Hawaii and decided to take your revenge out on her. Hell, you were the only one of us who was a substitute contestant."

At his harsh words, Marlie actually inched away from where Nancy sat. "You also said you lost it after you didn't get picked and just came to Hawaii anyway. Why? Why did you do that?"

The woman looked dumbstruck. She opened her mouth but nothing came out.

"What if this isn't about stolen jewelry at all?" Tommy speculated. "What if you're just a psycho?"

She gasped and shook her head. "I'm not. I didn't take revenge on anyone. I didn't. I didn't even know her. Evan knew her," she said pointing in the host's direction, then turned her finger back on her accuser. "And you had the stick and the protein bars in your bag. You're the cheater."

"Cheater but not a killer or a psycho. Big difference."

"Enough!" Talia covered her face with her hands and tried to will away the splitting headache behind her eyes. "This isn't getting us anywhere."

"Easy for you to say," Evan drawled. "You're the only one who's not a suspect."

The group quieted then as they studied one another, each of them considering the horrible possibilities.

"Look, I need to get Gus," Talia reminded them quietly. "I can't let him stay out there on his own overnight. It's not fair. Now, I can do this alone. As long as you all stay together you'll be safe. I'll be back in an hour."

With that she left the cave quickly before any more arguments ensued. Stumbling down the hill, moving as fast as she could without risking a fall, she retraced the path they had traveled.

Almost guiltily, she was happy to be away from everyone and have a little peace. It was easy to see that paranoia was taking over. And she couldn't blame anyone for it. Still, if they didn't get help soon, Talia feared what might happen. Thinking about help, she was about to reach for the radio to check the reception when she heard her name.

"Talia! Wait! Wait."

Freezing in her tracks, Talia looked behind her, shocked to hear Nancy's voice calling to her. Wearing one of the slickers, the pudgy woman bounced down the hill like a bright yellow ball with arms.

"What in the hell…" she muttered. Nancy had left the shelter where she had food, water and blankets. That didn't make sense. Suddenly everything Tommy had said reverberated in her ears. Could simple, simpering, pitiful Nancy actually be…crazy? It wasn't possible.

"Don't let appearances fool you."

Reuben's words surfaced next to Tommy's suspicions and Talia felt sick to her stomach. She put a hand up. "Hold it right there. What are you doing, Nancy?"

The woman struggled to bring her round body to a fast stop. Her expression was a picture of confusion. "I…"

"Nancy, if you know what's good for you, you'll turn around and head back to the cave now."

"Oh, Talia, please tell me you don't believe Tommy."

The problem was Talia didn't know what to believe about anything anymore. It was making her crazy. "Go back." When Nancy didn't immediately respond, Talia yelled, "Now."

Then Nancy was reaching under the slicker into the waistband band of her shorts. Talia braced herself for whatever was coming, but all she saw was a water bottle that the older woman carefully placed on the ground in front of her. "I just wanted to make sure you took some water for Gus. I saw you pack a protein bar, but not… Well, you know me. Always worried about water. I'll go."

She walked back up the hill. Cautiously, Talia moved forward until she stood over the innocuous bottle. Nancy was several feet away. Talia picked up the bottle and shoved it between the small of her back and her jean shorts. She felt guilty as hell.

"I'm sorry, Nancy," she called out. "I just…"

Nancy looked over her shoulder, a sad smile playing on her lips. "I know. Trust no one. You go and get Gus, dear, and bring him back as soon as possible." She continued walking until eventually, Talia felt comfortable turning her back to trek down the hill.

Stopping for a moment to rest, Talia wondered why no one had prevented Nancy from leaving the cave and how they were accepting her return. What if the next time there were more than accusations thrown around? If Tommy or Evan got violent, things could get ugly. Fortunately, Dino was there and seemed to be maintaining his calm. Once she brought Gus back into the mix, there would be another voice of reason to keep everyone's tempers cooled until help arrived.

She wished she had Reuben with her, watching her back. If she had known earlier that they would be able to find the cave and have access to all the food they needed, as well as the radio, she might have been able to convince him that swimming to the yacht was too dangerous. He might not be in the middle of the Pacific Ocean, drowning beneath the onslaught of the storm.

"Don't think like that," she muttered under her breath. "He's going to make it. He's probably on the yacht right now swigging a beer and pointing the captain in our direction."

"That would be sweet."

Startled, Talia jumped at the voice behind her. She whirled around to find Dino a few steps away with another yellow poncho in his hand.

"You know…drinking a beer."

"What are you doing?"

"I decided I'm coming with you."

Talia sighed. She didn't need this. Not after the showdown in the cave with Evan, then again with Nancy. She was worn down and frankly too tired to keep her guard up anymore. Which meant she needed to be alone because that was the only way she could be sure of her safety. "I just told Nancy—"

"I know. I passed her. She said you're wound a little tight."

"That's an understatement," she muttered.

"But you have to trust someone, Talia. You need help. Gus could barely walk when we left him. There's no way you're going to be able to get him to the cave on your own."

"I have food and Nancy gave me water. He's had a chance to rest and he's a tough old bird."

Dino shook his head. "I don't doubt it. I just think you can't do it all by yourself. All the time. Besides everyone back in the cave is cool with this. We'll go, we'll get Gus, let him eat stuff and then we'll take him to the bat cave and we'll all hang out until the boat comes. Did you use the radio yet?"

"No, I was going to when Nancy showed up."

"I think we should get Gus first. Don't you?"

Talia considered her options. If Gus was still as weak as he had been when they left, he would have a hard time managing the incline. And with only a few bites of protein bar sitting in her stomach, she knew she would need help dragging him up the hill.

"Here, I brought you a slicker. It will keep you drier than my windbreaker. It's got a hood."

Trust no one.

She was trying, but it was hard. She didn't necessarily have to trust Dino to use him. As long as he maintained some distance, she could manage. They weren't that far from Gus's cave. Another fifteen minutes, tops.

She had to believe that the two of them could handle fifteen minutes together.

"Okay." She unzipped the blue windbreaker and pulled it off. Rolling it into a ball, she tossed it to him rather than get any closer. He did the same with the slicker. She caught it and quickly donned it.

"Ready?" he asked once he had his own coat zipped over his round chest.

"Yes."

"You know where you left him?"

She gave him a baleful look, and he shrugged defensively.

"Sorry. I shouldn't have doubted you. You know, Tommy is right. You really are like some superhero."

"Hardly."

"No, seriously. Is there anything you can't do?"

That had her choking out a garbled laugh. "Sure. I can't get a job."

Walking a few paces behind her, she could tell Dino was struggling to make casual conversation. "I forgot what you said you did again?"

She opened her mouth to tell him, then stopped. Reuben had given her such a hard time about her occupation. In the beginning it seemed odd to her that he had such a difficult time accepting what was a life fact. She'd gone to school, she'd studied hard, she'd gotten her degree in a sensible field that offered a host of job opportunities.

But suddenly, when faced with a very basic question about what she did, the description wouldn't come. She could balance a ledger, locate loopholes in tax code and find creative ways to write off certain types of assets, but she wasn't an accountant. She could see that now. Vividly.

All those years of college trying to run away from something to be something else. What a waste. Her father was going to give her a hell of a time being proven right. Forget what Reuben would say.

"I don't know what I am." But she knew as soon as this mess was behind her, and she was safe at home on the boat with her father—the only place that she had ever truly called home—she was going to have to figure it out.

"I don't get it," Dino returned.

"Just promise me, if you ever see Reuben again you won't tell him about this. I hate the fact that he was right."

"I promise."

Shrugging off the fact that she was going to have to rethink her whole life, Talia concentrated on the present. Rain was now joining the ever-present wind. Glancing up at the sky, she could see dark gray replacing light and knew that the brief respite from the storm they had received was over.

"We need to move faster."

Dino didn't answer, but she heard him pushing past the brush behind her at a pretty good clip. She heard him trip, then curse, but he regained his feet quickly and continued to keep pace.

To take his mind off whatever was hurting, she asked her own questions. "So I guess you don't have my luck in the job department."

"Huh?"

"Because of Joe. I guess he looked out for you when it came to finding a job." He'd told her something to that effect when they had been on the beach together, standing over Joe's body.

"Oh, yeah. I was real lucky. I'd just gotten canned from this other job when I ran into him. The other guy who was supposed to work this job bailed and Joe was in a real bind. I guess you could say we sort of saved each other…." His words trailed off as it must have dawned on him what he'd said. Joe certainly hadn't been saved. "Wow. That's sort of weird. It's almost like I forgot that's he dead. You know?"

"That's because it is all so unreal. Don't think about it. Tell me something else. Tell me what were you doing before this?"

"Right. Don't think about it," he repeated. "I was shooting a film in Waikiki. This action-adventure flick. Your standard shoot 'em up, car chasing, explosions everywhere, massive budget, cookie-cutter stuff. It sucked."

Talia smiled, thinking his description was probably accurate. "Why did you get fired?"

"Oh, this bitch. She hated me. You know the type. First, she's all sweet and flirty. Flipping her hair and stuff and then bang, she dropped me the minute this stud actor showed up. She made Marlie look like Mother Teresa."

"That doesn't sound like an easy—" Talia's breath left her as his words began to sink in. He was on a film set. In Hawaii. A woman got him fired. Talia thought about how many people on a film set who would have the power to get a cameraman fired. A director, a producer…the star.

"I'm sorry, Talia. Really, I am. Because you're not like her at all. You're really nice and everything. Only you're too strong and superhero-like and… Well, I can't take the chance."

Slowly, she turned to find him extracting a pocket-knife from the blue windbreaker. The same one he'd shoved into Joe's back.

Chapter 11

Crippling fear rocked her body. Talia could hear her shallow breathing, feel her limbs going numb, and knew that she was slipping into shock.

Fight it, her will to live demanded.

Not him, she wasn't ready to fight him yet. She had to fight the panic first. There was a metallic taste in the back of her throat and her hands were shaking. She needed to stop that. Struggling not to pant, she managed to inhale a full breath. Like an elixir, it steadied her body and allowed her mind to function.

"You killed them." That much was evident.

Instantly, he shook his head. His expression so solemn so…innocent. It was hard to believe that she was looking into the eyes of a multiple murderer. That was until she remembered the stubby knife in his hand.

"I didn't mean to."

Flashes came back to her. Dino at camp, always around. She'd never really noticed because he'd been behind the camera. He easily could have tampered with the bucket. Then on Tommy's ladder during the challenge, how easy it would have been for him to cut the ropes on his way up.

But how did he get the knife back? Reuben had had the pocketknife. He'd taken it out of Joe's back and...and had handed it over to Dino to finish the second shelter. And it had been in the damn pocket of the windbreaker she'd been wearing for the past hour. She hadn't registered the weight of the knife in the too-large coat.

Here, I brought you a slicker...

Right. The slicker so he could get the jacket—and the damn knife—back.

Stupid, stupid, she mentally cursed herself. She should have been more cautious. She should have been more suspicious of the fact that he seemed so calm when everyone else was losing it. He'd never fired any accusations at anyone. Why? Because the whole time he knew who was responsible.

Her brain tumbled over itself until the facts and the details sorted out. All she was left with were questions.

"Where's the jewelry?"

Dino blinked at her question. "That's your first question? Not why?"

"You said why. Because she got you fired. Because, I'm guessing, you hated her."

"She said I was a nuisance on the set. She told everyone that I was making improper advances. Can you believe that? We were talking, flirting. Shit, she was squeezing my biceps wondering how it was that I could lift such heavy cameras on my shoulders. And when I wanted her to make good on that promise, she flipped out. She told the director she was afraid I was going to rape her."

"Did you?"

He dipped his head and averted his eyes. "She said she didn't want me. But she lied. All women lie. I didn't want to rape her. But she owed me."

"It sounds like she paid. Why did you take the jewelry?"

"She was famous! Everyone would know she was dead and they would come looking for me because of the fight we had on the set. I told her she was a tease. I told her she would get hers. Everyone would know it was me. I had to get away. To another country. And I needed money. I didn't have any. It's not like I took everything."

"I'm sure her family appreciates that."

"Shut up!"

"You can't deny what you did, Dino."

His head lowered again and she used the opportunity to retreat a small step. She needed to create as much distance as she could. The knife he carried in his hand was small, probably dull from use by now. It would be effective only at close range. She needed to keep him off guard, thinking about his deeds, rather than his next move.

"I hate to say this,.but it sounds like you have a problem with women," she noted. "Have you killed everyone who has rejected you?"

"She didn't reject me, she teased me!" he shouted. "There's a difference."

Talia watched as his face changed. Previously his features had seemed so nondescript. The perfect person to be behind the camera because there had been nothing noticeable about him that would hold anyone's attention. But he was changing in front of her eyes. The transformation was more frightening than anything else had been so far.

Gone was the round placid face. His lips were tighter, his nostrils wider and his eyes…they were empty. Even his chest seemed to expand, turning paunch into power.

"You have killed other women before," Talia concluded sickly, knowing that this mutation wasn't happening for the first time. How many women had seen his face last?

He tilted his head to the right and his lower lip pouted slightly. "Nobody else famous."

How ironic that Tommy turned out to be right, she thought. This wasn't about the jewels. This was about a psychopath.

A buzzing started in her ears and she tried to shake it loose. Her life was hanging in the balance and the only weapons she had were her strength and her wits. If she let fear overtake her, she'd be easy prey for him. She refused to let that happen. She wasn't going to make it as easy for him as Sam and Joe had.

"Why kill Joe? Why not kill Marlie first? She teased you."

"Marlie's a bitch," Dino snarled and wiped the blade of the knife against his thigh. Stroking it back and forth, to clean it or because he couldn't stop himself, she didn't know. "Did you see the way she was with me on the yacht? All giggling and laughing and posing for me so I would get her best side. You saw that, right? Tell me you saw it!"

"I saw it," she answered swiftly but her words were muffled.

Irritated, he took a step closer, which sent her stumbling backward. "I can't hear you! Say you saw it," he shouted.

"I did," she cried out and nodded, too, as she took another step away from him. Then another. At this point she would say anything to keep him at bay. "I saw how she treated you. She flirted with you and then she flirted with Tommy. And then Tommy wasn't good enough anymore so she turned to Evan. She's a horrible tease. I admit that. But there is something I don't understand. You also saved her life."

"I wasn't thinking then. I just ran and when I stopped I saw that I was still holding her arm. That didn't mean anything."

"So you were planning to kill her?"

"No, not really. I didn't want to hurt anyone. I swear."

"Just Joe and Sam."

"Joe found the necklace," he tried to argue. "Evan and Marlie were off doing it, and Nancy was busy collecting shells or something. I figured it was the best time to remove the spark plug from the boat's engine. I figured Evan would think that the boat wouldn't start or something and then we would camp out on the beach for the night. Once everyone was asleep I was going to take the boat and go. I wouldn't have had to hurt anyone. But Joe's battery ran out. He came back from the woods and he went into my bag looking for a spare and found it. Then he guessed everything so I had to do it. But that doesn't mean I wanted to."

"Of course you didn't."

Again he took a threatening step forward, closing the distance that she needed to maintain, but she feared that if she retreated from him now, he'd be compelled to leap for her.

"I didn't. He saved me. We had worked together a few years ago in LA. That's how he recognized me in Hawaii. He told me he had a job for me, but I had to leave right away. Can you believe that? It was fate."

Fate didn't work out so well for Joe on that one.

"I never would have hurt Joe if he hadn't realized what I had done. But he did. At first he said he could help me," Dino recalled sadly. "He said I could confess and they would say it was an accident or something. He was like that. Always trying to help."

"I didn't know him well, but he seemed like a good man."

Certainly a man who didn't deserve to die for reaching out to an old colleague. But the grieving process would have to wait. Talia glanced down quickly and inched her feet back while he spoke.

"Sam was, too. All I wanted to do was get away. If he'd only let me get away. But he must have woken up when I left and he followed me down to the beach, asking what I was doing. Then I guess he knew, too. He was really easy though. All I had to do was hold his head under the water until he stopped kicking."

Talia closed her eyes trying to shut out the terror that his words brought. Sam must have been so afraid, she thought. He'd hated the water. To die that way had to be so hard for him.

Her voice, thick with grief and anger, deepened. "Why didn't you just leave? You had what you needed, you'd already killed twice, why didn't you just take the damn boat and go?"

His round cheeks blushed pink. "I lost the plug. In the water while I was…you know while I was…"

Pushing Sam's head under water, holding it there, waiting until he died.

I'm so sorry I wasn't there, Sam. So sorry that you had the rotten luck to wake up.

A harsh gust whipped around them and had them both struggling to remain upright. Talia took a significant step and considered using the distraction as an opportunity to run. But Dino was right there with her, moving to within a couple of feet. Too close to risk having him reach out and catch her before she could escape. He looked down at the short knife in his hand. Probably wondering the same thing she was: what was he going to do with it?

"What's your plan now, Dino?" She watched his face react to her question. His brow creasing deeply with uncertainty. "You can't use the boat. The yacht will be coming for us, if it isn't in the inlet already. Reuben is a very strong swimmer. You know that. You saw him in the water. He could make it."

"Not possible."

She ignored that and continued to press. Her sense was that Dino wasn't so much evil or sinister as he was simply…nuts. It was hard to know which was worse. But the more buttons she pushed, the better her chances to destabilize him.

"You can't kill all of us. When I don't return to the cave, they'll know it's you. They'll fight you."

Stubbornly, almost childishly, he shook his head. "I'm not going back to the cave. You've got the radio. I'm going to take it and go to the beach to radio for help. When the yacht comes I'll tell them you're all dead."

"If I don't return soon, Tommy and Evan will search for me."

This time he managed to smile. A sickly sweet, condescending smile. "No, they won't. They're too scared to leave the cave. They have food, water and blankets now. Nancy thinks you're safe with me. No, they won't go anywhere until someone comes for them. It will be sad when no one does. You're the leader. I knew that if I could take you out, then I would have a chance."

"Gus will—"

"Oh, I'll kill him when I'm done with you. He's another one who might try to get in the way. Not the rest of them, though. They'll stay in the cave."

Talia detected a million faults in his plan. What if Reuben had made it? What if the boat was waiting already for them? Reuben wouldn't take Dino's word that they were all dead. The captain shouldn't, either.

However, she found no reason to point any of that out. If Dino thought his plan would work, then she would work with it. Her gut was telling her that her best chance to survive was to keep him outside. She'd have space to run and hide as soon as the moment came.

Hide for how long, though? What if something has happened to the yacht and it never comes?

Instantly, she shut those thoughts down. Doubts were not acceptable; they would only weigh her down.

Just take the dive one step at a time. Jump first, then somersault, then hands down. You know the routine. Execute.

Talia reached down under her slicker and grabbed the radio she'd clipped to her shorts. In the process, she recalled the water bottle tucked into the back of her shorts, her body suddenly tuning in to the uncomfortable presence of plastic pressed against her skin.

"Here, take the radio. You can go and leave me. I promise I won't follow." She tossed it to him, hoping he would drop the knife in the process. He grasped it out of the air with his free hand and quickly secured it to his own waistband.

His face flushed beet red and his lip curled in a snarl. She could see the wafts of steam floating off his bald head as the rain pelted them both.

"You think I would believe you? A woman? You're all liars and teases."

"You called me a superhero. A superhero wouldn't lie, would she?"

"Superheroes aren't real," he shouted. "Do you think I'm retarded?"

"No," she insisted quickly, clearly misreading the level of dementia he was suffering from.

"I'm not stupid. That bitch said I was stupid, but I'm not and you know how I know? Because she's dead and I've got millions of dollars of her jewelry." He cackled and once more Talia struggled to evaluate him.

Earlier she'd questioned how sinister he truly was, now she understood. Maybe he did feel guilt, if such a thing was possible in a man like him, over killing Joe and Sam. But he wouldn't feel the same about killing her, a woman.

And he wouldn't hesitate, either.

Another powerful blast of wind hit them, bringing debris with it, including a leaf that hit him flat on the side of his head. Knowing she wouldn't get a better opportunity, Talia reached for the bottle at her back and flung it at him as hard as she could.

She didn't wait for the sound of it making contact against his face before she was running down the hill at full speed.

"Ow," he hollered. "Come back here."

Talia weaved her way through the trees, leaping over the bushes at her feet as fast as she could. Briefly, she contemplated heading for Gus's cave hoping that he regained enough of his strength to help her fight off Dino. But it was too much of a risk. If he wasn't strong enough, then she would be trapped and Dino would be quick to take Gus out, as well.

The problem was she wasn't a fighter. She didn't know how to throw a punch or execute a martial-arts kick. She'd never taken self-defense classes because she'd never seen the need for it.

Dino had called her a superhero and she wanted to

laugh in his face for it. A real superhero would have been able to kick his ass. The fact that she could swim, dive and catch fish couldn't aid her now.

A weapon.

Images of Tommy standing over Evan with the stick in his hand flashed in her head. Evan had been fearful that Tommy would crush his skull with it. She imagined if the stick were thick enough, she could do the same to Dino.

Did she chance stopping to look for something appropriate? Concentrating on controlling her breathing, she tried to listen beyond the sound of the wind for signs of her pursuer.

"I can see you," he called, not more than twenty or thirty feet behind her. "Stop now and I'll try to make this easy. I promise."

She spun her head around to see if she could catch a glimpse of him, but couldn't in the thickening grass and trees. With the wind blowing, it was impossible to tell what was causing the movement of the leaves.

Jumping over a rotten log, she landed with her ankle at an odd angle and was unable to prevent the cry of pain that erupted past her lips. Somehow she managed to stay on her feet, but as she raced forward she could tell her speed was much slower because of the new pain.

"Now I can hear you, too. What's the matter? Did you fall? You fell when that waterspout was after you. I thought it was going to suck you up right then. But then you got up. Just like a bitch, won't die when it's convenient."

Talia was beginning to lose her sense of orientation.

They had been running downhill, obviously, but in which direction? They hadn't climbed this way. She didn't recognize any of the landmarks and the bamboo was so thick on this part of the hillside that she found herself having to squeeze her body through the reeds to move past them.

That's an advantage. He'll have to push his way through them. That will take time.

Realizing his size would slow him, Talia continued to weave her way into the heart of the reeds that shot up well past her head, thankful that her svelte figure allowed her to slide through the shoots easily.

For a second she paused to assess how far he was behind her.

The sound of bamboo being pushed aside and trampled let her know that her theory was right. He couldn't fit through them, which meant he had to knock them down.

But he sang out over the shrieking wind, "I still see you. Not too much longer now."

He saw her. How did he see her among all this green?

The poncho. It was typically yellow and impossibly bright. Pulling it over her head she left it hanging on a bush where the shoots were the thickest and continued through to a more evenly spaced part of the forest. Finally she was able to run at full speed, her sneakers eating up the muddy ground beneath her.

From a distance she could hear his strange singsong voice, although she could barely make out what he was saying. "There…are. That's… Hold… Damn it!"

She couldn't be sure, but she believed he'd fallen for

her decoy. But he also knew he wasn't looking for yellow anymore and was still on the move. All she could do was run—knowing that her life depended on it—and hope that he got tired first. The surrounding trees were too thin to hide behind. And he wasn't far enough behind her that she could risk slowing down to look for cover or a weapon.

Think! What now?

But her brain wouldn't respond. It was too busy keeping her body moving. To where, though, she had no idea. The mud was thicker now and causing her sneakers to sink below the ground so that she had to struggle to pull herself out of the bogs. It was the horrible realization of a dream—you knew you needed to move but your legs were stuck in molasses. This mud was thicker than that. With a pop, she pulled her left foot free and knew that she had to get out of this stuff or risk loosing any lead she had on Dino.

Checking the area, she found a log and stepped on it, following it for as long as it could keep her out of the thick stuff. When it ended she found another one she could leap to and kept moving. The fallen trunks didn't take her in a straight line, zigzagging slightly. And the time it took to balance herself on them, despite her innate sense of equilibrium, wasn't helping. However, she felt she was better off than in the goop that had become the forest's floor.

Another crash sounded behind her. She turned to check even though she knew it would cost her time. Dino was at the edge of the spot where the bamboo gave way to palm trees and mud. His right foot had sunk deep into the wet dirt, sending him sprawling face first to the ground.

He pulled himself up, his body covered in thick black mud, his eyes seemingly glowing whiter because of it, and stared at her.

"You can't get away. I'll find you no matter where you are. You're just postponing the inevitable."

Don't look. Don't listen. Just move.

She continued her path on the logs until they ran out. But when she hopped off from the last trunk, her feet found rock instead of dirt. Twisting her body once more to get a sense of where she was on the island, she realized that lava rock was dominating the area.

The lagoon. She was close to the lagoon.

An idea occurred to her and, finding new strength in her limbs, she made a dash for it. A tug in her thigh muscles told her that she was climbing again, but that could be a good thing. Pushing her way through a bush, she came to an abrupt halt.

Suddenly the forest was gone and the only thing in front of her was space. Glancing down, she saw that she was about ten feet above the outcrop where the waterfall poured down into the lagoon and fifty feet above the water.

Good thing you're not afraid of heights.

Catching her breath, she moved farther onto the rock overhang, careful and precise with each step. Her mud-slicked sneakers were making it difficult to keep steady footing on the wet rock.

Unsure of the wisdom of the next decision, but not seeing an alternative, she lifted her leg and used her hand to push off first one sneaker, then raised her other leg to knock off the second. Her bare feet gave her better traction on the smooth rock and the familiar feel of a wet surface under the soles of her feet cemented the idea that had taken root as soon as she'd figured out where she was.

Now it was just a question of waiting.

Looking over her shoulder, she tried to see the color of the water below her. But the remaining daylight had been sucked up by the darkening storm. Below her all she could see was an endless black abyss.

"That will be good to clean off under."

Reuben's words about the waterfall came back to her. Closing her eyes, she thought back to the color of the water and where it had been the darkest.

"I don't think you could stand under it. It looks like the surface drops severely," she had answered him.

It had better. Her life depended on it.

A sound different from the wind greeted her, telling her that her pursuer was getting closer. Her stomach dropped noticeably. He pushed through a bush, his momentum carrying him forward to the point where he might have gone over the edge had his hand not wrapped around a branch.

Bad luck for her.

He checked left and right then spotted her a few feet away, higher on the edge. He smiled and she wanted to cry.

Stay calm. You can do this.

"I…can't… There is nowhere left to go," she choked out. "You have the radio, you still have the jewels somewhere—why don't you just go?"

"You know I won't do that." He moved closer to her but stopped when his mud-covered Dockers slipped, giving him trouble navigating the slick rock.

"I've never lied to you, Dino. I don't deserve this."

"All women deserve it," he answered coldly.

Keep him talking. He could slip before he reached her....

His free hand reached out to grab her, but she pulled back. His forward momentum had him leaning precariously close to the edge, but somehow he managed to right himself before tipping over.

"Come here," he snapped, evidently tired of the chase.

"Not going to happen. You want me, you're going to have to come and get me."

He took another step forward. Then one more.

She was able to inch back, staying just out of range, taking her so close to the edge that her heels met space. Curling her toes tight, she clung to the rock with the balls of her feet and struggled to maintain her balance by shifting her arms out to the side.

Come on, Dino. A little closer. Let's do this one together.

"What are you doing? You're going to fall," he shouted.

"What difference does it make to you?"

"No, no, no," he whined, stomping his feet in irritation. "I have to kill you. I have to know you're dead or my plan is no good."

"That's your problem." Talia lifted her hands in the air, pantomiming a move she used to make when preparing for a backward dive.

The movement signaled her intent and Dino reacted as predicted. He rushed for her, lunging to try to grab her before she could topple over, but it was too late.

She felt him wrap one arm around her waist and saw him raise the knife to stab it hard into her stomach. But she was able to reach up and circle his wrist, keeping the knife away.

And then they were tumbling backward, the impact of his body into hers more than enough to send her over the edge of the cliff. With her hands still holding on to his wrists, and his arm still around her waist, he was forced to take the ride with her.

Comfortable in space, she brought her legs up as if positioning her body into a tuck position and used her knees as leverage to push against his thick belly. Then she released his wrist, arched her back, dramatically creating as much separation from him as she could. She felt a sting in her thigh before she was completely clear of him and knew that the knife had cut her.

It was pointless to focus on the cut, though. Certainly not in midflight. Talia relaxed her body and let herself fall easily, trying to find her spots among the darkness, trying to orient herself between the sky and the water. She didn't listen to Dino's shouting. She didn't think about what would happen if the water wasn't deep enough.

If this was going to be her last dive, she was going to enjoy it. Stretching out, she let her body embrace the wind as it gently pushed at her like a hand coaxing her in the direction it wanted to go. She felt the rain on her face and the warmth from the blood trickling down her leg.

She found that point where she needed to transition from falling to diving and arched until her body was again vertical. Gripping her hands, one on top of the other, tightening her muscles to brace for impact, she willed herself into a thin straight line.

The water came up to greet her and she cut through it cleanly, as she had so often in the past. As soon as her hands were underneath the surface, she pushed them in front of her trying to make her entry as shallow as she could. Her ankles smacked down behind her, she felt the whoosh of seawater that erupted above her in what she was sure was a significant splash.

But there would be no one to judge her this time. And the only thing she would win was her life.

Her body submerged completely and her hand bounced off a jagged edge that rose up from the lagoon floor just under the surface. She bumped up against another hard surface to her right, but knew that she'd hit a deep pocket of water as her body continued to sink. Rolling forward in a somersault to stop her momentum, Talia continued to drop without touching bottom.

After a final turn, her speed slowed enough for her to right herself. With nothing beneath her, there was nothing to push off from and she was forced to work her arms and legs to climb back to the surface. Only the faintest hint of light above her head gave her any indication that she was swimming in the right direction. But after a few strokes, just as her lungs started to get tight, her head broke above the water and she was able to breathe.

Instantly she searched for Dino, expecting him

somehow to have survived the fall while still holding on to the knife in his hand, but the water was flat except for ripples created by the raindrops. Squinting to penetrate the dark, she twisted her body a full three hundred and sixty degrees and still nothing.

Left with only one choice, she swam to the center of the lagoon where she knew she would be able to stand. Once on her feet, hopefully she would be able to survey the entire area more thoroughly. Dino was in the water with her somewhere, it was just a question of what condition he would be in.

Putting her face down, she reached her arm up over her head in a crawl and bumped into his fleshy round body. She opened her mouth to scream. Panicking, she used her legs to reverse her position in the water, kicking at him as she did and fighting to stay out of reach of his arms.

It wasn't until she was more than a foot away that she realized he wasn't coming after her. Using only her legs to hold her head above water, she splashed at the body that seemed to be floating on the surface. There was no reaction.

Appearances can be deceiving.

"Dino!" Still nothing. She hollered again, "Dino!"

Nothing. He didn't lift his head or turn his body. She pushed farther back, but her foot nicked another sharp rock jutting up from the bottom. The space she'd dived into was deep, but obviously treacherous. If he'd landed in the wrong spot...

"See, this is always the part in the movie when the girl thinks the killer is dead, but the killer really isn't dead," she chattered to herself.

The water was warm, but her teeth were clicking together sporadically, probably a result of shock. She couldn't forget the cut to her leg. There was no way to know how deep it was or how much blood loss she was sustaining. To reach the shallow part of the lagoon she was going to have to swim around him and she wasn't going to do that until she was positive he was no longer a threat.

Seconds ticked by while she continued to shift her position to keep what she deemed to be a safe distance between them. Then minutes. Suddenly, her overworked conscience sprang to life as she began to consider the possibilities that he'd hit his head. What if she was treading water, watching him while he drowned? He was a murderer, but she wasn't.

Cautiously she moved toward him with the knowledge that if he did move suddenly, he would be out of breath and she could move faster in the water than he could.

His body bobbed and she reached out to poke him. Then she moved closer and tugged on his arm, pulling him and turning him until he was face up.

"Oh my—" She lost her breath as she saw what was left of his face. His head must have connected with rock and the jagged shards had cut through skin and bone, leaving him a bloody mess.

Blood. A lot of it in the water.

She needed to get out of the water now. She put her head down, closed her eyes and her mouth, as she passed through the thicker, warmer fluid that she knew was remnants of Dino.

Once beyond him, she started kicking her legs furiously only to stop when she felt something, a vibration under the water, that rocked her.

What now?

Lifting her head up, she prepared herself for anything—a shark attack, another twister, maybe even a tsunami. What she didn't expect, couldn't hope to expect, was a large white yacht pulling into the inlet. The vibration she felt was the motor in the water and the sweetest sound she'd ever heard was the long pull of a slow, deep horn.

She swung her arms wildly above her head in the hopes of attracting the attention of someone on deck, but suspected it was pointless given the darkness. Ahead of her she could see a beam of light cutting across the water and she raced for it. She hit the shallows of the lagoon and got to her feet, running part of the way until she tripped and fell forward. She decided to swim the rest of the way to the inlet. The next time she lifted her head, she had to turn away from the blast of white light that was shining in her face.

She couldn't see anything, but if someone was looking they should be able to see her. Weakly, as her strength was beginning to ebb, Talia lifted her arms in the air hoping that the visual disturbance would garner the attention of whoever was piloting the boat.

"Please," she murmured even though she knew it was pointless. "I'm so tired."

In response to her plea, another shock of white sailed through the air and dropped beside her. Never had she ever thought that she would need to be on the receiving end of a life preserver.

"Come on," came a shout from above. "Swim for it."

"Easy for you to say," she muttered, not knowing if she had the energy to take her the last few feet to the floating doughnut.

"Sugar, don't tell me you're getting lazy on me."

It wasn't the words so much as the sarcastic drawl that had her smiling faintly. With a little more motivation now, she swam to the buoy and wrapped it around her body.

It was uncomfortable being hauled out of the water, the plastic pressing into her stomach, but it was so much better than being chased by a crazed killer and falling fifty feet into the water.

Arms reached out to her and hauled her over the railing. Someone tossed a blanket around her shoulders, and then two hands were gently cupping her face, tilting it upward. She opened her eyes and saw Reuben gazing down at her and knew that it was finally over.

"You made it," she croaked.

"Barely. Sorry it took so long. What were you doing in the water?"

"Trying to get away," she answered simply. "It was Dino."

"Was?"

"He's dead. We fell over the cliff into the lagoon. He hit a rock, I think. His face… There is no face anymore."

He blinked once, but other than that there was little reaction. "Okay. The captain and I will take it from here. Where is everyone?"

"In a cave in the interior of the island where the emergency supplies were kept."

"They're safe?"

She nodded limply.

"Good girl."

It was silly, she should have berated him for treating her like a child, but instead his approval of the job she'd done in his absence warmed her from the inside. Tears welled in her eyes and, after everything she'd experienced, she didn't try to stop them.

"Just like a woman to get all mushy after fighting off storms and a killer, and leaping over a fifty-foot cliff. All heart. No toughness."

If she could have, she would have hit him. Instead she let him pick her up and carry her inside to safety.

Chapter 12

"Dad! Dad, you onboard?"

Talia stood at the end of the pier across from her father's boat the *Slainte*. In his typically neurotic way, he'd left the plank up. No doubt a leftover precaution from his natural predator: Rocco the shark.

The white clapboard, somewhat neglected sign that read Mooney's Sport Fishing Tours hung from the rope that acted as a gate to the boat. If only there was a plank.

It was good to be home.

"Dad!" she yelled again.

He emerged suddenly from below deck, a beaming smile on his face.

"There she is! My star. My fearless daughter. My savior." Colin Mooney stood with his arms wide. His face, as always, was dark brown from the sun; his hair almost luminescent white—no doubt from the stress of being perennially in trouble. But his knees looked to be sound and she could spot the twinkle in his eye from ten feet away.

"I take it you got the money I wired."

"Did I ever get the money!" He moved quickly to push the plank out to the pier and Talia unhooked the rope gate that would never keep anyone out.

"Ah, ah, ah. What do you say?"

She stopped, groaning inwardly at the old ritual, but also heartened by the idea that so little changed here. Her heart beat heavy and she decided that, for all his faults, she wasn't ready to kill him after all.

"Permission to come aboard, Captain?"

"Permission granted."

She walked to meet him, her white sneakers perfect for maintaining balance on a wet plank. Instead of jean shorts, she'd opted for a short, breezy skirt and floral top. After living in the same getup for a few days, she'd never been so happy to get out of a swimsuit and shorts in her life.

Reuben had felt equally strongly about her need to disrobe.

She smiled at the memory, but then quickly tried to dismiss it since, ultimately, it made her sad.

After the police in Waikīki had questioned them, taking detailed statements, the surviving cast had been shipped off to L.A. for a meeting with the producers of *Ultimate Endurance,* all of whom were extremely nervous about lawsuits. So much so that they agreed to a half-million-dollar payoff for each of the contestants, including Iris who already had returned home.

With no family to leave it to, Sam's share went to support the Holocaust Museum in Washington, D.C. Everybody decided it was a good decision for a man who had wanted to be a hero so much. In the end, he'd found a measure of bravery he probably hadn't known he had.

After that, there hadn't been anything left to do but leave each other and return to their separate, albeit richer, lives.

Marlie had been too busy planning a shopping spree in L.A. to bother with an overlong goodbye, but she blew air kisses to everyone before hopping into a limo. Tommy surprisingly had seemed more sentimental than Talia would have thought, hugging her tightly and thanking her before he left. She could only hope that he could look back at everything that had happened on the island and grow from the experience.

Gus actually had gotten a little choked up after the last handshake. And, naturally, Nancy had bawled unceasingly until Talia had promised her that they would arrange for a reunion at some point in the future.

Evan never got to say goodbye. But at least they were all able to see him as he immediately started making the rounds of the entertainment news shows detailing the tragic events of the reality series gone wrong. Talia and Reuben had watched the various shows from their hotel bed fascinated by the TV host's rendition of how he'd held the group together during the most desperate hours.

Oh, Reuben had made a miraculous swim and Talia had done her part by identifying and taking out the killer, but, more importantly, without Evan's leadership at key moments the group would have fallen apart.

It made for excellent TV even if it was complete bullshit.

"Damn, I love reality TV," Reuben had quipped.

Neither quite ready to return to their normally scheduled programming, they'd spent two days sleeping and eating, two nights making love until they couldn't do it anymore. But at the end of that time, Talia had told him she was leaving.

Like nothing she had ever seen on reality TV, the scene that had ensued was all too dramatic.

"What do you mean you're leaving? The fuck you are."

"I can't stay. I have to go home and think about things."

"Think about what? We're together and we have a million dollars between us. We've got the whole damn world on a stick. We can be whoever we want, do whatever we want."

"I thought I wanted to be an accountant."

"So? You were wrong."

"And that's just so easy for you to say, isn't it? I spend four years working toward something—"

"You spent four years running away from something, sugar. Not working toward it. It's time you realize that. Hell, I thought you already had."

She might have. But she wasn't about to tell him that. She'd only known him for a couple of weeks and her reaction to him had been far too intense. The physical chemistry aside, their relationship—she hesitated to use the word—was born out of nothing more than extreme circumstances. It was a good bet that once they returned to actual reality as opposed to "television" reality, any tenuous connection they'd shared would be gone, ripped apart like a fragile spiderweb.

Besides, she had a plan, she reminded herself. First the serious job, then a serious husband who drove a Volvo and wanted to live a safe and stable life with her and their two children. *Serious* and *safe,* two adjectives she definitely would not assign to Reuben. No, he was absolutely nothing she thought she ever wanted…until now.

Now she didn't know what the heck she wanted.

Which was why she was standing on the deck of her father's mostly dilapidated boat hoping that he might have some answers. But even if he didn't, at least she could take comfort in her old home.

Some home, she mused, reacquainting herself with the old lady. At thirty-five feet and with two levels, technically it was big enough to be considered a yacht. But no one looking at her would ever mistake her for such.

"You look like you need a beer, girlie."

"I do."

"Stay here. I'll bring it up."

Once more he dipped below deck to the galley where she'd once eaten dinner with him and her mom, like any other normal kid would do except that they had special dinner plates that stuck to the table.

Growing up, it had never occurred to her to think her life was strange. And as a competitive diver, each kid had a life that was so geared to diving, nothing was considered odd. Not waking up at 3:00 a.m. to practice, not driving for days on end across states to compete in an important meet. That was the life.

It was when she'd gotten to college and had seen how things could be different that she'd imagined she wanted something else. Something steady and normal.

Staring out at the marina and the other boats bobbing in their slips, Talia felt her father's presence behind her. She reached her hand back, and he silently passed her the beer. The bottle was cold and felt good in her hand.

"Dad, how come you never remarried?"

"What sort of question is this?"

Without turning around, she shrugged. "I'm just curious."

"That's easy. I never came close to loving anyone like I loved your mother."

She shook her head slightly and took a swallow of the dark amber beer he preferred. "When I remember her, it's hard to imagine you two together. She was so different from you."

Her father came up alongside her and leaned against the rail. "No, she wasn't, girlie. You only think she was."

"Dad, no offense, but Mom's work ethic was slightly different than yours. She was always the one to make sure we did our chores. When we went camping, she set the camp, caught the food and cooked it. She was always pushing you to take on more customers so that you could expand the business. You…you would be happy fishing all day."

"That I would. That I would."

"I bet deep down she hated this boat. I bet she wanted a real house."

"Not so," he countered loudly. He turned to her, his face scrunched up in question. "Is that what you think? You think because your mother was a hard worker, which God rest her soul she was, that's all she was? You think she wanted a house? Or maybe a job? You think she would have been happy in one of those…accounting firms?"

Yes. That's exactly what Talia believed. She believed that not only would her mother have been happy, but she would have been running any business she'd worked for by a year's end.

"You don't?"

Colin laughed, a deep, full, belly laugh that never failed to make his daughter smile.

"Poor baby. Your mother right now is in heaven shocked that her daughter could be so misguided about her own mother. She was a worker, yes, but she was also an adventurer. She would pick these remote islands to camp on that I had never heard of just to challenge us as a family to find our way. She could dive for shellfish without any fins or snorkels for hours, holding her breath for lengths the likes of which I had never seen anyone do before. She loved the water. She adored this barnacle-laden boat. She was amazing."

Suddenly, he slapped his knee and his face brightened with dawning.

"Oh, I see now. All this time you've been afraid of your very nature because you think you're just like your dear old dad. Always needing a new challenge—"

"Always getting in trouble," Talia added.

Colin continued to smile. "'Tis true, I do tend to get in a wee bit of it every now and then, but to my way of thinking, that's part of the spice of life. But sweetheart, trust me when I tell you that the drive in you that pushes you physically and mentally is all hers. That makes you comfortable on a boat miles out to sea during a rough storm, or on a desert island where you have to hunt for food and find water. All of that comes from your mother. Don't doubt it."

"I made a mistake, didn't I?"

"Which mistake would that be, dear?"

She nudged him with her elbow. "You make it sound like I've made so many."

"A few that I could think of off the top of my head anyway."

"I picked a major in college not because I was really interested in it, but because I thought it was…. I thought it was something that Mom would have wanted for me."

"There it is," he whispered. "Doesn't that feel better to get that off your chest?"

No. It was frightening. All her life she'd had a purpose, first diving, then numbers and normalcy. Now she didn't have a clue what came next. The good news was she had plenty of cash, which meant plenty of time to figure it out, she supposed.

She took another swig of beer. "I don't know what I'm going to do next."

"You'll find something," he told her somewhat philosophically. "Maybe instead of fishing tours you could start up your own little business taking groups of people out camping on remote islands. It seems you're quite capable at that."

"And I suppose having a background in accounting isn't a bad thing for a person who intends to have her own business."

"Certainly not. Like I always say, a schoolroom education is never wasted."

She scrunched her face. "You never say that. You told me college was pointless."

"A man can learn."

Wrapping an arm around his waist, she leaned into him. "I love you, Dad. And I'm glad you didn't get your kneecaps smashed."

"As am I," he quickly replied. "As to that, though. It does seem what with your winnings and all that you do have some spare cash laying about these days."

She pulled away and glared at him. "Dad," she growled.

He held up his hands innocently. "I'm just saying we have a rare opportunity now to really go after some legendary treasures. Galleons that have been sunk off this coast for hundreds of years are just waiting for us to come and claim them."

"I take it back," she muttered. "I am going to kill you."

"Granted, we couldn't do this alone. I have the knowledge and the connections, you're a fair swimmer and all that, but I think we could do with a partner."

She gasped in disbelief. "Are you kidding? A partner? Dad, that's how we got into this mess, remember? I had to go back on TV, in a bikini no less, on an island with seven crazy castaways and, oh yeah…a killer. A psycho killer who chased me through a forest and over a cliff!"

"Now sweetheart, I understand you had a wee bit of a trial with all of that."

"It was more than wee, Dad. It was super wee!" She had no idea what that meant but he was fast pushing her into insanity.

Still Colin continued to speak calmly. "But I think I found someone who is perfect for us, dear. He's willing to try new things and he's an exceptionally strong swimmer and—"

"And he's not going anywhere so you better get used to the idea."

Reuben climbed up the three steps from the below deck wearing shorts, a white T-shirt, a ball cap and bare feet.

He looked so good she thought she might drink him.

"Yes, your mother and I," Colin reminisced. "Two adventurers we were. One more of a dreamer, the other more of a worker, but both of us were always heading in the same direction. I'll be below if you need me."

Practically skipping, her father left them standing on the deck. Reuben reached out and took the beer from her hand. He took a long, slow pull from the bottle and she was helpless against the wave of heat that surfaced just watching his Adam's apple bob up and down.

"What are you doing here?" she wanted to know.

"I said I wanted to open a bar. Granted, a beach place

in the Keys is a little more Jimmy Buffett than I had originally planned…but what the hell. I figure I can have my bar and have you, too. And your dad thinks we would make a great team."

She snorted. "My dad thinks someday he's going to find lost treasure."

Casually, Reuben shrugged. "He might."

"But he probably won't."

"But he might," he repeated. "I can see which one of us is going to be the dreamer versus the worker. For the record that's okay with me. You're better at catching fish than I am."

She shook her head, almost fatalistically, as he moved closer and circled one arm around her waist.

"You really are nothing I ever thought I wanted in a man," she stated even as she circled his neck with her hands. "This is never going to work." What a crazy twist of fate that she had fallen in love with him.

Stupid fate.

Undeterred by her feeble resistance, he smiled wide, his white teeth gleaming in the sun as he lowered his mouth to hers.

"But it might."

* * * * *

There are some days when it just doesn't pay to get up. Definitely, this was one of those days. It had been strange and weird from the beginning and showed no signs of improving.

My name is Whitney Pearl, but almost everyone calls me Pink. I'm a CPA, a certified public accountant—or Constant Pain in the Ass, depending on whom you're talking to. And the people I'd talked to today had done nothing to help my self-esteem.

A little before five, I left the office and headed for the grocery store. I needed some down time with just me and a pint of Bluebell Cookies 'n' Cream.

I pulled in at the Allbright's on Loop 250, because it was on the way home. With no list or real idea of what I needed, except for the ice cream and the salad for the tamale dinner, I grabbed a basket and began my long trek through the supermarket.

I'd been wandering around the store for quite some time before I noticed I was being followed.

In the canned-fruit section, while I checked the labels on peaches, looking for something without fifteen pounds of added sugar, I realized this guy was sort of lingering behind me, just to the right. It dawned on me, in a weird, lightbulb moment, that he'd been close by on the spaghetti aisle. He'd also been hanging out at the deli when I ordered a quarter pound of shaved turkey.

I'm convinced we all have some secret, inner alarm that goes into alert mode whenever something isn't quite right. Mine began to go off, right there in the canned-fruit aisle. I didn't look directly at him, but tossed a can of peaches in my basket and shoved off, headed for the cosmetics aisle. If he showed up there, I'd know for sure he was following me.

As I wheeled across the store, it occurred to me he might be a cross-dresser, in which case I guess he might logically be buying makeup. But from what I could gather out of the corner of my eye, I didn't think the guy was a cross-dresser. He was tall and kinda gnarly, with a crew cut and work boots, and his skin was a shade darker than mine.

A few minutes later, I felt relieved when he never showed up. I tossed some mascara and a new tube of lipstick in the basket and strolled off toward the produce section to look for salad stuff. I was kinda looking forward to having some real groceries at home. The past few months, my diet had mostly consisted of fast food and frozen dinners.

After I nabbed a bag of lettuce, I went to find a decent tomato. There, while I searched for one that wasn't too ripe, the man moved just next to me, reached out one tanned, rough hand and grabbed two tomatoes. When he pulled back, turned his basket and left, I saw he'd dropped something in the middle of all that red. With my hair slowly rising, I picked up the small piece of paper and read his note.

I was told that you would help me. If you want to aid your country, meet me in the bakery.

Now my mama didn't raise no fool. A gnarly guy follows me around, leaves this cryptic note in the tomatoes, and I'm supposed to go meet him? Yeah, I don't think so.

I hauled my ass for the checkout counter. Just my luck, there were only two lanes open, and each had at least five people in line. I debated leaving the basket and hitting the road, but I really wanted those groceries. It was the first time I'd picked up real food since I moved to Midland, and after spending all that time shopping, no way I wanted a repeat anytime soon. I hate grocery shopping. It's on my Top-Ten List of Things I Hate To Do, between filing my taxes and having lunch with Aunt Dru. No, I definitely needed to buy the groceries, so I decided to take my chances on the nutty guy finding me. If I was in line, he couldn't do anything, could he?

I had my answer about thirty seconds later. He came right up behind me and said conversationally, "Boy, what's with only two lanes? This time of day, with so many people stopping in after work, you'd think they'd have more checkouts open."

The lady in front of me nodded and added, "Last week, I had to take my own groceries to the car!" She said this as though carrying her groceries out ranked up there with superhuman efforts like swimming the English Channel or climbing Everest.

"The bakery's kinda falling off, too, if you ask me," the gnarly man said. He stared at me as he said it and I felt my scalp tingle again. Then he picked up the *National Enquirer* and studied the front page for a time. I kept my focus on the chewing gum selection until he tapped my shoulder and held the paper toward me. "I'm always pretty skeptical about their articles, but they are sort of intriguing, don't you think?"

The lady was still looking at us, and I couldn't ignore the guy without appearing boorish. Miss Manners took over, and I glanced at the cover. He'd attached another note to it.

I understand you think I'm crazy. Santorelli gave me your name—said I could trust you if I got in a bind. Just give me two minutes.

Santorelli? My Santorelli? The senator from California who could kiss like nobody's business, who had an off-the-wall sense of humor and awesome suits? I looked up, into the man's eyes, and couldn't miss the sincerity there. Along with a small amount of fear.

"You know," he said to no one in particular, "it seems to me that with this many shoppers, they'd have more people working. There's a whole crowd over on the pickle aisle sampling some new kind of olives."

"I tried those!" the lady in front of me said. "Stuffed with garlic and jalapeños and the like." She looked at me. "Did you try one?"

"No, I guess I missed that." But I didn't miss the stranger's point. The store was crowded. I wasn't in any danger, and what could it hurt to hear what he had to say? Sighing because I knew I was gonna regret it, but my curiosity was killing me, I pulled back my cart. "I'll check it out."

The stranger said, "Yeah, I think I'll pick up a jar of the sardine ones. Gotta love sardines."

I pushed my cart toward the pickle aisle, über-aware of the sardine-loving guy right behind me. I slowed down next to the kosher dills, several feet away from the small crowd gathered around the olive company representative, a short guy who was giving away ceramic olive boats. They were pretty cool, and I decided maybe I'd get one, too, as soon as Mr. Gnarly explained how he knew Santorelli and how I could aid my country.

While the olive rep went on about the olives as he passed some around on toothpicks, the mystery man angled his big body toward me, bent his head as if he was studying his grocery list and whispered, "I don't have much time, so I can't give any explanation, but I need you to pick up a cake in the bakery and deliver it to someone. It's imperative that you get it to the right person, that you not allow anyone else to get it. Make everyone believe it really is a birthday cake for a little boy."

I consider myself a quick study, but I was thoroughly confused. The guy coaxed me to the pickle aisle to tell me about a birthday cake for a pretend little boy, to be delivered to one particular person? What did this have to do with aiding my country? Or Senator Santorelli? Maybe I was having a blond moment, but I didn't think so.

He retrieved a jar of sweet gherkins from the shelf and studied the back while he whispered, "I'm with the CIA, and my cover's blown. I've gotta get out of town immediately, but I have to get the information that's in that cake to the right people. I can't take it myself because I'm being followed, and I'd lead them to my contact, which would blow his cover, as well." He cast a quick glance over his shoulder, then continued, "I waited for you to come out of your office, then followed you. I'm trying not to be obvious, but at this point, I believe they're watching every move I make. If their guy sees me talking to you, they'll think I passed the information off to you and you'd never get out of here with it. That's why I put it in the cake. Nobody would think to look in a cake."

For the very first time, I started to believe maybe he was on the level, that maybe he wasn't smoking crack. "Where is their guy?"

"I don't know. He could be anybody in this store, or

I may have lost him and he isn't anywhere near here. Don't trust anybody and don't give the cake to anyone but the man whose name and address is inside the cake. It'll be ready in about thirty minutes."

"How do you know Santorelli?"

"He gets briefed about money-laundering. This has been an extremely dangerous assignment, and he said if I got in a bind, I could trust you to lend me a hand."

Before I could ask more questions, a large, older woman with a tiny dog in her bag parked her cart next to him.

Acting as though we'd been chatting it up all along, he said in a normal voice, "What kind of cake are you picking up for your friend?"

"A birthday cake, for her son. They said it would be ready in about thirty minutes, so I'm killing time."

The man nodded. "My nephew just had a birthday and his cake had a Spider-Man action figure on it. He loves Spider-Man because he always gets the bad guys."

The big lady chuckled. "Spider-Man's not just for boys. My little girl is crazy for him."

The gnarly guy smiled at her then said to me, "Interesting name your friend's son has. Can't think I've ever heard of a boy named Santa. I bet the kids tease him about that."

Santa? What the hell? Couldn't he have dreamed up a better name for the pretend boy? I cast about for an appropriate comeback. "It's a nickname, actually." Leaning close to him, I pointed at a block of fresh mozzarella in his basket. "Is that brand any good?" I asked aloud, then asked beneath my breath, "Who's laundering money?"

"It's excellent," he replied, "especially with a ripe to-mato, fresh basil and a bit of olive oil drizzled on it."

"I like it with balsamic vinegar, as well," Big Mama said.

Mr. Gnarly nodded in her direction, then focused on the olive dude. After a few moments, he whispered, "Al Qaeda."

Maybe I sucked in a breath. Or perhaps I actually made a small noise in the back of my throat. I admit, it's all a bit fuzzy now. But I know I must have made my shock and horror known, because the man looked panicked and his expression warned me to be cool. I swallowed back the lump of fear in my throat and began to back away from him.

Suddenly, the simple task of picking up the cake and delivering it to someone became very dangerous. Was I up for it? Did I really have a choice? I was keenly curious to know more, and most especially, to know what was hidden inside the cake. Only one way to find out, and that was to agree to deliver it.

"You know, I don't really need more stuff in my apartment, even an olive boat. I think I'm gonna head for the bakery. It was real nice talking to you."

He'd been staring at the big lady, but when I spoke, he turned and his dark eyes crinkled at the edges as he smiled at me. I had the fleeting thought that he was a lot better looking with a smile on his harsh face. "Hang on and let me give you something." He shot a quick look at Big Mama, who was now absorbed in the olive rep's spiel, then reached inside his right jeans pocket. But be-fore he could withdraw his hand, the lady's little dog went ape-shit and started barking it's head off. Well, barking is a little strong. Did I mention the dog wasn't much bigger than a rat? It's barks were more akin to yips. High-pitched little squeaks. In the middle of his conniption fit, his tiny body convulsing with hysterical yips, he scrambled out of the bag, hit the floor and took off.

Big Mama bumped into Mr. Gnarly as she ran after the dog, her long caftan billowing out behind her. The olive crowd parted like the Red Sea, but the olive rep wasn't fast enough to get out of her way. She upset his tray as she rushed past and suddenly, olives skewered with toothpicks rolled drunkenly across the shiny linoleum.

Mr. Gnarly leaned down and I swear to God, I thought he was going to pick one up and eat it. I was just about to be grossed out, when I realized why he was bent over. While I watched in stupefied horror, his big body crumpled to the floor. I rushed to kneel beside him, yelling at the top of my lungs, "Call an ambulance! This guy's been stabbed!"

eHARLEQUIN.com

The Ultimate Destination for Women's Fiction

For **FREE online reading,** visit
www.eHarlequin.com now and enjoy:

Online Reads
Read **Daily** and **Weekly** chapters from
our Internet-exclusive stories by your
favorite authors.

Interactive Novels
Cast your vote to help decide how these
stories unfold...then stay tuned!

Quick Reads
For shorter romantic reads, try our
collection of Poems, Toasts, & More!

Online Read Library
Miss one of our online reads?
Come here to catch up!

Reading Groups
Discuss, share and rave with other
community members!

For great reading online,
visit www.eHarlequin.com today!

INTONL04R

If you enjoyed what you just read,
then we've got an offer you can't resist!

Take 2 bestselling love stories FREE!

Plus get a FREE surprise gift!

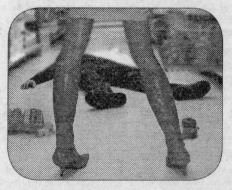

COMING NEXT MONTH

#53 DEVIL'S BARGAIN by Rachel Caine
Red Letter Days

Desperate to clear her partner of a murder conviction, former police detective Jazz Chandler made a deal to start her own P.I. agency. The agreement included a loose-cannon new partner and one all-too-sexy lawyer—and making any case that arrived via red envelope top priority. The seemingly innocuous cases soon threw her into a shadowy world of clandestine societies and hidden agendas where Jazz would have to choose between two evils to save them all.

#54 RARE BREED by Connie Hall

Young, idealistic Wynne Sperling put her life on the line every day working as a park ranger in Africa. Protecting the endangered animals she loved was certainly better than pushing paper in Washington. But when Wynne's attempts to thwart a deadly poaching ring got her into hot water, would her trusty slingshot and help from a mysterious smart-mouthed Texan be enough to prevent *her* from becoming extinct?

#55 SHE'S ON THE MONEY by Stephanie Feagan

She should have known better than to take on a client called Banty. But Whitney "Pink" Pearl couldn't say no to billable hours—and now the fearless CPA was knee-deep in trouble and sinking fast. Seems the oil-well scam she was uncovering led to secrets someone would kill to keep. And with death threats, tangled paper trails and two amorous suitors to juggle, it would take some bold moves to keep Pink out of the red.

#56 THE PROFILER by Lori A. May

A serial killer was on the loose in New York City, and FBI agent Angie Davis was on the scene. But this case was straining even Angie's highly developed profiling abilities...not to mention trying her patience. It was bad enough that she had to work with maverick NYPD detective Carson Severo, but as the body count rose, an unsettling pattern emerged—the victims all shared a connection to Angie. Was she next on the depraved killer's hit list?